# In Plain Sight

**Other books by Lorena McCourtney**

**The Julesburg Mysteries**
*Whirlpool*
*Riptide*
*Undertow*

**The Ivy Malone Mysteries**
*Invisible*

BOOK 2

An
Ivy Malone
Mystery

# In Plain Sight

## Lorena McCourtney

Revell
Grand Rapids, Michigan

Published by Fleming H. Revell
a division of Baker Publishing Group
P.O. Box 6287, Grand Rapids, MI 49516-6287

Printed in the United States of America

ISBN 0-7394-5518-4

Cast all your anxiety on him because he cares for you.

1 Peter 5:7

# 1

In spite of the threats, I'd held on to a small hope that the danger would, given a little time, fade away. The phone call I'd just received squashed that hopeful fantasy.

The Braxtons are not fading away.

Because of my role in convicting his brother of murder, one mean, beefy Drake Braxton vowed at the end of the trial to make roadkill out of me. There are apparently more Braxtons eager to help in this endeavor. Their homicidal intentions were made all too clear when my house caught fire, with me in it, a couple of weeks ago. Intentions thwarted in the small-blaze stage only because of the observant eyes of my good—and nosy—neighbor, Magnolia Margollin.

Although I recently discovered that I have aged into a semi-invisible state, I'm afraid I may not be invisible enough to evade the Braxtons' murderous intentions toward me. This phone call that threatened dire damage to various parts of my anatomy was further proof of those intentions. The prudent action at this point appeared to be to remove myself from the danger zone for a time.

Ever since the death of my best friend, Thea, my niece DeeAnn Harrington had been urging me to stay with her and her family in their big house near the small town of Woodston, Arkansas. She'd also suggested I should consider living with, or close to them, permanently.

I'm reasonably certain I don't want to make a permanent move. Harley and I bought this house here on Madison Street in Missouri many years ago, and, though Harley is gone and the area has deteriorated in the past few years, it's still home to me. But I've been talking it over with the Lord, and a temporary visit down there in the lovely Ozarks appears to be a fine solution to my problem.

Fourteen-year-old grandniece Sandy answered when I dialed DeeAnn's number.

"Oh, Aunt Ivy, you should see what I just crocheted! It's a candy-pink top that's just awesome. I can't wait for some nice spring weather to wear it."

I'd helped Sandy learn to crochet the last time I was down for a visit. Now, with a certain apprehension about teenage apparel, I asked, "Does it show your belly button?"

"Of course!"

"Does your mother know?"

"I'm going to show it to her." Considered pause. "Soon."

I didn't intend to jump into the middle of *that*, so I just said, "Could I speak to DeeAnn, please?"

"Are you going to come visit us again? Oh, I hope so! But you need to come right away, before—"

"Maybe," I cut in.

8

"Okay, I'll get Mom. She's upstairs sorting through some towels and stuff to pick out things that match."

That seemed odd. DeeAnn is a good enough housekeeper, but she doesn't usually fuss about such things as whether her towels coordinate. She came on the line a minute later.

"Aunt Ivy, how good to hear from you! I heard on the news that they sentenced that awful man who murdered your neighbor, but I couldn't get you when I tried to call. And everything has been in such an uproar here that I didn't get around to trying again."

*Uproar* was the usual state of existence in the Harrington household. The twins, Rick and Rory, were off at college in California now, but DeeAnn was financial secretary at their church, created puppet shows about Korman the Klutzy Kangaroo for the Sunday school kids, and kept books for several small businesses in Woodston. Sandy practiced gymnastics in an upstairs hallway, zoomed around on her skateboard, kept in touch with people from Arkansas to Zanzibar on the Internet, and sometimes had the guys in a local Christian rock band over to practice. Husband Mike did executive things with an expanding roofing manufacturer and was up to his elbows in activities aimed at keeping the teens in a church youth group busy.

"Maybe I can help," I said to DeeAnn. "There have been some, uh, unforeseen developments here, and I'm thinking I might take you up on your invitation to come visit for a while."

"Oh, Aunt Ivy . . ."

It didn't take extrasensory powers to hear the dismay in her voice.

"If it isn't convenient now, maybe some other time," I amended hastily.

"Oh, Aunt Ivy, I feel so bad about this. It isn't that it isn't convenient, and we'd love to have you. But we're moving. Mike has gotten a promotion, but it's also a transfer. To Hawaii!"

"Hawaii," I echoed in astonishment. I finally gathered my wits together enough to add, "Well, this is so exciting! And wonderful news for all of you. Congratulations!"

"It is wonderful news, and we are excited. But it's all happening so fast. We're leaving in less than a week, and there's all this sorting and packing and everything that has to be done. I didn't realize we had so much *stuff*."

I was glad I hadn't mentioned my Braxton problem. Dee-Ann would feel worse than ever if she knew about that. "Throw things out," I advised. "That's what God designed moves for. To make us get rid of our excess baggage."

"Hey, I know what let's do. As soon as we get settled over there, you come stay with us! Sandy has been researching all this stuff about Hawaii on the Internet. We'll eat fresh pineapple and go body surfing and roast a whole pig in a luau!"

A whole pig sounded a bit intimidating, but, in general, a trip to Hawaii might be a fine idea. If the Braxtons didn't roast *me* first. "Maybe I can do that," I said.

"Aunt Ivy, is something wrong?" my ever-perceptive niece asked. "You aren't thinking we don't *want* you to visit, are you?"

"Well, of course I think that," I said with pretended huffiness. "I'm sure you've invented this wild story about Hawaii just to keep me from coming. I venture to say you may even go so far as to move to Hawaii to make the story convincing."

DeeAnn laughed. "There's one woman I've done some bookkeeping for whom I'd consider moving to Mars to escape from, but not you, Aunt Ivy. Never you."

"I know. And I appreciate that."

"But there is something wrong, isn't there?"

I considered how to phrase my situation in order to be truthful but not cause DeeAnn concern. "Since the trial, things have felt a bit . . . edgy here. I was just thinking it would be nice to get away for a while. But don't you worry about it. I'll be fine. I'll just go spade up my garden and plant some spring peas. Now tell me all about Hawaii."

DeeAnn bubbled on about how the company had leased a house for them in Honolulu, and how they'd already had welcoming emails from relatives of friends in their Woodston church. "Sandy has mixed feelings about the move. She's excited about Hawaii, but she hates to change schools in the middle of the year. And leave her friends, of course. I've found homes for all my houseplants. We're down to only one cat at the moment. Celery. And Mrs. Grandy from church is taking her, so no problem there."

Celery, their stub-tailed calico cat, so named for one of her odd food preferences, was a stray that had wandered in a couple of years ago. I've always suspected there must be some sign in generic animal language announcing "Free food! Nice folks! Come on in!" posted on the back steps of the Harrington house.

"But we haven't decided what to do about the house, whether to put it up for sale or rent it. I do love this old place . . ."

"I'm sure everything will work out fine. Well, I'll just let you get back to your sorting and packing. We'll talk again before you leave, okay?"

I didn't mean to cut her off, but I had some thinking to do here. With Plan A shot down and the Braxtons gunning for me, it was time to move on to Plan B.

Unfortunately, I had no Plan B.

# 2

I stood at the window looking out on my backyard garden area. *Now what?*

The yard, under a drizzle of spring rain, looked as dispirited as I felt. Straggly weeds. Puddles and mud. Soggy dead leaves. In spite of my cheery words to DeeAnn, I felt no urge to go out and dig. Actually, I've been considering giving up gardening. My vegetables too often bear a disconcerting resemblance to an experiment in plant genetics gone awry.

Even my trusty old '75 Thunderbird, parked in the driveway because the garage door was stuck, looked as if it was losing its grip on elegance. The dent in the rear fender that had been barely noticeable seemed more pronounced now. And when had I lost that left front hubcap?

An old car. Getting ever older. Like me. Both showing our age and dents.

*Okay, enough with the pity party,* I decided, annoyed with myself. *I can do all things through Christ who strengthens me.* True, as the years have shown me. And the Lord always lives up to his promise never to forsake us. *But I could use some help with details here, Lord. Any suggestions?*

A cruise? With the gray rain drizzling down, sea and sunshine beckoned. Yet a cruise would severely strain my limited budget and not put me out of reach of the Braxtons for more than a couple of weeks.

Take refuge with my young friends, police detective Matt "Dix" Dixon and his new bride, Haley? They'd invited. And they'd successfully hidden me out to protect me for weeks before the trial. But they had a life to live, and not one on which I wanted to intrude.

Sell the house, pick up, and move far, far away?

Probably the most effective long-term solution, but the thought of abandoning my home forever gave me a jolt inside. Surely so drastic a step wasn't necessary! And it would also be too time consuming. Selling the house and moving could take months, and I needed to get away—now.

I heated leftover spaghetti in the microwave for supper, washed up the dishes, and was just settling down in front of the TV when the phone rang. I considered not answering it. My good neighbors the Margollins were off in their motor home now, and Dix and Haley were visiting her parents. I couldn't think of anyone except another telemarketer likely to call, and I was not in the market for vinyl siding or windshield repair.

Yet someone with my "mutant curiosity gene," as Dix once grumpily termed it, is genetically incapable of *not* answering a ringing phone.

DeeAnn spoke before I even had a chance to say hello. "Aunt Ivy, Mike just got home, and he has the most wonderful idea! You can come live in the house even if we're not going to be here!"

"Really?"

"Of course. It's perfect. We don't want to sell the house yet, not until we know how things work out in Hawaii—"

"You could rent it out. It's a nice big house, right there beside the lake. It should bring a good rental price."

"I know. But we're concerned that renters might not take care of things. And if you live here I can just leave a lot of this stuff and not worry about it. Your being here will be a big help in this move."

I suspected she might be exaggerating the "help" factor, but I felt a huge swoop of relief. "That sounds great!"

*Thank you, Lord.* Even after all these years I'm still sometimes surprised at how fast and efficiently he can solve problems.

"There's just one thing. Not exactly a *drawback*, but—"

"Mother!" I heard Sandy wail in the background.

"And you don't have to do it, of course," DeeAnn added hastily. "It won't make any difference."

"Umm," I said, carefully noncommittal.

"The thing is, as I mentioned earlier, Sandy would rather not change schools this far along in the year. She'd like to stay here with you until school lets out."

Shock waves. I didn't want to hesitate. I love my grand-niece Sandy. She's bubbly and fun and smart and dependable, a committed Christian. I enjoy her. But she is a teenager, and what do I know about the current teenage generation? "What do you think of the idea?" I asked cautiously.

"I have to admit, I find it a little scary."

"Scary?" Not reassuring. "Scary how?"

"Scary for you. Everyone knows teenagers are the scourge of the universe. Scary for Sandy. She's never been away from us for more than a couple weeks at summer camp. And scary for us too. We've just gotten used to Rick and Rory being gone, and then to leave Sandy behind . . ." Her voice wobbled.

"It's less than three months until school lets out for the summer," I pointed out. "It's not as if you're looking at a permanent empty nest yet."

"Yes, that's true. And not having to cope with a mid-year

14

school transfer would make the move easier for us too." Ever the woman to whip away the clouds and polish the silver lining, DeeAnn suddenly turned upbeat. "Hey, it might even be fun. Just the two of us, like being newlyweds again!"

Noise in the background. Sandy gagging at the thought of her parents as playful newlyweds?

"But it's just fine if you'd rather not," DeeAnn repeated. "We want you to come and live here as long as you want, no matter what. Why don't you think about it and let us know in a day or two?"

DeeAnn is too good and generous a woman to be resentful or insulted no matter what my answer. A no wouldn't change our relationship or their offer of hospitality.

Yet, with my first jolt of shock absorbed, I peered a little further into the situation. As a librarian and Sunday school teacher, I'd always enjoyed children. And I've never wanted to be isolated in some antiseptic, no-kids-allowed system. Sandy was mature enough that it wouldn't be like a baby-sitting job.

*What do you think, Lord?*

I've never been on the receiving end of advice chiseled into stone tablets by the Lord. No sonorous voice has ever boomed in my ear and told me exactly what to do in any given situation. Which, I must admit, I've sometimes wished would happen. But somehow the Lord has usually managed to guide me, and just now I had the definite feeling this was the way to go.

"I'd love to have Sandy stay with me," I said firmly.

"Really? Aunt Ivy, that's wonderful. You're a jewel. I'll tell her—"

Sound of a small scuffle, then Sandy's victorious voice as she claimed the phone. "Hey, Aunt Ivy, we'll be almost roomies! We'll have a great time."

"I'm looking forward to it."

15

"I accidentally bumped into this Internet chat room of old—" Abrupt break while Sandy apparently considered a tactful rephrasing. "This chat room of senior citizens, and I'll show it to you, and you can meet all these interesting men. One of them has a yacht!"

I'm afraid I have a strong suspicion of Internet males bearing yachts, but we could discuss that later.

"Are you sure about Sandy staying?" DeeAnn interrupted.

"Absolutely."

"She'll have strict instructions that she's to help with the cooking and housework. That she isn't to fill the house with herds of noisy teenagers. That she has to keep the same curfew she has when we're here. That the rock band can come over only when and if you say it's okay. That you aren't some full-time chauffeur for her. That just because Skye wears all that makeup and those outrageous outfits doesn't mean Sandy can. That—"

"I'm sure we'll be fine," I cut in hastily. Much more of this list of eye-opening possibilities for errant teen behavior and I'd be thinking the Braxtons looked like the safer alternative.

"Will you be able to get here before we leave? If not, I'm sure Sandy can stay with someone for a few days."

"I'll be there by the end of the week."

Yet there was one other thing. I'd convinced myself that staying with DeeAnn and Mike wouldn't put them in any danger, that even the hostile Braxtons wouldn't gallivant all the way down to Arkansas to do me in. Especially if they didn't know where I was. Mike was also a big guy not even the Braxtons were likely to outsmart or push around. But if it was just Sandy and me there alone . . .

By then I really wanted Sandy to stay. But Mike and Dee-Ann, and Sandy too, had a right to know that the possibility of danger existed, so they could judge for themselves if they wanted her to be with me. Or, for that matter, if they even wanted me in the house.

"Are you still there, Aunt Ivy?" DeeAnn asked, and I realized the silence had stretched to an awkward length.

"I'm here." Finally I said, "There's a . . . detail I need to talk to both you and Mike about."

DeeAnn must have heard the worry in my voice, because she immediately said, "Mike can get on the other phone."

So Mike did that, and I explained everything about Drake Braxton's threat and, even though the police hadn't come up with any definite proof, the strong probability that he or his clan had something to do with my house fire.

"You mean you're on some kind of hit list with these people?" Mike asked, sounding astonished. An understandable attitude, I suppose. How many little old ladies with possum-gray hair wind up on a homicidal hit list?

"Even though the Braxtons do have this hostile attitude, I honestly don't think they'll come down to Woodston after me. I'm hoping they'll figure running me out of town is sufficient."

Finally Mike said, "Let us think about this and do some checking, and we'll call you back, okay?"

I spent the night berating myself. I never should have involved them in this. I should have simply packed myself off to a cheap rental in the middle of nowhere and hidden out for a few months. Why hadn't I thought of that in the first place? In the morning I got out Harley's old road atlas and started studying places out West with names such as Remote, Lizard Valley, and NoWhere.

When the phone rang I was prepared to hear Mike say, in a diplomatic way, of course, that they'd decided to take

Sandy with them and rent the house out. I figured that by now, any renters, even people with eight dogs, a collection of junk cars, and a taste for barbecuing possum in the fireplace, would look preferable to one LOL on some killer/arsonist's hit list.

But what Mike said was, "Okay, we've talked to an acquaintance in the county sheriff's department, Sgt. Yates, and he got in touch with some contacts up there in Missouri. He says that Drake Braxton has big legal problems with his construction and land development business. There's a criminal negligence charge hanging over him, and the definite possibility of prison time. So he's probably too deep in his own problems to worry about hunting you down and getting revenge for helping convict his brother."

"Which doesn't mean he won't make time for a little road-kill action on the side. And there's the rest of the Braxton clan to worry about too."

"That's possible, of course. But we've also contacted a security company, and they're coming this afternoon to install a good alarm system. If you're careful not to leave a trail behind for the Braxtons to follow—"

"I won't! I intend to make it look as if I've disappeared off the face of the earth."

"Good. So we think the danger is minimal."

"What does Sandy think? Is she scared?"

"Sandy loves the idea." Mike sounded mildly exasperated with his adventurous daughter. "She's already thinking about all these *Home Alone*–type schemes in case the bad guys show up. I don't think we could drag her away now."

"I'll take good care of her. I promise."

"I think she figures she'll take good care of you. Not that we'd consider doing this at all if we thought there was really any danger."

I put in a forwarding address at the post office and arranged to have the phone, electricity, and water disconnected. I decided I wouldn't arrange for yard upkeep. I'd just let the place look abandoned, like the other empty houses on Madison Street. The city officials might get up in arms about this eventually, but hopefully I'd be home before that.

I followed the advice I'd given DeeAnn about using moving time to get rid of excess baggage. Out went polyester pants that refused to wear out and apparently intended to march into eternity with me. Shoes so pointy-toed they'd fit into keyholes. A dark suit with shoulder pads large and square enough to deter a halfback tackle.

On the last morning, I left a noncommittal note on the Margollins' back door and sent an equally vague note to Dix and Haley. I didn't want them to have the responsibility of actually knowing where I was in case the Braxtons pressured them.

I took a final tour through the house. I got teary in the kitchen where I'd baked Harley's favorite pot roast and apple cobbler so many times, and real tears flowed in the bedroom Harley and I had shared for so many years.

The house already looked sad and forlorn when I scooted into the T-bird and started the engine. A window blind drooped like a tired eyelid, and the windows needed washing.

Good. I wanted the Braxtons to think I was gone forever.

Although this was, I assured myself as I backed out the driveway, only a temporary move. I just wished it didn't feel so much like a permanent good-bye.

# 3

I ate dinner on the road and arrived at the big house outside Woodston about 7:30 that evening. The yard light was
on, shining on an unfamiliar red car in the driveway. Rain
and darkness hid Little Tom Lake, but I could hear the wind
driving rough waves against the small dock down below the
walking trail that separated the house from the narrow beach.
Branches on the big old black walnut tree creaked overhead.
Rain bounced off the flagstones of the walkway, but a pleas-
antly woodsy scent rose from the damp bark mulch around
the shrubs. Sandy, unmindful of wind and rain, dashed down
the front steps to meet me.

"Aunt Ivy, thank you, thank you for letting me stay!"
Sandy is small and compact, but gymnastics makes her lim-
ber as a coil of spring steel, and she wrapped me in one of
her surprisingly powerful hugs. "Mom and Dad are over at
church, finishing things up. I think they're glad to be rid
of me and can't wait to get away!" Her pert nose wrinkled,

but the sparkle in her blue eyes belied any concern about abandonment. "I'll carry your stuff in—"

"The suitcase on the front seat is all I need tonight. We can haul everything else in tomorrow."

She ran out to the car for the suitcase. Another girl was standing under the coach light on the covered front porch. She looked a little older than Sandy and considerably more sophisticated. Tall, slim and willowy, dark-haired, very pretty even though wearing enough eye shadow to turn her eyes into smoky caverns.

This had to be Skye of the "outrageous outfits," I decided. Her slithery, psychedelic-print skirt swirled around her ankles, but it hung so low on her hips that the bones jutted out like coat hangers. Enough bare skin separated the skirt and a skimpy knit top to invite pneumonia in this weather. She smiled, but her manner was reserved.

"Hi. I'm Sandy's friend, Skye Ridenour." She held out her hand, a formality I didn't expect, and we shook. I tried not to look at her belly button, but, since it had a gold hoop attached to it, I found it difficult not to.

"I'm always pleased to meet Sandy's friends. I don't think we've met before."

"I've only been in Woodston since last fall. I came here to live with my father then."

Sandy came up the walkway with my old Montgomery Ward suitcase banging against her knees. "We've been making brownies for you, with pecans and chocolate-mint frosting!"

Skye looked at the watch on her left wrist. I'm not on time-keeping terms with expensive watches, but I'd guess she could buy an armful of my Timex for what that one cost. "I'd better get home."

"Don't run off because of me—"

"Oh no, it isn't that. The Dumpling told me I had to be

21

home by 7:30 to sit with Baby so she could go to the health club. I'll get my jacket."

Since it was already 7:35, it appeared that Skye wasn't overly concerned about the deadline. I wondered who or what the Dumpling with a baby was, but I didn't want Sandy's friends to think I was a nosy LOL, so I didn't ask.

Inside, Skye picked up a jacket in camouflage colors lying on the sofa. It, in contrast to the clingy top, was as bulky as a sleeping bag, with enough pockets to arouse a kangaroo to envy. She waved as she went out, fingernails flashing sparkly glitters.

"She's walking home in the dark?" I asked, concerned.

"That's her car out there."

"Her *own* car?"

"She's sixteen," Sandy said, as if that explained everything. Which I found a little scary.

Sandy carried the suitcase across the living room, where a fire crackled in the fireplace, and up the stairs to the corner room I always occupied. The big old house has four bedrooms and a bath upstairs, plus the master bedroom downstairs.

A four-poster bed covered with a multistar design quilt centered the far wall of my room. Around it was a comfortable hodgepodge, everything from a rolltop desk (maple, imitation antique) to a beanbag chair, a cane-bottomed rocker, and a genuine antique trunk as a nightstand. Underfoot were three old-fashioned braided rag rugs, courtesy of Mike's grand-mother. An appliquéd quilt, this an aunt's handiwork, hung on one wall, a watercolor of an empty cross on a distant hill on another. I'd always felt at home in this room.

By the time I unpacked a few things and went downstairs, Mike and DeeAnn had returned. We ate brownies, delight-fully tasty in spite of the odd pecan and mint combination, and had a lovely visit. They showed me how the new alarm system worked. I suspected it might deter my entry more often than that of any prowling Braxtons, but computer expert Sandy blithely assured me it was no problem. I decided I'd just let her manage it. Mike said he was leaving his impressive collection of mystery novels behind, which meant I wouldn't run out of reading material for a long time. A sad note was news of the death of an elderly neighbor, Lois Watkins, a sweet and chatty woman whom I usually stopped in to visit when I was here.

We discussed possible dangers from the Braxtons, but Mike and DeeAnn were confident everything would be okay, or, as they'd already pointed out, they wouldn't be leaving Sandy here.

The 'bird was still full of my stuff, so we used DeeAnn's Buick to take Mike and DeeAnn to the airport in Fayetteville the next morning. Both Sandy and DeeAnn were teary when they said good-bye, but Sandy was upbeat and chatty on the way home.

"Well, here we are, Aunt Ivy. Just you and me!" she said cheerfully when she unlocked the house. She poked buttons on the new control panel when we stepped inside so the alarm system wouldn't consider us intruders and alert the police.

I, however, was suddenly uneasily aware of how close the thick woods grew around the house—plenty of cover for creeping Braxtons. Of how big the house was—plenty of space for hiding Braxtons. Of how noticeable my white T-bird, sitting out there in the driveway, was—a vehicle with which the Braxtons were undoubtedly quite familiar.

*Okay, get off it,* I told myself grumpily. The Braxtons had no clue where I was hiding out, and my biggest problem here would probably be deciding how to fill my time.

Not a problem those first few days.

That afternoon we lugged my stuff upstairs and unpacked. Sandy gave me a quick introduction to her computer and

Internet system, although I begged off on chatting with cyberspace Romeos with yachts. Later, a half dozen teenage friends came over to play ping-pong in the basement and eat popcorn. Mike and DeeAnn called to report a safe arrival in Hawaii.

By next morning, when Sandy phoned to see if Skye wanted to go to church with us, the weather had metamorphosed into glorious spring. Skye was still in bed and didn't go, but I'd been to Mike and DeeAnn's church before, knew a few people, and felt comfortable and welcome. Afterward, DeeAnn's friends urged me to join a Thursday morning women's Bible study, which I gladly agreed to do. But I put off an invitation to join a quilting group. An earlier venture into quilting had made me think I'd as soon try working a crossword puzzle in Russian.

That afternoon Sandy and I dragged the aluminum skiff, which had been stored behind the garage for the winter, down to the water. A couple of young guys hiking on the public pathway, and taking interested notice of Sandy in her cutoffs, helped when we got stuck. I suspected young male help would appear if Sandy were stranded on an Antarctic ice floe.

The trail bustled with activity, hikers and joggers and dog walkers all out to enjoy the spring day, everyone talkative and friendly. The trail begins at the city park and follows all along the west edge of the lake, far past where the houses end.

We took turns rowing. Little Tom isn't a wide lake, but it's long, so we covered only the south half of it. I seldom venture into shorts, but Sandy had urged me into them today, and the sun felt good on my bare legs. Glittery rays reflected off the water into our sunglasses, and the faint breeze brought scents of damp earth awakening and squeals of children on the trail. From our vantage point out on the water, the shoreline was a misty green haze of bushes in fresh new leaves.

The far side of the lake, which had been wild woods when DeeAnn and Mike first moved here, was now divided into what Sandy said was called "Vintage Estates." A building requirement for the area was that all the houses must be "period" style. Exactly what period was apparently up for grabs, as they ranged from Victorian to Craftsman—and even one in antebellum plantation style. It looked as if Scarlett O'Hara might stroll out of it at any moment. All were huge. Sandy said most of the residents were new, not local people. On this side of the lake, Sandy said, unlike over on the less-exclusive side, people owned right down to the water's edge and there was no trail for public use.

The lawns weren't lush yet, but they sloped gracefully from big houses to the water, with elaborate boathouses and private docks sticking out into the lake like manicured fingers. The boathouse at the plantation-style place matched the house, right down to white columns. Two peacocks graced one lawn. A guy sitting shirtless in a gingerbread-trim gazebo gave us a friendly wave. I decided if he wasn't concerned about exposing his hairy belly to the world, I shouldn't worry about my legs in shorts.

By the time Sandy gave my tired shoulders a rubdown that evening and supplied bubble-gum-scented bubble bath for a long soak in the tub, I wondered how I could have hesitated for a moment about having her here with me.

She went to school on Monday, of course, but I had plenty to keep me busy. I washed DeeAnn's Buick and put it away in the double garage, alongside the SUV. The company was furnishing them with a car in Hawaii. Then it was such a great day that I washed the T-bird too and prudently parked it where it wasn't quite so visible. Just in case.

But I really wasn't feeling any ominous vibes from hostile Braxtons, and at about 3:00 I went for a walk. The trail wasn't busy this weekday, and I met only one hiker. A jogger, actually, a lean woman with a blonde ponytail swinging out the back of a baseball cap. She jogged by me both coming and going, and I was impressed with her stamina. Although I couldn't say that she looked as if she was enjoying herself much.

I saw her again the following day. This time I said hello. She gave me a distant nod and kept jogging. On the next day I tried again, adding, "Beautiful day, isn't it?" Not even a nod today.

I was surprised and a bit vexed. Arkansas people, and especially Woodston folks, are usually so friendly. Unless she actually hadn't seen me, of course. I am, by charitable description, petite and slender, an inconspicuous older woman. Less charitably, I am short and scrawny, an invisible little old lady (ILOL in this age of abbreviations). That invisibility, though disconcerting when I first discovered it, can be quite useful.

I didn't see how this woman could have totally missed me on the trail, however. If I'd stuck out a foot she'd have fallen flat on her face.

On Thursday morning, before Bible study, I had another odd encounter. Sandy and I had left the skiff tied at the dock, and I decided to go down and check on it. Brush concealed the short dock from the house, so I was at the beach end of the warped boards before I realized a man was down on one knee at the other end. I didn't really intend to sneak up on him, but something about his odd, almost furtive, position made me curious, and I stopped before my foot touched the dock.

Now I could see that he was holding binoculars to his eyes. I squinted, trying to see what he was studying so intently.

Birds? I'd spotted a cardinal the day before, and an owl had hooted out back of the house last night. Yet there was something oddly stealthy about the way he suddenly lowered the binoculars, took a quick glance around, and then raised them again.

When he looked around, his gaze skimmed right over me. Maybe it was because my green sweats blended into the haze of green bushes. No need for alarm, I told myself, just because he seemed to be acting a bit peculiar. But I realized I was uneasily fingering the emergency whistle that always hangs on a cord around my neck. It was a gift from my departed friend Thea, who gave it to me after an older woman was mugged in a parking lot back home.

But my uneasiness was surely foolish. This was broad daylight, and the man was simply . . . what?

When in doubt, I advised myself, ask.

"Anything interesting out there?" I called out.

The guy jumped to his feet as if I'd jabbed him with a barbecue fork, and for a moment I thought he was going to tumble off the dock. But he managed to right himself, and he turned and looked at me as if he thought I'd deliberately snuck up on him. He was good looking, in a sharp-faced way, but his deep tan struck me as out of place for this time of year in Woodston.

"I didn't mean to startle you. It isn't a private dock," I added, because he'd wedged the binoculars against his chest as if trying to hide them. His wrinkled slouch hat was pulled down low, three fishing lures snagged above the droopy brim. His khaki pants ended high on his ankles, exposing heavy work boots. Blue suspenders crisscrossed his red plaid shirt and held the top of the pants well above his waist.

"It's okay to use the dock. Everyone in the houses along here does. That's my niece's boat," I said, pointing to the skiff. "The other one belongs to the neighbors."

"Okay, thanks." He turned his back to me, hesitated a moment, and then put the binoculars to his eyes again. They didn't appear to be focused anywhere in particular.

"Beautiful day for bird-watching," I suggested, mostly fishing for information.

"Yeah, it is."

He raised the glasses higher and scanned the sky with so much speed that he couldn't have focused on a flying elephant. I'm not familiar with bird-watchers, but somehow I doubted this was standard technique.

"Are you doing one of those bird count things?" I asked.

"Just looking." After about thirty more seconds of rapid sky searching, he muttered something about not seeing much today, jammed a pair of mirrored sunglasses over his eyes, and hurried back up to the trail.

An unsettling thought suddenly raised goose bumps on my arms. Something didn't feel right here. Could the Braxtons have gotten wind of my whereabouts and sent this guy to reconnoiter? Was all this looking around on the lake just a ruse, and his real purpose was to spy on *me*?

# 4

*Get off it*, I chided myself. *You're on a one-way route to Para-noidville.* Sure, the Braxtons were underhanded, tricky, and clever, and I was certain this guy was no bird-watcher. But his binoculars had not been aimed in my direction, so whatever he was doing had nothing to do with me.

Unless he was just playing it clever . . .

Paranoidville. Right at the city limits.

I went on to the Thursday morning Bible study, with a lively discussion on Corinthians. By that afternoon a light drizzle had started, but I got my umbrella and went for a walk anyway. Would Ms. Standoffish be jogging on a day such as this?

Yes, indeed. And no more friendly than before. I deliberately stood in the middle of the pathway, thinking she'd have to acknowledge my existence then. But she jogged around me as if I were one of the bushes dripping puddles onto the trail.

People have problems, I reminded myself, and perhaps she was too absorbed in hers to be aware of anything else.

But that evening, after I'd picked up Sandy at the gymnastics studio where she had after-school practice three times a week, I was still fretting about the woman. Was she that unfriendly to everyone, or just me?

Sandy, Skye, and I were at the breakfast bar eating homemade chili, salad, and corn bread I'd jazzed up with bits of bacon and jalapeno. Skye had been with Sandy at the studio, which is only a couple of blocks from the school. With minimal urging, she'd come home with us for dinner.

"There's this woman I see jogging on the trail every afternoon. I was wondering if either of you know who she is. Tall, blonde, no makeup but quite elegant looking, rather like a young, more athletic Grace Kelly?"

The comparison with Grace Kelly drew blank looks from Sandy and Skye, who were no doubt more familiar with blondes named Britney or Christina.

Sandy suddenly got a lightbulb-turning-on look. She lifted her spoon. "Expensive velour sweats, some designer brand, a different outfit every day? Jogging shoes that cost, like, two hundred dollars? Friendly as a shark?"

I'm not familiar with shoes in that price range, but I could tell this woman's footgear was beyond the $9.98 area of my purple tennies. And "friendly as a shark"? Bingo.

"You know her?" I asked.

She and Skye looked at each other. "Leslie Marcone," they said in unison.

"Has to be," Sandy added. "She's a mystery woman. She bought that big Southern plantation place across the lake a year or so ago, but no one knows much about her."

"Does she have a husband or children?"

"Not unless she keeps them stashed in the basement or attic. Which she might, she's that weird. But I've never seen

30

or heard anything about them." Sandy looked at Skye, who nodded agreement.

"You mean she lives there in that big place all alone?"

"I heard she has a housekeeper and a gardener. And that she goes all the way into Little Rock to get her hair styled." Skye held out a strand of her own hair, eyes turned sideways to study it disconsolately. "I wish I could go to Little Rock. That woman the Dumpling sent me to destroyed my hair when she cut it."

Her hair looked lovely to me, long and dark and shimmery, like something out of a conditioner ad, but at the moment I was more interested in the mystery woman than Skye's hair problems. Leslie Marcone had appeared to be in her late twenties. Why in the world would a young, healthy woman living alone have a housekeeper?

"She's a real exercise nut," Sandy added. "She's out there jogging almost every day, and in the summer she swims back and forth across the lake. Or sometimes she goes out and rows for hours."

My own thought was that she could do her own gardening and housework, get plenty of exercise, and save the expense of hired help. But someone who has money enough to buy a place on the "estate" side of Little Tom probably has a different agenda.

"The Dumpling says she showed up at the health club a few times when the weather was really bad," Skye said. "And she actually *does* something, of course, when she's there."

The Dumpling again. And I heard a certain snideness in Skye's crack about actually doing something. As compared to someone—the Dumpling, perhaps?—who went to the health club and *didn't* do anything? I made a mental note to ask Sandy about all this later.

"I'll bet she doesn't have more than 15 percent body fat," Skye added, her tone admiring. "After taking a look at that crummy little health club, she probably set up her own exercise room at home. Hey, there's my dad!" She pointed to the TV in the living room, where the local news from a Fayetteville station had just come on.

"Really?" I looked closer.

"I guess I forgot to mention it." Sandy sounded guilty for not having informed me of this celebrity status. She grabbed the remote and flicked the sound to a higher level. "Skye's dad is the anchor for the local news. His name's Brad Ridenour."

"They call him 'the Big Brad,'" Skye said with obvious pride.

We all watched Skye's father tell about a weekend fire in Fayetteville. He had an excellent voice, deep and mellow, good, clear enunciation. He didn't get maudlin about the two dogs that were lost in the fire, but he sounded as if he cared. Though a moment later he was kidding with his coanchor about her frequent changes of hair color.

Skye must have inherited her dark-haired, willowy good looks from her mother, I decided, because I couldn't see any resemblance between her and this husky, blond guy with the cleft chin. "The Big Brad" definitely fit him. He was good-looking too, but in a heavy-necked, ex-football-player kind of way. I also saw no resemblance between Skye's quiet reserve and the way Brad Ridenour bantered and kidded with the coanchor and the weather girl.

"He's going to be the speaker at our high school commencement ceremonies in May," Sandy added, as if to make up for not giving the man his proper due earlier.

"He's into all kinds of civic activities," Skye said. "It's good for his image. Some people have been suggesting he should consider politics, and he'll probably run for state representative in the next election."

After the local news ended, Sandy lowered the sound again, and I went back to the subject of the mystery woman.

32

"Does this Leslie Marcone work somewhere?"

"If she does, it must be nights, because she's out there exercising like a maniac in the daytime," Sandy said. "Except I sometimes see lights on at, like, 5:00 in the morning over there, so it looks as if she's home."

"A home business?" I suggested.

"Maybe. Mom did some work for her, but I don't know what it was about."

There was nothing in particular to make me think so, but a hint of disapproval in Sandy's tone made me wonder if this was the client DeeAnn had said she'd move to Mars to escape from.

"I think she's fascinating," Skye stated suddenly. "Rich and beautiful and mysterious—"

Just as suddenly Sandy stated an opposite opinion. "I think she's a stuck-up snob."

I was mildly shocked by Sandy's hostile comment. Usually Sandy goes out of her way to look for the good in people. Apparently my surprise showed.

"She is a stuck-up snob," Sandy repeated, though now her tone held a defensive note. "She acts like she owns the trail. She jumped all over some little kids last fall, just because their dog came out of the water and shook on her. Elly, who did Mom's hair, told Mom that Leslie got up and stomped out because she had to wait about five minutes for her appointment. I guess that's when she started going to Little Rock. And Mom said she practically went into riot mode over some little two-dollar photocopy charge on the bill Mom sent her for the bookkeeping work."

Okay, those weren't particularly likeable traits, and I could understand Sandy's defensiveness about her mother, but the vehemence of her announced dislike for Leslie Marcone seemed out of proportion. I looked to Skye for her reaction.

33

"I still think she's fascinating," Skye said. "And you can tell just by looking at her that she isn't from around *here*."

Skye's *here* dripped enough scorn to relegate Woodston to the outskirts of civilization, something out of those old *Beverly Hillbillies* reruns where the swimming pool is called a cement pond.

"I hate those black-eyed peas and hog jowls everyone here thinks you should eat on New Year's Day," Skye added. She rolled her eyes. "And those burgers at that Biff's Burgers place downtown taste like they're made out of roadkill."

I looked at Sandy again, wondering how this scornful attitude about Woodston sat with her. I also considered inquiring of Skye just how much roadkill she'd sampled in order to make this judgment but decided better of it. Sandy scowled and squashed her napkin with uncharacteristic ferociousness, but she didn't say anything.

I couldn't help asking, "I take it you don't like it here in Woodston, Skye?"

"I wouldn't even be here except my mother got this cool new job in New York and had to move back there in a hurry. As soon as she gets settled, I'll go live with her." She paused, small frown between her perfectly arched dark brows. "Though being with my father is great too, of course."

I suspected what her problem was. She saw wanting to be with either parent as somehow disloyal to the other. "What does your mother do in New York?"

"She's editor of a new magazine called *Edge*. It has cool fashion and makeup and decorating articles." She didn't ask if I'd ever read it. I suppose it's obvious I'm not on the cutting edge of fashion. Skye held out her hand, slender fingers spread to show her pale blue nails with silvery sparkles. "This is the nail polish the cover model was wearing last month. My mom sent it to me."

"That was nice of her."

"She's going to set me up with the same modeling agency when I get to New York."

I glanced at Sandy. She was busy buttering a chunk of corn bread. I had the distinct impression things were not quite as they appeared on the surface here, but I'd made myself a promise not to be a nosy LOL with Sandy's friends. I went back to the original subject.

"So, if this Leslie Marcone doesn't have a family or job, does anyone know what she does in her big house all the time?"

"Yeah, I wonder. What *does* she do all the time?" Sandy said.

Skye leaned back in the chair and looked off into space with a dreamy expression. "I think she's into something sophisticated and glamorous, but she keeps it secret because she wants her privacy."

"Like what?" Sandy asked skeptically.

"Oh, maybe she used to be a model, and now she's a fashion designer who's famous under a name we'd all recognize if we heard it. Or maybe she's a best-selling author, but her books come out under a pen name, so no one here knows. Whatever it is, she must make tons of money."

"Maybe she married some rich old guy and grabbed all his money in a nasty divorce," Sandy said, a suggestion that rather startled me with its hint of worldly cynicism. Her expression brightened. "Or maybe she embezzled millions of dollars and is hiding out here. But the FBI and CIA and everybody are about to catch up with her!"

Sandy seemed to find that prospect appealing, if not necessarily plausible, because it ended on a giggle.

After a moment, Skye said, "But her hair will look great, and she'll be slim and gorgeous when they put the handcuffs on her," and giggled too.

I was relieved that the difference of opinion about Leslie Marcone was apparently no real rift between them.

But this talk of embezzlement and handcuffs suddenly made me think about that phony bird-watcher down on the dock again. Now I targeted something else about him that bothered me. He wore those hayseedy clothes, but he'd never fit in with the genuine farmer types down at the Woodston Feed & Seed. Combined with that deep, non-Woodston-looking winter tan and nervous jitters, the clothes were too much like a carefully chosen costume. An outsider's idea of what an Ozarks hayseed would wear.

And the way he'd jammed those mirrored sunglasses over his eyes, as if he didn't want me to get a good look at his face . . .

Okay, I'd semi-canceled him as an agent of the Braxtons up to something nefarious concerning me. But that didn't mean he wasn't up to *something*.

The question was, what?

# 5

The answer came to me like one of Harley's old fly-fishing lines zinging across a creek to hit a target in the water.

Those binoculars hadn't been aimed upward to look for birds. At least not until the guy latched on to my suggestion that he might be a bird-watcher. They'd been aimed straight ahead. At Leslie Marcone's imitation Southern plantation. Was there some connection between the man and the mysterious woman?

"Does anyone know where this woman came from?" I asked.

"California, I bet. Or New York," Skye said, with an air that said anybody who was anybody came from one of those two states.

"Skye's from California," Sandy added.

"I used to spend practically all summer hanging out at the beach. 'N Trouble and their friends came to the same beach to surf sometimes. I talked to Nick LeClaire a few times."

This was obviously important name-dropping, but I was

not knowledgeable enough to be properly impressed. I looked to Sandy for explanation.

"'N Trouble is a rock group," Sandy said. "Nick LeClaire is the lead singer."

From her hothouse complexion I wouldn't have guessed Skye to be a beach girl. But maybe Little Tom's narrow beach, without a rock star in sight, didn't meet her eligibility requirements for outdoor activity.

Skye went home a few minutes later, and Sandy ran upstairs to start packing for her trip. Spring vacation was next week, and she was going with a mixed group of teens and adults from church to a small town just across the Mexican border for a project at a mission orphanage. The trip had been planned for some time, and Mike and DeeAnn had taken care of all the permissions and paperwork before they left.

I put the leftover chili in cartons for the freezer and then went upstairs to see if I could help Sandy. "Don't forget sunscreen," I offered as she stuffed denim cutoffs in a duffel bag.

"Right, I'll need that." Sandy rummaged in a dresser drawer and came up with a blue plastic bottle.

"Is Skye going on the trip too?"

"No. I asked her, but she thought she'd be spending spring break with her mom in New York."

"Which isn't happening?"

"She said her mom had to fly over to Italy for some last-minute fashion shoot thing."

"But she is going to go live with her mother before long?"

"Her mom's been in New York since last fall. How long can it take to get 'settled'? Skye thought she was going to New York at Christmas too, but then her mother had to go to London and sent a bunch of presents instead."

Including an expensive watch, I suspected.

Sandy held up a pair of red thong sandals. Apparently they fell short on some rating standard that escaped me, and she tossed them aside.

"Skye's older than you, isn't she?" Their relationship rather surprised me. I'd thought older girls considered it beneath them to hang out with younger ones.

"I'm a freshman and she's a junior. But all Woodston has is an elementary school and a four-year high school, so Skye and I have one class together." Sandy hesitated, as if she was uncertain about confiding something to me, but finally she added, "Skye isn't too popular with most of the kids."

"She's very pretty. And she has a car of her own."

"But she's always talking about how much better everything in California is, and how she's going to be a model and everything. People would like her a lot better if she'd just . . . you know, be herself, instead of acting so phony and superior."

I wondered if "being herself" *was* the problem, that what you saw with Skye, shallow and self-centered, was exactly what she was.

"Does she go out on dates?" Mike and DeeAnn weren't letting Sandy date yet, but Skye was two years older.

"With any of the guys here in, as she calls it, Hillbilly Heaven?" Sandy scoffed. "She'd rather eat hog jowls, and you heard how she hates them."

"Sounds as if she's her own worst enemy."

"She's really not so bad, down underneath all the name-dropping and stuff," Sandy said with what I thought was admirable compassion, given how Skye had trashed Sandy's hometown of Woodston. "Mostly I think she's just scared."

"Scared?"

"Her folks toss her back and forth like a Frisbee. She'd never admit it, but I think she's afraid that neither of them really wants her. So I've tried to be friends with her and tell her about Jesus. I try to make her feel . . . not so alone and shut out."

I was ashamed of myself then. Fourteen-year-old Sandy had looked deeper into Skye than I had and was conscientiously trying to help her.

"And I like her. I mean, we're not Velcroed or anything, but she can be fun. Though I'd like her better if she'd try a little harder with the other kids. And with her stepmother too."

"The Dumpling?" I guessed.

"Right."

"Maybe it's because of the baby. Maybe the baby makes Skye feel insecure, or like an outsider."

"Baby?" Sandy gave me a blank look. "What baby?"

"The stepmother's baby. Skye said that first night I arrived that she had to go home to take care of the baby while her stepmother went to the health club."

Sandy burst out laughing. "It isn't a baby like with bottles and diapers. It's Baby."

"It's not a baby, but it's baby?" I was beginning to feel as if we were stumbling around in some old Three Stooges routine.

"Baby is—oh, you'll just have to see Baby for yourself," Sandy said, still laughing. "Just don't try to put a diaper on him. Though he's so sweet he probably wouldn't mind."

"Fine," I muttered, feeling a bit miffed that I seemed to be out of the loop. "So, tell me more about the Dumpling. I assume she has a real name?"

"Tammi."

"She and Skye don't get along?"

"Skye doesn't give Tammi much of a chance. I mean, Tammi can be a pain all right, but she really tries to be nice to Skye. She isn't one of those evil stepmother types."

"So what's the problem?"

"Tammi's, well, I guess you can tell from what Skye calls her, a little plump—"

"If plump is a crime, half the country would be guilty."

"Tammi buys all these exercise and diet books. They're scattered all over the house. She has a new one that must weigh ten pounds. And she has all these gadgets. Stretch bands you're supposed to exercise with. A huge ball that you're supposed to roll around on or something. A thing she calls a slantboard, and all kinds of weights and stuff."

"If she wants to lose weight, exercise is important."

"Right. But Tammi never actually *does* anything with all that stuff. It's like she thinks she's going to drop pounds just by reading the books and buying the equipment. It drives Skye crazy."

"But the stepmother goes to a health club, doesn't she? Maybe she does her real exercising there."

"We sneaked in and watched her one time," Sandy admitted. "She walked about ten minutes on the treadmill and then went out for a double latte."

Not a program for successful weight loss, I had to agree. But still, hardly enough to warrant the level of Skye's apparent antagonism. "That's all Skye has against her? That she's plump and doesn't exercise enough?"

"Oh, Skye gripes about other stuff. Like all the eggplant and tofu Tammi is always trying to feed her. Tammi wants to be a vegetarian and make Skye one too, but then Tammi gets a burger attack and runs out and scarfs down about three double cheeseburgers. And Tammi wanted them to get matching outfits one time." Sandy rolled her eyes, apparently sympathizing with Skye on that point. "And she is, well, you know . . . a stepmother. Skye doesn't say it, but I think she wishes her folks would get back together."

"I think many children of divorce feel that way."

"But Tammi tries, and Skye won't give her a chance. I'm

sure she's the one who talked Mr. Ridenour into letting Skye have the car." She paused. "I think maybe she even paid for it. Skye said Tammi inherited a bundle of money from her grandmother."

Two mothers competing to see who could buy Skye's affection? I wondered if, perhaps subconsciously if not deliberately, Skye wasn't playing the two women against each other to see what goodies she could collect from both sides.

Motherhood can be a rough game.

"Who makes the decisions on Skye's wardrobe?" I asked.

"Well, uh, Skye mostly. Tammi's pretty lenient."

"Whatever became of that crocheted top you made?"

"Mom told me it required some, umm, alterations before I could wear it." Sandy gave me an unexpected look and smile. "You're really curious about people, aren't you, Aunt Ivy?"

Oh dear, caught. "Any time I ask something that's none of my business, you just tell me," I said hastily.

The van came for Sandy and her gear Saturday morning. Before I could get lonely, however, a guy who identified himself as Jerry from the Christian rock band called to ask if they could come over and practice that afternoon. I said Sandy was gone for the week, and he apologized for calling. I had a few qualms, but I said, "Why don't you come over anyway?" And they did.

Their basement music was loud enough to rattle my four-poster bed upstairs, but after the first few ear-splitting, floor-shaking minutes—and the shock of their trademark blue hair—I rather enjoyed them. And they seemed to enjoy the nachos I fixed. I invited them to come again.

Just after they packed up their instruments and left, a

man I didn't recognize arrived in a black pickup and rang the doorbell. I considered not answering. Could this be a Braxton scheme to lure me out? But that old mutant curiosity gene got me again. I couldn't just let the doorbell ring. Although I did put my ear to the door and say "Who is it?" rather than just flinging it open.

"Mrs. Malone? Is that you? Sgt. Yates. I just thought I'd stop by and see if everything's okay."

I opened the door then. This was the deputy from the county sheriff's office whom Mike had contacted to check up on Drake Braxton, although the deputy was in jeans, not a uniform, today. A long and lanky, brown-haired guy, forty-ish but with a face that would have looked almost boyish if not for a nasty scar cutting through his right eyebrow. Bullet wound? Knife? Whatever, it gave him a tough, don't-mess-with-me air that I found both intimidating and reassuring.

"Thank you. I appreciate your concern."

"You're getting along okay? Nothing suspicious going on? No strange cars or people in the neighborhood?"

"No . . ." I momentarily thought about telling him about the man with binoculars down on the dock, but the guy certainly hadn't threatened me in any way, and I didn't want Sgt. Yates thinking I saw boogeymen around every corner. And I didn't want to cause some innocent guy problems. "Although there are a lot of people walking by on the trail, of course. Especially on weekends. And a couple of times cars have pulled into the driveway and just turned around and left." I hadn't thought much about the car incidents at the time, but who knows?

"I'll just take a look around, then, if it's okay with you."

I followed as he circled the house. He paid special attention to the windows, parting the shrubs and bending them back so he could inspect the ground underneath. Looking for tracks, I supposed. Mike and DeeAnn used to have a lawn, but several years ago they'd taken out the grass and put in shrubs and decorative rock and bark for easier maintenance. It makes for a nice, woodsy ambiance, but the shrubs and bushes could also offer concealment for evil-intentioned Braxtons.

"Been getting any strange phone calls? Hang-ups, anything like that?" Sgt. Yates asked as he studied an indentation in the bark mulch.

"No. Nothing unusual. As you may know, Mike and Dee-Ann had a security system installed." Guiltily I realized I hadn't set it since Sandy left. "They've called several times and really seem to like Hawaii."

He checked the windows fronting the porch, tested the roll-up and side doors on the garage, and peered under the tarp covering the wood for the fireplace. When we were out front again, he said, "Well, I don't think anyone's been prowling around the house. Though it wouldn't hurt to have some of those shrubs near the windows trimmed back."

"I'll see about that."

"And give me a call if anything makes you uneasy, okay?" He handed me a card listing office, cell, and home phone numbers.

At the last minute, just as he was opening the pickup door, I changed my mind on holding back about the man on the dock. If the guy was up to something concerning Leslie Marcone, it would be unfair of me to keep quiet just because I didn't want Sgt. Yates thinking I had a boogeyman complex.

So I told him what I'd seen. For the first time an innocent explanation of the man's concentration on Leslie Marcone's house occurred to me. "Of course, maybe he was just interested in the architecture of the house. It is a rather unusual place. Especially that matching boathouse."

"Could be," Sgt. Yates said with the skepticism of one who

takes nothing for granted. He took out a well-worn black notebook and asked me to describe the man.

I couldn't tell him much beyond the hayseedy clothes. The slouch hat had covered the color of the man's hair and the sunglasses the color of his eyes. "But he was about medium height, with a stocky build. His face was rather narrow, and he had a really deep tan."

"Would you know him if you saw him again?"

"I'm not sure," I had to admit. "Maybe."

"Did you see a vehicle?"

"No. Most people walking the trail leave their cars at the city park."

"Anything else?"

"Nothing except that he seemed awfully nervous and jittery for a man who wasn't . . . up to something."

"Okay, we'll keep him in mind in case anything unusual happens." Sgt. Yates flipped the notebook shut and put it back in his pocket.

"Do you know the woman who owns that house?" I asked. "I often see her jogging on the trail, but she seems somewhat . . . aloof."

"No social butterfly, from what I hear. But about all I really know about her is that she doesn't have a criminal record."

"You checked?" I asked, surprised.

"A neighbor across the road complained that she'd stopped him from using the boat landing on her place. The previous owner had always let him use it to put his boat in the water and tie up at the dock."

"Was stopping him illegal?"

"Not as far as I know. We told him it was a civil not criminal matter and that if he thought he had rights to use the boat landing he should contact a lawyer. He got quite irate and had a number of uncomplimentary things to say about paying his taxes and not getting any service, bureaucrats feeding at the government trough, etc., etc." Sgt. Yates's smile was wry, as if neither complaint was unfamiliar.

"I wonder why she stopped him?"

"I suppose she figures it's her boat landing and her dock, and she's entitled to private use of it. But the neighbor said he suspected she was doing something illegal on the property, drugs or something, and the reason she wouldn't let him in was because she didn't want him to see what was going on there."

That thought startled me. Could some illegal activity be why Leslie Marcone was so aloof and unfriendly? And why the man with binoculars was studying her house?

"Did you search her place?"

"No. We hadn't sufficient evidence of possible illegal activity to ask a judge for a search warrant."

"Could this neighbor simply have been trying to make trouble for her?"

"Certainly a possibility. As it turned out, he wound up in more trouble than she did."

"Really?"

"After we didn't rush out to tell the woman she had to let him use the boat landing, he took matters into his own hands and rammed her gate with his pickup. He denied it, but paint from the pickup was all over the gate, and dents in the pickup matched the spokes in the gate. He didn't have a record either, however, and with this being a first offense, he didn't get any jail time, just a fine for malicious mischief. He replaced the gate with a new one, and I haven't heard of his having problems with any other neighbors, but the man has a mean streak, that's for sure."

"Could the man I saw on the dock have been him?"

"The description doesn't match."

"It sounds as if it could be a rather scary situation for Ms.

Marcone." This gave me a different perspective on her un-friendly attitude. Perhaps her wariness with strangers was justified. "I understand she lives there alone?"

"I believe so."

"She's apparently rather wealthy."

"Given what those Vintage Estates places cost, I'd say that's probably true."

"Did you use fingerprints when you checked on her criminal record?"

"No. We didn't have any reason to ask for them." The scarred eyebrow lifted. "You suspect her of something?"

"Well . . . a pretentious taste in housing, if nothing else."

He laughed. "Agreed."

"Does she have a job somewhere, or maybe an office at home?"

Sgt. Yates tilted his head and crossed his arms. "Mrs. Malone, are you pumping me for information?"

"Now why would I do that?" I put a hand to my chest in righteous indignation.

"Good question. But since you're the woman who sent a killer to jail, after first putting him in the hospital with a concussion . . ." He gave me a speculative appraisal, as if wondering how a harmless-looking LOL had managed to do that.

"But there's no dead body involved here," I said. A non sequitur, I suppose, but I couldn't think of anything more appropriate.

"True. So let's keep it that way, shall we? No dead bodies."

"I'm all in favor of that."

"And if any of this Braxton clan show up, you remember that it's our job to take care of them, not yours, okay? You call me if you see or hear anything."

I waved his card and smiled brightly to show I was prepared to do exactly that.

"I'll stop by again in a few days," he said.

I watched the pickup disappear down the driveway. A nice man. Concerned. Caring. Helpful. But with a hard core of no-nonsense lawman.

Good. Exactly the type of person I wanted keeping an eye on me.

It was church on Sunday, of course, and afterward some ladies invited me to dinner with them at an all-you-can-eat chuck wagon place. Since I feel financially obligated to eat as much as possible in such eating establishments, I spent the rest of the day in an overstuffed state of lethargy. On Monday I tackled a job I'd brought along, identifying and organizing jumbles of old photos into an album.

But by Tuesday afternoon I was feeling rather at loose ends. Little cooking to do for just me. House all vacuumed. Laundry all washed and folded. A steady drizzle had started. It might be a jogging day if you were a Leslie Marcone, but I didn't want to get out in it. Then I remembered something my mother did every spring, and on impulse I decided it would be a good job for today.

I strung a clothesline across the covered patio between the house and garage, then dragged down the braided rag rugs from my bedroom and draped them over the line.

I didn't have a regular old rug beater like my mother always used, but I got out a broom and started whomping. Oh my, did the dust fly! Whomp, whomp, whomp. Even though the rugs had been vacuumed, whomping gets way down deep where vacuuming never penetrates. And there's a satisfaction in whomping that mechanical vacuuming can never provide.

I'd done the first rug and was starting on the second when

48

I got that peculiar feeling you get, that prickle between your shoulder blades that tells you someone is watching.

The prickle spread to a tightening of my scalp. I paused, broom held upright. When you have Braxtons after you, a feeling of being watched is not good. In a best-case scenario, it means they have your whereabouts targeted. In a worst-case scenario, it means one of them is standing behind you ready to bash you with a 2x4 or put a bullet in your back.

I sprinted through my limited options. Run for the door and lock it? Make a dash for the T-bird and floor the throttle? Drop to the ground and scuttle like a crab to the woodpile?

No time for any of that. Not if my watcher was as close as my between-the-shoulder-blades radar warned.

I took a firm grip on the broom handle and whirled.

# 6

"I saw you from down on the trail. It's a pleasure to see someone taking such a conscientious attitude toward her work. I haven't seen anyone actually beating rugs since I was a little girl at my grandmother's. Did Mrs. Harrington tell you to do this?"

"No, I just thought it needed doing."

"That's very commendable. I admire initiative and hard work."

I lowered the broom and stared in astonishment. The Mystery Woman, who had looked through me before, was now studying me with a faint hint of warmth in her ice-blue eyes. She wasn't actually smiling, but she was speaking to me. In cordial tones.

"Well, uh, thanks," I said.

"You're Mrs. Harrington's housekeeper?" At my blank look, she added with a certain impatience, "This is the Harrington house, isn't it? DeeAnn Harrington, the bookkeeper."

"Yes, but—"

"How much is she paying you?"

I blinked at the blunt question. I could see now that she was somewhat older than I'd thought earlier. At least midthirties.

"Well, uh—"

She waved a dismissive hand, apparently impatient with my stumbling. "My former housekeeper is no longer with me, and I'm looking for a replacement. I believe you would be suitable. Not many housekeepers are industrious and dedicated enough to do what you're doing here. I can offer you more than the Harringtons are paying," she stated, although I'd still given no indication of what my position as the "Harrington's housekeeper" paid.

"You're offering me a job?" I was astonished on several counts, not the least of which was the nerve I felt it took to snatch a housekeeper out from under a current employer's nose. Not that I was an employee, but she thought I was.

"Five hours a day, 9:00 to 2:00, perhaps a little longer if I need you. Six days a week, Sundays off. The usual housekeeping duties, plus you'll prepare my midday meal at 11:30, which I take as the main meal of the day. Eleven dollars an hour. Cash. No health insurance or other benefits."

Having never been a hired housekeeper, nor been in the position to employ one, I had no idea if this amount was paltry or exorbitant. "Don't you want references?"

"My last housekeeper had excellent references. References can be deceiving. I've decided to trust my instincts. I have confidence that a person who beats rugs will do a thorough job in other areas of housekeeping."

"I see."

"You're rather older than I had in mind . . ."

She looked me up and down, as if I were a used refrigerator with a bad dent in the door. But if she thought I was going to supply my age, she was mistaken. Once I arrived at Social Security eligibility, I'd decided further details were unnecessary.

"But it isn't heavy work," she went on. "A cleaning company does the windows."

I stood there holding my broom like a grounded witch, rather astonished that I found myself actually considering accepting Leslie Marcone's unlikely offer. The thought of looking for a job hadn't even occurred to me. A retired librarian is not a hot item in the employment market. Also, given Sandy's view of her and what I'd seen already, I wasn't convinced Leslie Marcone would be an ideal employer.

But there were several good reasons to seriously consider the job. The top one, of course, was the extra money. I am not on easy street with Social Security and a limited amount of CD interest. I did a quick calculation and came up with the fact that I could earn over three hundred per week for what I did all the time anyway. I had extra time on my hands, and if I didn't do *something* I might find myself trapped into quilting.

But I may as well admit the number one reason I was really considering the job. Plain old curiosity. Rampant curiosity, to be honest.

This was, however, the woman who had argued with Dee-Ann over a two-dollar charge on her bill. Did I want to put up with that nitpicking? I tossed out a challenge. "Fourteen dollars an hour."

She split the difference as if she were cutting a diamond. "Twelve-fifty."

At the moment I was making $00.00, and I saw visions of healthy donations to several missionary groups I try to help out occasionally, and maybe a trip to visit DeeAnn and Mike in Hawaii. "Okay. I'll do it."

"I'll be out of town tomorrow. Be at my place at 9:00 on Thursday. Wear quiet shoes. It's that one." She pointed to the white-columned mansion across the lake. "The address is 2742 Vintage Road. I'm Leslie Marcone." She didn't offer to shake hands.

I noted that she also didn't inquire about my transportation or how I planned to handle the matter of leaving my "employer" on such short notice. Not her problem.

But I was, it seemed, now gainfully employed.

With Sandy gone, I didn't have anyone with whom to share my news. On impulse I dug out Dix and Haley's email address and sent them a message through the computer. I doubted the Braxtons could hack into email, but I wasn't sure, which was why I hadn't emailed Dix and Haley before this. I also didn't tell them where I was, just that I was fine and had taken a job. I asked them to pass the message along to my Madison Street neighbors, Magnolia and Geoff, who were computer-less.

That night I had a scare. I woke from a sound sleep to hear a strange moaning, a rustle and whisper. If I believed in ghosts, I might think one had just moved in. I didn't believe in ghosts, of course, but I did believe in Braxtons.

A rasping or scraping. Perhaps even a grating. And there, wasn't that a thud? Grating, scraping, thudding Braxtons? It occurred to me that I'd again forgotten to set the security system for the night.

Sgt. Yates came to mind, but there was no phone on the second floor. I eased out of bed and grabbed the first item I came to on top of the chest of drawers to use for protection until I could reach the phone. I crept out the door and down the hallway toward the sounds, weapon in hand. *Rasp. Whisper. Scrape.* Then I bumped into one of the mattresses Sandy puts down in the hallway for gymnastics practice, and it fell with a gigantic *whoosh*.

I held my breath, waiting for a reaction.

Another scrape. A softer sound. Breathing? I could feel air coming under the closed door to an unused bedroom. An open window? It would take a long extension ladder, but the Braxtons were nothing if not inventive, so access to a second-story window wasn't impossible. Cautiously I opened the door. Faint light filtered through the window from the yard light, revealing a tangle of discarded furniture. An old chimney from before the house was remodeled went through the wall here. The wind was blowing, I realized now. Waving branches flickered shadows outside the window.

I stopped and sorted out the sounds. Vines growing on the back side of the house rustling and scraping against the wall. Wind moaning through the old chimney and slipping around the loose window. A branch whapping against the roof.

No intruders, just the old house making windy-night noises. And me, wandering on the outskirts of Paranoid-ville again.

I went back to my bedroom, stopping along the way to wrestle the mattress upright. I turned on the light, embarrassed to see that I'd grabbed a curling iron as my weapon of defense. What would I have done if I'd actually met an intruder? Curled him into submission? Probably not. But perhaps I could have scared him into flight with threat of a beehive hairdo.

The following morning, with the windstorm passed over and sunshine blazing, I rummaged around in the shed attached to the garage and found a pair of hand clippers. I attacked the bushes Sgt. Yates had said should be trimmed. A very satisfying job, watching bits of shrubbery fly. No Braxtons were going to hide here!

Standing back to appraise my work when I finished the last bush just before lunch, I realized I may have overdone it a bit with the clippers. These bushes now had a buzz cut worthy of the Marine Corps. But certainly they'd offer no concealment for Braxtons.

Then I was really annoyed with myself. *Enough with the Braxtons!* I'd let them disturb my sleep last night. I'd let them color my attitude toward every stranger. Because of them, I'd scalped these poor shrubs down to baseball size.

Yes, I was hiding out here, but I was not going to let the Braxtons monopolize my life. *Braxtons, be gone!*

After a fruit and yogurt lunch, during which I contemplated Leslie Marcone's remark that she would be away for the day, I came up with a perfectly sensible reason to take a jaunt over to Vintage Road. I wouldn't want to get lost tomorrow morning and be late for my first day of work, would I?

Vintage Road was paved and turned out to be easy to find—the specific number, 2742, less so. Most of the estates had imaginative and impressive address markings. Numbers burned in rustic wood, etched in bronze on a plaque across a wagon wheel, printed on a heart-shaped sign held aloft by a fiberglass bear. Some places had names: Hickory Acres. Barringer House. Digby's Retreat. But the only identification on 2742 consisted of tiny white numbers painted on a black mailbox by a wrought iron gate—no name. Just beyond that was a glossy No Trespassing, Violators Will Be Prosecuted sign.

Now I understood why, if the man with binoculars was trying to get a look at Leslie Marcone's place, he'd done it from across the lake. From here, all that was visible of the house were some indistinct splotches of white through a tangle of trees and vines and brush, apparently native growth left in place when the house was built.

Across the road a man wearing a protective white mask was attacking vegetation along the road ditch with a noisy weed eater. I uneasily wondered if this was the ill-tempered gate rammer, but his back was to me, and I didn't have to pass him to turn in at the asphalt driveway on Leslie's place. So, hopefully, he wouldn't notice me. A stand of pretty spring flowers disappeared under the roaring machine as I watched.

A gate barred the driveway, and, confirming what Sgt. Yates had said, it looked new. At least eight feet high, spiked on top, and anchored by impressive brick gateposts, it appeared to have a system where you had to either punch proper numbers for entry into a pad or speak into an intercom box so someone inside could release an electronic lock. The long driveway went straight down toward the water, apparently to the disputed boat landing. A ribbon of asphalt curved off to the right, circling the house. I already knew the house faced the lake.

The gate appeared to be more precautionary than high security, however, designed primarily to keep unwelcome vehicles out. The white boards of the fence angling away from the gate would be easy enough to crawl through.

I was strongly tempted to do that. After all, this was my new place of employment, and the no trespassing surely didn't apply to me. Shouldn't I become familiar with the grounds? While I was still considering that, however, a mechanical apparition suddenly appeared at my window. I jumped so hard the seat belt almost cut off my breathing.

I touched my throat when the apparition, which I now realized was the working end of a weed eater, was replaced by a florid face with sour lines that sagged into heavy jowls. The protective mask now dangled on an elastic cord around the man's neck.

Warily I rolled down the window a few inches.

"You the lawyer from Little Rock?" he demanded through the narrow opening.

If he hadn't just scared the wits out of me, I might have been less tart with him. As it was, I snapped, "Do I look like a lawyer from Little Rock?"

"Well, no," he acknowledged. He also apparently hadn't noticed my Missouri license plates. "But that Marcone woman said she was hiring a woman lawyer who was gonna sue the shirt off my back."

The shirt off his back hardly looked worth suing for. It was grass-stained denim, his equally grass-stained work pants held up by a length of dirty cord. However, assuming he owned property here in Vintage Estates, even if it wasn't one of the pricier waterfront places, he must be better fixed financially than the clothing would indicate.

Just to be certain who he was, I said, "And you are . . . ?"

"A neighbor. Milo Eagan. Been here for thirty years, long before all these people with more money than sense moved in. The owner here and I have had some . . . ah . . . differences."

"So I've heard."

"I've already paid for her new gate." He shot the offending metal barrier a baleful glance. "But she says I caused her mental anguish and stress and all that baloney."

"I see. Well, I hope everything works out satisfactorily." I wanted to maintain a neutral status. If he'd attack a gate with a pickup, maybe he'd take on a Thunderbird with a weed eater.

"I don't know who you are, lady, but whatever dealings you got with this barracuda, watch out," he growled.

"I'm the new housekeeper. I was just . . . locating the address today."

"Maybe you oughta find out what happened to the last housekeeper," he suggested darkly.

I changed my mind about an excursion beyond the gate and put the car in gear. "It's been nice meeting you," I said brightly.

"Shyster lawyers aren't the only way to settle things," he muttered and strode away, weed eater roaring to life again when he reached the far side of Vintage Road. Another stand of purple flowers bit the dust.

And I drove home, wondering, *What did happen to the last housekeeper?*

# 7

I wasn't certain what Leslie Marcone meant about "quiet shoes," but my brown oxfords had never made any impertinent remarks, so I hoped they would be satisfactory.

I allowed myself plenty of time and arrived at 2742 Vintage Road at 8:50. I waited seven minutes before getting out and approaching the intercom box. Instinct told me Leslie Marcone would rank lateness down there with slothfulness, but for all I knew perhaps she would find earliness equally objectionable. I was relieved that Milo Eagan and his formidable weed eater did not jump out of the bushes at me.

I spoke into the box and identified myself. The box didn't answer, but after a few moments the gate swung open. I drove through. The gate closed behind me. I squelched the uneasy image of a dungeon gate clanging shut.

The long driveway wasn't steep, except for a sharp dip at the bottom near the water, but a careless or disoriented driver might easily barrel directly into the lake. Especially with that boathouse, which looked uncannily like a shrunken-head version of the main house. I took the loop that went around the house, parked in back under a dark pine, and rang a bell. A fairly long interval passed before Leslie Marcone opened the door. Here at home she was in a blue cable-knit sweater that almost shouted an expensive price tag, but her faded, baggy jeans and scruffy slippers looked more like Goodwill discards.

"If this arrangement proves satisfactory, I'll provide you with a remote control for the gate, and you may enter the house by this door without ringing the bell so as not to disturb me. I'll have it unlocked for you."

She led the way into the kitchen, which, in contrast to the untended jungle between the house and road, was almost surgically sterile. Spotless white cabinets with the narrowest of gold trim, gray granite countertops, an enormous central work island surrounded by a pale hardwood floor. No colorful decorations, no bright curtains at the windows, not a live green plant in sight. Not even a phony plant, for that matter.

I wasn't certain I could operate the enormous kitchen stove. It looked as if it might require an engineering degree. I wondered where the refrigerator was located, since I couldn't see one. Leslie opened a side door into what I'd call a pantry, although architects may give it some more upscale name now. The shelves were almost bare. Leslie Marcone obviously was not a worried survivalist stocking up for coming disasters.

She led me farther into the house while outlining my duties. I would daily vacuum the areas of the house in regular use; once a week would suffice for the unused rooms. She waved a hand toward a grandly curved staircase, the only part of the interior of the house that truly seemed to go with the Southern-plantation exterior. Apparently the unused rooms were up there somewhere.

"You are not, under any circumstances, to answer the

phone," she said sternly. "If it rings and I don't answer it, just let it ring."

A bit peculiar, but none of my business. I also didn't see any proliferation of phones to ring.

The floors were all bare hardwood, not even a throw rug. I now saw the point of quiet, non-squeaking shoes. Those hardwood floors were to be waxed every two weeks, kitchen floor waxed at least twice a week, equipment for waxing purposes in a utility room off the kitchen. The living room furniture was mostly white leather, the draperies a pale peach. No bright throw pillows. A huge, sterile-looking fireplace was also white. A few paintings, which appeared to have been chosen mostly for their size and wall-covering capability rather than their generic landscape content, decorated the walls. An enormous chandelier made of dangling spears of crystal hung over a bleached oak dining table with matching chairs for twelve. A railed balcony overhung the living room. The ceiling was so far away I wanted to cup a hand around my mouth and call "Yoo-hoo, anyone up there?"

The far side of the lake was visible through the expanse of windows, but I couldn't pick out DeeAnn's house. Its earthy coloring and shake roof did not stand out from the woodsy setting like the plantation white of this house did from the other side of the lake.

The master bedroom did have carpet. White, of course. A quilted satin bedspread in ice blue covered the king-sized bed. The bed was unmade, although its unmussed state suggested that Leslie didn't churn around in her sleep the way I did. I wondered if the sheets were also satin. I'd soon find out, because Leslie informed me that the sheets should be changed twice a week, starting today. The walk-in closet would make roomy quarters for a dozen homeless people. And the white-and-gold, marble-floored bathroom with whirlpool tub would do nicely for communal bathing and showering.

"I bought the place already furnished and decorated," Leslie said with a small furrowing of brow, and I couldn't tell if she was apologizing or congratulating herself. I was also coming to the conclusion that she wasn't really familiar with household staff and their duties. Her attitude was definitely imperial, but there was also a certain defiance in it, something that said "This may not be the way you've seen it done in other rich households, but this is how I want it done."

I thought about inquiring about the former housekeeper, but I decided that was probably none of my business and confined my questions to work duties. I didn't see any braided rugs that needed beating, so it seemed my talents in that area were superfluous.

One room surprised me. Here, dramatic hunter green drapes decorated the windows, and dark shelves lined the walls. A library, obviously. The shelves were bare, but dozens of boxes of books were stacked around the room and on the dark mahogany, library-style table. I wondered if Leslie had done what I understand some people who have more money than literary preferences do: buy books by the yard to fill up their shelves.

"My father's library," she said, relieving me of that unkind suspicion. "I inherited it a couple of years ago. Books were his passion."

Something in her tone gave me an unexpected vision of a lonely child ignored by a father who preferred books to little girls.

In a rare moment of uncertainty she frowned and added, "I haven't decided exactly what to do with the books or how they should be organized and shelved. There's a master list of the titles and authors around here somewhere. Some of them are trash, but a few are worth a fair amount of money."

"Perhaps I can help." I surreptitiously peered at a title visible in an open box. Jack London's *White Fang*. Very old looking. Maybe even a first edition! I felt a surge of excitement. "I was a librarian up in Missouri for some thirty years before my retirement."

"Oh? Well, we'll see. Your housekeeping duties come first."

I caught the translation: don't waste time in here with books when the toilet bowl needs cleaning.

"Did I mention that you may take a fifteen-minute break at midmorning?"

"Thank you. Do you like to read?"

"I read some useful nonfiction occasionally, but I've never been the reader my father was. I consider novels a waste of time. And these paperbacks certainly aren't worth bothering with."

She picked a John Grisham out of a box of paperbacks and flicked through the pages with disdainful scorn. She tossed the book back in the box. Obviously we wouldn't be discussing my favorite mystery authors. We moved on.

The only room that actually looked lived in was what she called the den, obviously more accurately an office. It held an imposing array of computer equipment, a file cabinet, a couple of large folding tables, a fax machine, a scanner, and a large, professional-looking copier. (No more two-dollar charges from insubordinate bookkeepers?)

But it was the messy array of papers and scattered manila folders that really startled me, so unlike the pristine sterility of the other rooms in the house. I mean, this room looked as if a mischievous child had been playing paper Frisbee. A rumpled blanket and pillow on a sofa suggested Leslie even slept in this room occasionally. She did not offer to explain what she did here, of course, but I was mildly relieved by the clutter. It suggested Leslie Marcone had a human streak after all. Maybe she even forgot to shave her legs occasionally.

I could tell from the steady green light that the computer

was on, but the screen was dark, not revealing what she'd been doing.

"You needn't bother cleaning in here unless I specifically request it," she said, dousing any hopes I might have of finding out what the clutter was all about.

Back in the kitchen, she repeated what she'd said when offering me the job, that her midday meal should be served at 11:30. "I'm up by 5:00 or earlier, so I prefer to eat early. This also allows sufficient time between the meal and my afternoon exercise."

"You're a very dedicated jogger. I've seen you on the trail almost every day."

"Oh?" She looked down her nose at me, figuratively if not literally, and I suspected I wasn't the first trail walker she'd ignored. "I don't care to interrupt my exercise with irrelevant chitchat."

Equal-opportunity snubbing. Very democratic.

Back in the kitchen, she reached for a handle on one of the cabinets, which turned out to be the hiding place of the refrigerator. I mentally marked its location, afraid I might not be able to find it again in the long expanse of cabinetry.

"I'll handle the grocery shopping myself. You will not be involved with that. I prefer my meat rare and my vegetables crisp. A fruit-based dessert two or three times a week is acceptable." She tilted her head, as if considering something, and finally added, "On rare occasions, perhaps something chocolate."

Another I-am-human-after-all streak. I was pleased.

I'd pegged Leslie as a vegetarian. It seemed to go with her spartan exercise routine. Not so. From the looks of the immaculate refrigerator shelves Leslie was definitely a red meat eater. Steak, chops, a small roast, all very lean. Canadian-style bacon, again very lean. The vegetables were ordinary, non-exotic varieties: lettuce, tomatoes, green peppers, cucumbers, broccoli, cabbage. Although there was some green stuff I didn't recognize, and I figured those out-of-season peaches in the crisper must have cost a fortune.

Leslie Marcone, I decided with some bemusement, was a woman of unexpected contradictions in all areas of her life.

She went back to her computer, closing the door behind her. After figuring out the central vacuum system, I vacuumed, dusted, cleaned the bathroom, and changed the sheets on the bed. No, the sheets were not satin. But definitely a more expensive cotton than my Penney's variety. None of the cleaning appeared to me to really *need* doing. I had no idea how long she'd been without a housekeeper, but dirt had not accumulated. But then, I suppose I'm a bit on the dirt-tolerant side; I had dust bunnies under the bed back on Madison Street that could have applied for old-age pensions.

For her meal, I broiled the sirloin steak, dressed up a baked potato with bacon bits and cheese, and made a salad. I tossed in some of the unknown green stuff after testing and finding it had a nice peppery taste. Apple tart for dessert.

She made no comments about the meal, but she left nothing uneaten on the plate, so I took that as approval. She didn't say what I was supposed to do about my own lunch, so I skipped it. I asked if she'd like me to prepare something and leave it for her supper. She said no, but I did wrap what was left of the tart and put it in the refrigerator.

At 2:00, after I managed to locate and use the dishwasher, I knocked on the closed door of the den. "I'll be leaving now, unless you need me to stay longer . . . ?"

"Not today. After this you needn't inform me when you're leaving."

On my way out I peeked in the garage and saw a light blue Mercedes parked in a space that would easily hold four vehicles. It looked lonely in there all by itself.

The same could be said of Leslie in her big house.

I had to go through town to get around to the far side of the lake, which took me past the roofing manufacturer where Mike had been employed. I splurged on a Hawaiian pizza for a late lunch, chatted with some folks from church at the pizza parlor, and picked up a few items at the grocery store. Out of curiosity, I detoured through the city park on the way home. Leslie's Mercedes was there, imperiously angled across two parking spaces to keep other vehicles from getting too close.

I looked at the clock when I got home. Three-thirty here. Which meant it was . . . what in Hawaii? Midmorning? I dialed DeeAnn's number. She was in the middle of trying to figure out what to do with some poi she'd acquired, but she said it could wait. "Maybe it will improve with age," she said philosophically. "Right now it tastes like that old flour-paste goop Sandy and I used to mix up when she was about four years old."

We chatted for a few minutes about Sandy's trip and other doings here, and then I got down to the real purpose of my call.

# 8

"You did some work for this rather mysterious woman who lives across the lake, didn't you? Leslie Marcone?"

"Oh, yes." I heard a roll of eyes in her tone.

"Would it be breaking any confidences to tell me about her?"

"Why would you want to know about her?"

"Because I'm her new housekeeper."

"Housekeeper!" DeeAnn echoed. "Leslie Marcone's house-keeper?"

She sounded as if she wouldn't be any more astounded if I'd announced I was the new bartender at a local tavern. In a miniskirt. I explained how this had come about and added what I thought were the magic words. "She's paying me twelve-fifty an hour."

"Well, that is generous for Woodston," DeeAnn conceded. "Did she have you fill out any forms, such as a W-4 for the IRS?"

"No."

"Figures. That was the sticking point between us. What I did was help her set up a system to keep track of her stock market purchases and sales—"

"Oh, that's what she's doing in there on the computer all day!"

"She isn't actually one of those high-powered day traders, but she does a considerable amount of buying and selling."

"Doesn't the broker keep track of all that?"

"I should think so. Unless discount brokers on the Internet operate differently. In any case, she wanted her own record-keeping system as well."

"I don't think Leslie is a very . . . ummm . . . trusting person. I'm sure she'd want to have her own records so she could check everything down to the penny."

"My sentiments exactly." After a thoughtful pause she added, "Makes you wonder, doesn't it? Is she untrusting because someone betrayed her trust? Or because she betrayed someone else's trust and figures everyone is out to do the same thing to her?"

I hadn't thought that deeply about Leslie's peculiarities, but it did make me wonder. Though careful record keeping could have nothing to do with trust and mean only that she was a cautious person.

"Anyway, that part of our business relationship was more or less okay, although she was so secretive that it was difficult getting enough information out of her to set things up properly. Then I learned she was hiring a new housekeeper."

"How often does she do this?" I asked, alarmed.

"My impression is that she flips them like hotcakes. But, as you know, my attitude toward Leslie is not exactly unprejudiced. Anyway, I asked if she'd like me to make sure her records were set up properly to take care of taxes and Social Security and everything for an employee. She said no, that wouldn't be necessary. I pointed out that, legally, she had to keep records and pay her half of the employee's Social Security. I photocopied some of the regulations and gave them to her."

Which probably explained the two-dollar charge that had Leslie foaming at the mouth.

"She said that was ridiculous, and that if I weren't such an incompetent bookkeeper I'd know how to get around such bureaucratic nonsense. At that point, I decided it would be best to terminate our relationship. I didn't want to find myself implicated in any questionable maneuvers concerning employees or stock transactions. I suppose I also took exception to being called incompetent."

"Can I keep track of my earnings and take care of the taxes and Social Security myself?"

"That should keep you out of hot water. Though I don't know that it will help Leslie if they catch up with her." Dee-Ann hesitated a moment and then added, "Watch out for her. I wouldn't put it past her to—"

She broke off, and after a moment of silence I prompted her with, "To what?"

"Oh, I don't know." DeeAnn laughed as if embarrassed about her melodramatic warning. "Just be careful, okay? She's sharp. And not above bending—or breaking—the rules."

"Do you know how she acquired all her money?"

"No, and I have to admit I've certainly wondered. Not on the stock market, because she hadn't been into trading for long when I set up the bookkeeping system for her. I thought maybe she received a big inheritance."

Possible. That theory went along with what Leslie had said about inheriting her father's library. Although she didn't strike me as having come from old money. The thought then occurred to me that she may have won some huge award in a lawsuit. She'd apparently been quick enough to think "sue" in relation to the gate-ramming neighbor. And there was always Sandy's theory about her grabbing some "rich old guy's" money in a divorce. "You wouldn't happen to know who her former housekeeper was, would you?"

"She's had several, but the last I heard Cass Diedrich was working for her. Cass brings her kids to Sunday school sometimes, but she doesn't usually stay for church."

"Maybe I'll look her up."

"Everything going okay for you otherwise?" DeeAnn asked. "No problems with the Braxtons?"

"I'm not even thinking about Braxtons these days," I assured her.

"Good. Tell Sandy to call when she gets time."

Friday and Saturday also went fine at Leslie's. By Saturday, when the remainder of the tart still hadn't been eaten, I tossed it and made a mental note for future reference: Leslie did not eat leftovers.

I also made another discovery. While doing the once-a-week requisite cleaning of the unused rooms upstairs, I found, as Skye had once speculated, one room equipped with enough exercise machines to turn a whole herd of Dumplings from fat to fit. I could identify a treadmill, but how the other machines worked escaped me. They had weights and pulleys and springs and belts. Probably, I decided, for muscle groups I didn't even possess.

Checking with Leslie first, I managed to spend a few minutes in the treasure trove of boxes in the library on Saturday. Oh, my. Everything from Dickens and Longfellow to Steinbeck and Ellery Queen!

She'd told me I didn't have to notify her when I left, but I ventured a peek through the door at 2:00 to say I'd see her on Monday, in case she'd forgotten I didn't come Sundays. The office door was open today, which I presumed was because the stock market was closed on Saturday and her privacy and/or concentration were not such a high priority.

"I appreciate that I have Sunday off," I added.

She picked up an envelope on her desk and handed it to me. It rustled nicely. My partial week's pay!

"Thank you."

"Oh, and this—" She reached in a drawer, pulled out a dark oblong thing that looked a little bit like a TV remote control, and handed it to me. "It's for the gate. I mentioned earlier that I'd give you one."

Yes, if our arrangement proved satisfactory. No word about the status of my work, but, with Leslie, I suspected this gesture took the place of words. I felt quite elated.

"There's a numerical keypad on it," she added, "but it's programmed and all you have to do is punch that button at the top."

"Thank you. I was thinking . . . I go to Woodston Community Church. If you aren't already attending somewhere else, it's a lovely little church, everyone very welcoming and friendly—"

"I get up early six days of the week, so on Sundays I allow myself to sleep in. If the weather is good, I sometimes jog in the morning instead of the afternoon. The trail is less crowded."

Obviously a no, although it came with an explanation, which was unusual for none-of-your-business Leslie.

"In the eternal scheme of things a relationship with the Lord is more important than rising early or extra sleep. Or even exercise," I offered gently.

"I don't believe in eternity."

And the door closed in my face.

A discouraging reaction, but not necessarily final, I decided optimistically. Yet I couldn't help feeling sorry for her, as I do

71

for anyone who doesn't live with the wonderful expectation of eternity with the Lord.

On the way home I saw a pickup parked at the house where elderly Lois Watkins had lived before her death. A man was lugging a couple of bulky garbage bags from the house to the pickup. Her son, I assumed, with the sad task of sorting through her things.

On impulse, after I got home, I walked over to express my sympathies.

I introduced myself, identifying my connection with Dee-Ann and Mike and motioning to their house down the road where I lived now. He identified himself as Hanson Watkins, the son. We shook hands, his a solid, big-handed grip that swallowed mine. He was fiftyish, a large man with an over-hanging belly, balding head, and an open, good-natured face that showed lines of wear and tear at the moment.

"I'm so sorry about your mother. I didn't know Lois well, but I usually stopped in to see her when I was visiting here. She was such a sweet woman, always so cheerful even though her arthritis must have been painful. She was very proud of you."

"Yeah, the only son. To Mom I could do no wrong." He smiled ruefully. "But I keep thinking now that I did do wrong. I should have insisted she come out to California and live with Marianne and me. Then maybe this wouldn't have happened."

"Most of us cling to living in our own homes, even if to an outsider it looks as if we'd be better off elsewhere. Lois was happy here. She never thought she was neglected."

"That's kind of you. You're the one I see driving around in that great old Thunderbird, aren't you? When I was a teenager, that was my big dream, to own a T-bird."

"It's been a little balky at times lately. I'll probably have to take it in for a checkup."

"Maybe I can take a look at it while I'm here. I'm no expert, but I can tell an oil filter from an air filter and fix a few little things."

"Will you be here long?"

"The house needs some repairs before we put it up for sale, so I'm working on that. But I have to take care of things with my plumbing supply business back home in San Bernardino too, so I'll be flying back and forth."

"Sounds difficult."

"I have to see about selling Mom's old motor home too. She hadn't used it since Dad died, of course, but she never wanted to get rid of it. And then there's all the lawyer stuff." His disgruntled tone offered a wordless commentary on "lawyer stuff," and I could sympathize, having been through some lawyer stuff when Harley died.

"But the legal end shouldn't be too complicated," he added. "Mom had already transferred almost everything to me."

"That should help. It's been nice meeting you. Again, I'm so sorry about your mother."

I walked home on the road so I could go by the mailbox at the end of the driveway. Most of it was for DeeAnn and Mike, of course, items I'd stick in a larger envelope and send on. A few pieces had been forwarded from the Madison Street address for me: a final bill for the electricity on the house, a solicitation from a charity and several other advertisements, and a postcard. From Mac.

The picture side was a photo of a car standing upright, nose to the sky, tail end buried in the ground. Behind it were several similarly half-buried vehicles in kind of a vehicular Stonehenge arrangement.

On the opposite side of the card Mac had written: *This made me think of you.*

A half dozen vehicles with their rear ends buried in the

dirt reminded him of me? I didn't get the connection. And wasn't flattered by whatever it was.

Then I looked more closely at the vehicles. Thunderbirds! Old Thunderbirds, every one of them, along with a title: Texas T-Bird Ranch. I smiled then. Thunderbirds had reminded him of me. *Okay.*

The remainder of the message said that he would be in Missouri to do an article on Lake of the Ozarks sometime in the next few weeks and would give me a call.

I'd met Mac MacPherson through Magnolia and Geoff back on Madison Street. They had met him on one of their many excursions into genealogy by motor home. He lives full time in his motor home and wanders the country doing articles for travel magazines. We had what I thought was a nicely companionable relationship. Then, with some abruptness, he took off for Montana, and all I'd ever heard from him since was another postcard and a copy of one of his travel articles.

Magnolia, who knew other RV people who knew him, eventually muttered that he had "commitment issues." Frankly, I found this a bit insulting. He was afraid I wanted to wrap him in a wedding ring and apron strings? We were barely more than acquaintances!

So now he was going to be in Missouri in a few weeks. With nothing more than a Texas postmark, no return address or other contact information, I had no way to tell him I was *not* in Missouri.

*Well, so much for Mac MacPherson,* I thought with mixed feelings of regret and relief that I wouldn't be seeing him and having to muddle around in awkward "commitment issues."

Thinking of Mac reminded me of another man back in Missouri. Jordan Kaine was a retired lawyer I'd met through mutual involvement in a vandalism situation at a rural cemetery. We'd had a brief but budding relationship that was cut short when I had to go into hiding before the murder trial, the trial that brought on the Braxtons' thirst for vengeance.

The phone was ringing as I unlocked the door. I started to fumble with the security alarm panel, realized guiltily that I'd forgotten to set it again, and headed for the phone.

"Hi! May I speak to Sandy please?"

"I'm sorry, but Sandy is gone for the week. She won't be home until Sunday evening."

"Oh, I didn't know! Skye didn't mention it."

She sounded dismayed, so I said, "Could I help with anything?"

"Oh, I don't suppose so. This is Tammi Ridenour."

"Skye's . . ." I hesitated momentarily and then decided not to split hairs. "Skye's mother?"

"Yes, that's right!" Tammi sounded delighted with the identification, perhaps mistakenly concluding that Skye had referred to her as a mother. "Oh, you must be Aunt Ivy!"

Tammi apparently had an oversupply of exclamation points and intended to use all of them.

"Yes, that's me. Ivy Malone."

"Skye went in to Fayetteville with Brad this afternoon. He's trying to interest her in TV as a career. I just now decided it would be great fun to run in and surprise them so we could all have dinner together after the early news! But I need someone to sit with Baby. That's why I was calling Sandy."

Maybe I was feeling adventurous. Maybe the evening ahead looked a little lonely. Maybe it was just that troublesome curiosity gene again. "I'd be happy to sit with Baby."

"Would you? Oh, that would be marvelous! I need to leave in about an hour and a half, so . . ."

"Just give me directions to the house."

She did that, and then I cautiously asked, "Is there, uh,

anything special I need to know or should bring for . . . sitting with Baby?"

"Not that I know of." She sounded mildly puzzled.

"I've never met Baby, you know," I said, fishing.

"But you've heard all about him, I'm sure!" she said gaily and hung up before I could admit that I had no idea if Baby was animal, vegetable, or mineral.

I speculated, of course, as I followed Tammi's directions to 422 Hickory an hour later. Something in the animal category, surely. But perhaps on the unusual side? A monkey, maybe? Parrot? Iguana?

The thought occurred to me that perhaps I should have pinned down this detail before blithely leaping into this.

# 9

The house on Hickory was low and rambling, an L-shape built around a big backyard with a high board fence. The height of the fence alarmed me. Perhaps Baby belonged in the giraffe or camel category? A coppery-colored Lincoln sat in the driveway.

I rang the bell, and a plump woman who had to be Tammi opened the door. But the woman was instantly eclipsed by the animal beside her. A dog? It did have the usual doggy attributes. Four legs, furry body, wagging tail, soulful brown eyes, and a damp nose instantly thrust into my hand.

Although this animal could almost as easily have thrust his nose into mine.

"This is Baby," Tammi said with obvious pride. "And the first thing everyone wants to know, of course, is, how big *is* he? So I'll tell you! He's 31 inches tall at the shoulder and weighs 260 pounds! And if he stands on his hind feet, he's taller than you or me!"

Here her oversupply of exclamation points almost seemed justified.

"He was only six weeks old when we got him. And he was such a soft, adorable little butterball that we just had to call him Baby. And then the name stuck."

"He's certainly . . . impressive. Is he . . . uh . . . some particular breed?" Or perhaps some mad-scientist combination of dog and pony? His tan hair was short but thick and rough rather than slick, his tail a darker bushy flag, his face and neck mottled with irregular splotches of brown.

"Mostly English mastiff, although he has smidgens of various other breeds. We think the brown may come from some St. Bernard blood. Although no one knows where that tail came from! His mother weighed only 175 pounds, and none of his littermates turned out nearly as big as he is."

"I hope he's good-natured?"

"Oh, he is! Baby loves to chase balls and wrestle on the floor and play with his teddy bear. And Baby loves everybody! Tell Aunt Ivy hello, Baby."

Baby, very dignified, offered me a huge paw. With some reservations I shook it, although I noted that his nails were nicely manicured. Tammi stood back and motioned me inside the house. By now, after the initial shock of Baby's size, I noted that Tammi was dressed for dinner. The tight, bright red dress complemented her fluffy dark hair, but . . . oh, dear . . . also emphasized every one of those plump pounds. Spike heels, apparently meant to slenderize her legs, unfortunately turned her feet into chubby stubs. But she also had a lovely, warm smile, a rose-petal complexion, dazzling white teeth, and, overall, was something of an adorable butterball herself.

"It's so nice of you to do this!" She squeezed my arm. "Brad usually stays in Fayetteville between the early and late news shows, so we don't often have dinner together. And it just seemed like a lovely idea to run in and join them, the three of us together!"

I wondered if Skye had perhaps been counting on dinner alone with her father, but I only murmured, "Yes, a lovely idea."

"We didn't talk about a sitting fee, but I always give—"

I waved a hand in dismissal. "That isn't necessary. I'm glad to do it." Although a thought occurred to me, now that I'd met Baby and he did seem like such a polite, well-mannered gentleman. "Why does Baby need a sitter?"

"Baby is very people sensitive." She gave his big head an affectionate rough-housing. "If anyone is home, he's quite happy to run and play in the backyard by himself. But if everyone leaves, he *knows* and immediately protests! Quite loudly, I'm afraid."

Deep-chested Baby looked as if he could make enough noisy protest to start an earthquake.

"Which the neighbors object to, I suppose?"

"Very much so. As if their children don't sometimes raise enough ruckus to—" She rolled her baby blue eyes and smiled. "Well, never mind. In any case, it's better that Baby not be left outside when no one is home."

"And inside?"

"Inside, he tends to . . . ummm . . . take out his frustration at being left behind on the furniture and carpet. He does love to go riding and stick his nose out the window."

*In what?* I wondered. Did they keep a Hummer in reserve for dog entertainment?

"But Baby can smile." She stretched her mouth, baring her teeth, and Baby did the same. I'm glad I knew it was a smile, because there seemed to be an extraordinary number of teeth in Baby's oversized mouth.

"And he's just the biggest, sweetest, friendliest baby ever! Show Aunt Ivy your caterpillar walk."

I appreciated that, in spite of all the exclamation points, Tammi was not into baby talk. She moved back a few steps and trailed her hand—bright red polish, big diamond engagement and wedding rings a little tight on her plump hand— along the carpet. Baby immediately dropped his belly to the floor. With legs stretched out behind him, front paws digging into the carpet, he scooted toward her, along the way cheerfully wiggling across whatever got in his way, which included my feet and a ragged teddy bear that was apparently one of his toys.

"His food is on the counter in the kitchen. You can give it to him about 8:00. He'll let you know if he wants to go outside. Otherwise, just enjoy! There are people snacks on the counter and in the refrigerator. Help yourself to anything!"

"Thank you."

"The TV remote is over there on the sofa. Baby will probably want to sit with you and put his head in your lap while you watch. Or there are magazines and books there on the coffee table if you'd rather read. I have tons of books, but they're mostly on diet and exercise, and I can see you don't need that!"

She bustled around gathering up purse, cell phone, and jacket. Baby watched her, tail swishing softly on the carpet. I wondered uneasily if the minute she was out the door he might turn into a rabid psycho-dog, a Woodston Cujo. But Sandy had Baby-sat him, apparently without disaster.

"My cell phone number is over there on the end table by the phone. Don't hesitate to call me if you need anything." She patted her purse where she'd tucked the cell phone. "I won't stay in town for the late news, so I should be home by 10:00 or so. Bye, Baby." She leaned over and nuzzled the big dog's face. Not many women, I suspected, would be so agreeable to a slurp of doggy tongue across fresh makeup.

At the door she turned and gave me a little wave, looking

as excited as a teenager going out on a date. "You know, we just *love* Sandy! She's such a good influence on Skye."

I watched the Lincoln pull out of the driveway, and then Baby and I regarded each other gravely. He offered his paw again, and I shook it. No, no psycho-dog here, just a big sweetie.

We watched TV together. I hadn't realized that when Tammi said he'd sit with me, she meant exactly that. Draped right beside me on the wildly flowered sofa with his head and one big paw in my lap. I suspected sofa cushions had to be replaced regularly here, but if Tammi and husband didn't mind, I certainly didn't.

After a while Baby wanted to go out in the backyard. Stacked lumber and concrete blocks suggested some ongoing building project. Perhaps an oversized doghouse for Baby? He brought me a ball to throw, and he romped and played with surprising agility for his size. Later I fed him the dog chow Tammi had put out, and while he ate I snacked on cheesecake squares.

I flipped through several of Tammi's diet and exercise books piled on the coffee table. Everything from Pilates to the Atkins diet, with a bizarre offshoot into *Weight Loss Secrets from Atlantis: Amazing Discoveries from a Lost Continent* with a svelte mermaid on the cover. The book that looked as if it might be the most effective at weight reduction, however, was the heavyweight one Sandy had mentioned. It featured a cover model of a sleek cat and weighed, if not the ten pounds Sandy had claimed, at least six or seven. If Tammi lifted that book overhead enough times a day, she'd surely change some fat into muscle.

Tammi was home at 9:50, coming in like a tornado of bubbles to first greet Baby as if she hadn't seen him in a month and then to give me a hug.

"Oh, we had a marvelous time! I'm afraid I may have

overdone it just a wee bit on the shrimp pasta." She touched her tummy and rolled her eyes. "But I'll make up for it with a zillion stomach crunches next week. Thank you so much. I can't begin to tell you how much I appreciate this!"

"My pleasure," I said. And it really was. Even at 260 pounds, Baby was still an adorable butterball. "Maybe I'll have to fight Sandy for the privilege of sitting with Baby next time."

Sandy returned home Sunday evening, bubbling with news of all they'd accomplished at the orphanage, plus their adventures with a blown transmission on the van, a bout of something called Montezuma's Revenge, and her encounter with a scorpion. In which she was, blessedly, the victor. She now had a smattering of Spanish tucked in to her chatter. She also had a black and blue thumbnail courtesy of an encounter with a stray hammer, a glowing tan, and the email addresses of half a dozen new friends.

I had my news too, and she stared at me open-mouthed when I told her I was working for Leslie Marcone.

"She really seems quite nice." That sounded a little lame, since Sandy's expression said I may as well have started housekeeping for the creepy woman in that *Misery* movie "And she pays well. And promptly!"

"Yeah. Well, uh, that's nice. I didn't know you wanted a job."

"I didn't either. But then she offered, and I thought, why not? And then Tammi called and I also Baby-sat."

Sandy's faint scowl brightened. This met with her approval. "Oh, don't you just love Baby?"

"Yes, and Tammi's nice too. It's too bad she and Skye aren't closer."

"Oh, that reminds me. I want to call Skye."

Sandy dashed off to make the call, and I picked up the oblong of paper that blew off the counter as she rushed by. Mac's postcard. I felt an unexpected twinge of regret. Okay, so he might have a skewed view of my intentions toward him, but it really would have been nice to see him again. We'd had fun at the Meteor Daze over in Clancy last summer.

At 9:00 on Monday, I was back at work. On this day a gardener came and industriously clipped and mowed on the grounds between house and lake. Leslie apparently liked the manicured look there rather than the tangle of au naturel jungle between house and road. Today I used my fifteen-minute break to stroll out on the dock, where I hadn't ventured before.

Up close, the imitation Southern plantation boathouse looked even more pretentious and ridiculous than it did from the house. A brass padlock on a chain guarded the door. I peeked through a crack around the door and saw only a small boat, no bigger than Mike and DeeAnn's skiff, inside. It was suspended above the water in a kind of webbed cradle. Like the lone Mercedes in the huge garage, it looked undersized and lonesome.

The water got deeper much faster here than it did on the other side of the lake, I realized as I peered into the greenish depths at the end of the dock. From here, I could pick out DeeAnn's house on the far side of the lake. Someone was standing on the tiny dock there. Could it be the man with binoculars again?

I doubted that. He hadn't liked my catching him spying; he wouldn't use the dock for such purposes again. But I was still thinking about him when I was Windexing a smudge on the living room window a little later. Then I was surprised to see binoculars on a small table by the window. Had Leslie also been watching something?

There were plenty of things to watch, of course. Boats. Birds. Deer. Trail walkers. It was one of the benefits of lakeside living. Maybe she'd even been curious about me over there at the house. But Leslie didn't strike me as having much curiosity about such mundane objects. Especially me.

It occurred to me that she might, however, be interested in the fact that someone had been studying her place. I'd thought a time or two about mentioning this to her, but she hadn't encouraged conversation of any kind. Now Leslie's own binoculars seemed an appropriate lead-in. I waited until she finished her midday meal, then broached it with her just before she returned to her office.

"I noticed the binoculars in there." I motioned toward the living room. "Before I started working here, I happened to see a man down on the little dock in front of the house where I'm living—" Another wave, this time toward the house across the lake.

"You *live* at the Harrington house?" she interrupted before I could finish the sentence. She sounded surprised.

"Actually, DeeAnn is my niece. I'm staying there temporarily." I rushed on, not wanting to blunder into the fact that I'd never actually been a housekeeper for anyone but Harley. "Anyway, this man had binoculars and appeared to be looking at this house."

She hadn't been interested, but now she turned so sharply that her shoe squeaked on the bare floor. "What sort of man? What did he look like?"

The unexpected intensity of her interest startled me. "Medium height. A stocky build, but a very narrow face, with sharp features. He was wearing hayseedy looking clothes, pants too short, with suspenders and a plaid shirt. But *he* didn't look hayseedy, if you know what I mean."

"I'm not sure I do. Please explain."

"He had a really dark tan, and he suddenly got out a pair of mirrored sunglasses, some expensive designer brand, I'm sure, and put them on. He just didn't . . . look as if he was from around here," I finished a little lamely, thinking I sounded all too much like Skye.

"A dark tan can come from anywhere. Mexico. Hawaii. The Caribbean. Even a tanning bed. The local health club has a couple of them." She spoke sharply, as if she were trying to convince one of us that a dark tan could have many sources.

"Oh. I didn't think about that kind of tan."

"Or there are all those tanning lotions. They're much safer than actual tans."

*Irrelevant chitchat,* I thought. Very unlike Leslie.

"Did you talk to him?" she finally asked.

"I asked him if he was bird-watching. He kind of pretended he was, but I don't think that's what he was doing. I think he was looking at your house."

"Lots of people are curious about the houses on this side of the lake. Sometimes people out on the water actually stop their boats to stare."

"They're all lovely homes." *Ivy Malone wins the gold star for vacuous remarks.*

She turned and went into her office, and I thought that ended the subject, that she'd lost interest. But she didn't close the door, and a minute later she returned. With a photograph.

# 10

She held the photograph out to me. "Does that look like the man you saw?"

I'd told Sgt. Yates I might not recognize the guy again, but I didn't have to look twice to know this wasn't him. This guy was too tall and husky, too square-jawed, a big-screen handsome guy with a smile that hinted at a daredevil recklessness.

But I certainly recognized the other person in the full-length photo. Leslie. In a white wedding gown and bridal veil.

"You're married?" It came out in a surprised gasp.

"No. We're divorced." She dismissed the subject on a note of impatience as if annoyed that I chose to pick this detail out of the photograph.

"I'm sorry." To me a failed marriage is a cause for sorrow.

She ignored my sympathies. Or perhaps she thought I was apologizing for my obvious curiosity.

"This photo was taken . . ." she paused, as if running some time line through her head, "about six years ago, so he'd look

86

older now. His hair is probably shorter. And maybe darker, since he was bleaching it then."

"You looked different then too." Then I mentally kicked myself for the insensitive comment. But it was true. Even the beautiful wedding gown and veil couldn't hide the fact that she was considerably heavier in the photo than she was now. "I didn't see the hair of the man with binoculars," I went on hastily. "He had a droopy old hat pulled down on his head. But this definitely isn't him."

"Did you see a car?"

"No. I figured he'd probably parked in the city park like almost everyone who walks on the trail does. You think your ex-husband may be in the area?" I added cautiously. I knew I was overstepping housekeeper bounds here, but I asked anyway.

Not that it did me any good. She ignored the question. "Describe the man you saw to me again."

So I did. I wished my subconscious would toss up some helpful tidbit I'd missed before, but my subconscious must have been snoozing that day.

"Did he ask any questions?"

"Not a one. Actually, once he realized I'd seen him, he seemed anxious to get away as fast as possible."

"Nothing unusual about his voice? No accent or anything?"

I considered that suggestion thoughtfully. Perhaps my subconscious hadn't been totally asleep. "Now that you mention it, maybe a smidgen of British accent. But he didn't say more than a half dozen words, so I can't say for certain."

I had the impression that my description of the man, skimpy as it was, meant something to her. Especially the deep tan and British accent details. I thought she might go back in the office and produce a different photo. Another husband? An unfortunate possibility, in these days of fast-food marriages.

But she just stood there, frowning slightly as she tapped the wedding photo with the back of a forefinger.

"Does he sound like someone you might know?" I asked.

She didn't ignore that question. She lifted her head and gave me a cool stare that put me in my place. I thought she was definitely annoyed by my curiosity, but she came out of her office just before 2:00, shortly after I heard the phone ring, and astonished me by handing me a key.

"I'll be gone one night this week. I don't know yet which night it may be, but the house will be locked when you arrive in the morning, so you'll need a key to get in. I'll expect you to put in the same hours as usual. If you have spare time, you can work on the books in the library."

The door was indeed locked when I arrived Friday morning. I let myself in with the new key, rather looking forward to being on my own for the day. Not that I had all that much contact with Leslie on any day, and she certainly never hovered over me. But the day suddenly felt looser, like the freedom that came with removing an old fifties-era girdle.

Yet when I stepped inside, I stopped short. The house felt . . . odd. Not the silence. Leslie never had music from radio or CD player blaring. Not the lack of homey scents. Whatever Leslie ate for breakfast never left any lingering scent. Not the closed office door. It was always closed when I arrived. Not even the emptiness. Unless Leslie was in the same room with me, which wasn't often, I was barely aware of her presence.

I rushed to the door that connected with the garage. Empty. The Mercedes was gone.

So, nothing strange here. Leslie had simply gone away

overnight, as she'd clearly said she planned to do. What had I expected from the odd feeling of emptiness—a mystery-novel scenario? Her body dramatically sprawled on the curved staircase or draped over the satin bedspread? A kidnapper's note?

I put on the coffeemaker and filled the kitchen with lovely scents of the mocha blend I'd found in the back of a cupboard. I turned on the unused radio hidden in a cabinet in the kitchen, and Alan Jackson sang about the Chattahoochee. I opened the windows and let in spring air and the cheerful chatter of a couple of blue jays.

And then I had this awful urge to snoop. I'd been almost everywhere in the house. It was my duty to poke into corners and clean medicine cabinets and put away fresh laundry. But I'd never been beyond the doorway of the office, and the urge to open the door and prowl was like a Godiva truffle pulling a chocoholic. I wanted to open drawers. Peer in the file cabinet. Examine those manila files and papers scattered all over the room. Turn on the computer and mouse-click into secrets.

I was appalled. How could I even think such a thing? I instantly plunged into a whirlwind of vacuuming, dusting, scrubbing, and laundering. I didn't even try the office door to see if it was locked. *Lead us not into temptation, Lord!* By noon, I had the necessities taken care of and dug into that treasure trove of books, which finally put the unacceptable urge to snoop to rest.

I spent a wonderful four hours there, because, without Leslie present, I granted myself permission to stay a couple of hours extra to luxuriate in the books. I found the master list she'd said existed and checked off books as I found them. William Faulkner and F. Scott Fitzgerald and Pearl Buck. But also Zane Grey, Louis L'Amour, and even a Frank Peretti. Nonfiction ranged from astronomy to botany, philosophy to ancient history. I started shelving fiction alphabetically by author, separating the hardcovers and paperbacks. There was no better system for organizing nonfiction than the good old Dewey Decimal System used in libraries, but I'd have to refresh my memory on the numbers.

I was strongly tempted to take a Mary Higgins Clark mystery home to read, but I decided that wouldn't be ethical without asking Leslie's permission first. I set the book aside so I could ask later.

Leslie hadn't yet returned when I left for the day. I was burning with curiosity, of course, wondering where she'd gone and what she was doing. Financial business? Conference with an out-of-town lawyer about the gate-ramming neighbor? Male friend? Or had this something to do with her ex-husband or the man I'd seen on the dock? Or maybe she just liked to get away and shop and take in a bit more culture than Woodston offered. Fayetteville had all the activities connected with the University of Arkansas.

She did not inform me where she'd been when I went to work the next morning, but the trip certainly had not put her in a good mood. This day, although the office door was closed, she was on the outside of it. She prowled the house like a cat looking for some unsuspecting mouse to pounce on. And complaining.

She asked would I please clean the stain out of the cabinet in her bathroom. She spoke as if it had been there for weeks, although I knew the cabinet had been spotless two days ago. She called somewhere and went into what Sandy calls "riot mode" because some mechanic couldn't take the Mercedes for servicing until next week. She complained that a soiled blouse I'd set aside for dry cleaning didn't need that expensive handling, and why wasn't I hand-washing it? She complained that I hadn't put the chair in her bedroom back where it belonged when I vacuumed.

Right. It was at least six inches away from where it usually stood.

By this time I was ready to shove her in the office and nail the door shut.

I was relieved when she finally did disappear into the office after lunch. I cleaned up the kitchen and started the dishwasher, thankful that I could now spend a few minutes with the quiet, uncomplaining books. But when I crossed the living room I was startled to look out and see someone sitting—no, lounging, as if he owned the place—on the broad curve of front steps.

His back was to me, so all I could see was his green windbreaker and a baseball cap. I wavered between yelling at the guy to beat it and telling Leslie there was a trespasser out there. Even with her present surly mood I settled on the latter and tapped on the closed office door.

"There's someone sitting on the front steps. Should I call 911 or the police? Or—"

Leslie threw open the office door and marched to the double doors opening onto the lake side of the house. She jerked one door open, and I assumed she intended to order the intruder off the property in no uncertain terms. Perhaps even bodily eject him. But she stopped so short that I almost whammed into her.

"What are *you* doing here?"

Leslie was not one to gasp, but this was definitely a gasp. She apparently recognized the guy from the back. When he turned and grinned I realized who he was. The ex-husband in the photo. With the same cocky grin.

"I figure there's enough of my money in this Tara of the Ozarks where you've been hiding out that I'm entitled to a spot on the steps. Great view," he added approvingly.

Always icy calm, Leslie now sputtered like an overheated

teakettle. I had the impression she was so furious she didn't know which of his statements to attack first.

"I haven't been hiding out," she snapped.

"No one's known where you were. Although you're lookin' good, Les. Very good. Down . . . what? Sixty pounds, maybe even seventy?"

She ignored the weight numbers. "I've been living here exactly like any other resident."

"But using your maiden name," he pointed out. Which gave me no clue as to *his* name, of course.

About that time I realized I probably shouldn't be standing here eavesdropping on this conversation. But no one said anything about my leaving, or even seemed aware I was present. So who was I to jump to the conclusion that I should remove myself?

"My maiden name *is* my name. I've had it longer than I had . . . yours. In any case, everyone here knows who I am."

"Yeah. Right. The mysterious lady in the Scarlett O'Hara house."

"And you, the guy who successfully hacked into the Pentagon, didn't have any problem coming up with my address, of course."

"Well, I wouldn't say it was no problem. You've done a fair job of cutting yourself off from the gang. And it took me a while to come up with the phone number." He recited a number that, from the angry tightening of her mouth, had to be her unlisted number.

"How did you get it?"

He grinned. "Vee haf our ways," he said with a waggle of eyebrows.

Leslie was not amused. "Did you try to call me?"

"I thought, just for old time's sake, a face-to-face visit would be preferable. Although your hospitality technique could use a tune-up," he added reproachfully.

"Did you send Michael to look for me?"

"Michael? What makes you think that?"

"Someone reported seeing a person of his description over on the other side of the lake. Michael never did know when to quit with the tan. One of these days his skin's going to look like a steak left too long on the barbecue. He was watching this place with binoculars."

"Actually, I haven't had much contact with Michael or either of our other partners since the demise of a certain dot-com company. If Michael has been watching you, he's done it on his own. We're not working together. Maybe he's a bit . . . ah . . . *miffed* about what you did."

The sarcastic emphasis on *miffed* implied a considerably stronger emotion than that moderate word suggested.

Leslie crossed her arms across her chest. "Okay, so you're here. So what?" she challenged.

The guy rose from his sitting position on the steps and lounged against one of the front pillars. He pushed the baseball cap back on his head, revealing a tumble of blond curls. "A lawsuit comes to mind."

"I didn't do anything illegal, and there's no money of yours in this place. It's all mine, money, house, everything. Fair and square."

"Fair and square?" He quirked a blond eyebrow. "That's a matter of opinion. California has community property laws, you know."

"All that was settled in the divorce. You got your share of Cy-berPowerAds; I got mine. The sale of my share of the company was after the divorce. No community property involved."

"Perhaps some high-powered lawyers and a judge will put a different spin on things. Perhaps concealment and inside information during the divorce settlement should be considered."

"You had as much inside information as I did. You were just too stupid, or egotistical, to use it."

"I see your sharp tongue hasn't lost its edge. That may get you in trouble one of these days."

"Oh, woe is me." She put a hand to her throat. "However will I live with myself, knowing my sharp tongue may have wounded you."

He ignored the mock melodrama, although the cocky grin had disappeared. His head tilted thoughtfully. "At the very least, you have to admit that what you did was unethical."

"Being smart is unethical?" She laughed suddenly, no humor attached. "*You* are lecturing *me* about ethics?"

"I have ethics." He managed to sound offended.

"Oh, really? Is that what you and the redheaded bombshell were doing in her apartment all the time, discussing ethics? I hired a private investigator, in case you didn't know."

"You and I were divorced by the time Rhonda and I—"

"What you did after the divorce is not now and never has been of any interest to me. I don't know anything about a Rhonda. I'm talking about a Wendy, and we were very much married then." She studied him with an open sneer. "What do you have, a Redheads-R-Us to provide a steady supply?"

He ignored the taunt. "In any case, our personal differences didn't give you the right to sabotage the company."

"I didn't sabotage the company! I simply got out when the getting was good. If the rest of you wanted to ride CyberPowerAds off into some cyberspace sunset or wherever it is dead dot-com companies go, that was your business."

"You took the other partners in the company, including me, for almost two million bucks!" he yelped. "We all went up to our ears in debt to buy you out."

"As I recall, all of you jumped at the chance to buy my share of the company. I think, in fact, there was some glee about putting something over on me. Perhaps taking advantage of the situation of my not wanting to be in partnership with *you* anymore."

94

"A belief you fostered."

"A smart investor knows when to get in and when to get out. I'm a smart investor. You're not. Now get off my property before I call the police. There are No Trespassing signs all over the place. Which you ignored."

He hesitated, his fists clenched, and for a moment I thought something more than words was going to explode between them. Then he lifted the baseball cap, ran his fingers through the curly blond hair, and replaced the cap. The cocky, daredevil grin returned. "Expect to hear from my lawyer."

"Expect to hear back from mine."

He looked at her warily. Her confidence probably told him, as it did me, that she had her legal bases covered. "There's more than one way to settle the score," he said finally, with a stare as frigid as the inside of Leslie's enormous freezer. "No lawyers involved."

"Are you threatening me?" She hesitated, as if for the first time wondering if it was possible that she didn't hold the winning hand here. "I remember you used to have a gun—"

"Sweetheart, I'd have to stand in line to take a shot at you." He blew Leslie a kiss and sauntered off, taking his time before disappearing around the corner of the house.

I expected Leslie to snap something at me standing there practically open-mouthed, watching and listening to everything, but she brushed past me as if I didn't exist. She disappeared into her office and didn't come out again before it was time for me to leave.

I went home feeling both curious and unsettled. And when I got there I received a surprise of my own. Apparently this was a day for unexpected visitors.

# 11

I recognized the vehicle immediately, and my visitors were a more pleasant surprise to me than Leslie's ex-husband had been to her. Who else owns a behemoth with an enormous mural of a bumblebee hovering over a huge magnolia blossom emblazoned on the back?

Magnolia Margollin, my neighbor from back on Madison Street, rushed out of the motor home the minute my Thunderbird rolled into the driveway.

"Ivy!" She wrapped her arms around me and gave me one of her big, bosomy hugs, all-enveloping as a wraparound pillow. "It's so good to see you! Running off without a word—"

"I left a note on your back door. And I told Dix and Haley to get in touch and tell you I was fine."

She stood back, still holding my hand, and looked me over critically. "Well, yes, you do look fine."

Magnolia looked fine too, her robust, Victorian-style figure and creamy magnolia complexion radiating vigor and good health. Her hair was a ripe tomato now, piled into a coronet on top her head and decorated with a silk magnolia in back. Her earrings were also magnolias, of course. Her gauzy caftan swirled around her in a dreamy mist of leafy green. As had occurred to me before, when I first discovered my own aged-into-invisibility status, flamboyant Magnolia would never be invisible.

Husband Geoff came out of the motor home, his wiry figure in tan pants and khaki shirt a conservative foil for Magnolia's splendor. He's much more reserved than she is, but he gave me a hug too. I was so glad to see them, and yet I couldn't help but feel dismay that they'd located me without apparent difficulty.

"I didn't think anyone knew where I was. How did you find me?" I asked, trying not to sound ungrateful that they were here.

Magnolia laughed. "Oh, Ivy, where else would you be, except down here in Arkansas with the only family you have?"

Well, no high-tech detective work involved here. Thirty seconds of thought, and Magnolia and Geoff had it figured out. And they were right. Where else would I be except here with niece DeeAnn and family? An elemental fact that the Braxtons, with minimal investigation, might also deduce.

That brought me up short. But then I reasoned that if they hadn't zapped me yet, they probably weren't going to. No reason for them to delay if they had some lethal scheme in mind.

I invited Magnolia and Geoff in, and they told me about what was going on back on Madison Street. A shoddy place called the Exotic Flower Club had closed down, which we all agreed was good riddance. A rumor was going around that some big chain wanted to buy up everything in the area and put in a motel and conference center. The Margollins' personal news was that they were on their way to a powwow in Oklahoma. Magnolia, in her enthusiasm for genealogical research, had discovered that she may have a few drops of American Indian blood, and she was rushing off to claim any distant relatives. I was sometimes afraid Magnolia would be soundly rejected by some newfound "relative," but she was so enthusiastic and good-hearted that so far it hadn't happened.

Mac MacPherson's name came up briefly, but they hadn't heard from him and I had only that vague postcard, so there wasn't much to say.

We all went to watch Sandy practice at the gymnastics studio that evening. She didn't put in the kind of practice hours that Olympic hopefuls do, but she had a big gymnastics meet in Fayetteville coming up shortly and was practicing harder than usual now. She looked incredible to me, strutting and balancing on that narrow beam, flipping across the mat like some acrobatic butterfly, whirling around on those parallel bars until my head spun just watching her.

The following day was Easter Sunday. Skye had spent the night with us, and she and Sandy and I got up early for sunrise services. Later, Magnolia and Geoff, though not frequent churchgoers, accompanied us to services at the regular hour, stayed for a ham dinner, and left about 4:00. One thing about a motor home, your bed is right there with you, so you can pick up and move any time of day or night. They planned to park at a rest area or shopping mall somewhere along the way that night.

I cautioned them again before they left about not letting anyone back home know where I was.

On Monday, Leslie said nothing about the confrontation with the ex-husband. I went about my duties as usual both then and on Tuesday. The most notable incident that day was when I broke the cord on the whistle I always carry around my neck. It happened when I was dusting the banister beside the curved staircase.

Dusting it how? That's a bit embarrassing.

It was a spur-of-the-moment thing. If I'd thought about it, common sense surely would have issued a resounding veto. But I was standing at the top of the stairs fully intending to dust the long, curving banister the customary way, when this other, considerably more fun way leaped into my head . . .

The anemic *no* of common sense was no match for the rush of adrenaline as I looked down the inviting sweep of banister.

And then there I was, gleefully throwing one leg over the railing and scrambling atop it. I'd never had a chance at a banister as spectacular as this a child, and who knows? I might never have another chance. Which proved prophetically true, although I wasn't thinking about that as I shoved off.

Whee! Down I went, polished wood singing hot against my pants, body plunging around the curve like a race car on a track. The room below spun in a dizzying whirl of white furniture. The chandelier in the dining room flashed a glitter of spinning jewels. I swooped on a roller-coaster ride! I flew like a bird!

I also crunched my tailbone hard against the newel post at the bottom, and I had to clutch the railing to keep from tumbling off it in a dizzy spin. But a small price to pay for such a glorious ride!

Then I peered around guiltily, thinking I'd surely see Leslie standing there tapping her toe and looking at me with blue ice in her eyes.

But no Leslie. No sound or movement anywhere. I hastily scrambled off the railing, and that was when I snagged the cord holding my whistle on the wooden ball atop the newel post. The whistle flew through the air and pinged on the polished floor.

*If that was the only casualty of my impulsive slide, I am indeed fortunate,* I thought as I retrieved the whistle. The cord was repairable; if I'd taken the kind of fall my foolish escapade probably deserved, I could have broken something considerably less fixable than the cord on a whistle.

I put the whistle in a kitchen drawer for safekeeping, intending to take it home that afternoon and replace the broken cord. Which I forgot to do, so I took a length of sturdy cord to work with me on Wednesday morning.

Where I immediately encountered a Leslie who pounced on me quicker than a principal encountering a tardy student in an empty hallway. "Mrs. Malone, I'd like to talk to you."

My first thought was, *Oh dear, she knows about my banister adventure and just waited until today to make an issue of it.* Then I saw the paper in her hand and the ice in her eyes and knew the wild ride was probably the least of my problems.

"I've been looking at what you've done with the books in the library."

"I haven't had time to do much so far—"

"Oh, really?" A sarcastic comment, not a question. "It appears to me that you've been quite busy."

"I don't understand," I said warily.

"Come with me, please."

She headed for the library with her long strides. I followed with my short ones. The books were not the way I'd left them. The cartons had been opened and books haphazardly dumped everywhere. I looked around, bewildered. What had happened here? A break-in? Vandalism? Surely she didn't think I'd done this.

Leslie, however, did not seem disturbed by the mess. "You see the names of these books with the *X* mark on the left side?" She thrust the paper at me, which I immediately recognized as the master list of the boxed books.

"I didn't make those marks." I had, in fact, wondered what they meant. "I've only been making that tiny check mark on the right as I identified and shelved each book. Right there, see?" I pointed to my pencil marks, then waved at the shelved books.

"I had an expert go through the list several months ago. Those Xs mark the books that he identified as old and particularly valuable, probably collector's items. As I'm sure you as an experienced librarian recognized."

"I've never had experience with books of collectible value—"

"Really." More sarcasm. "I've been going through the books." She waved a hand at the disorganized mess, which apparently was her doing. "At least five of those marked with an X are missing."

It didn't take diagrams to see what she was getting at. "You think I took them?"

"The books are on the list. They are not among the books now in the library."

"But there are any number of people who could have taken the books! Some previous housekeeper or other employee. The movers who brought the books here. Someone getting into them after your father died and before you got them. Someone who had access before you moved the books here. Someone—"

"You seem to have a rather ready list of 'someones' to blame. As if you had it already prepared."

"That's ridiculous." I was getting rattled now. "Innocent until proven guilty" didn't seem to mean much in this situation. "I mean, it's obvious any number of people could—"

"It's obvious to me that you're the only one who has ever shown any interest in these books, the only one who has ever expressed a desire to get her hands on them, the only one who has any knowledge about books. And the only one who's had access to them when they come up missing."

"I like books, but that doesn't mean I'd take them. In fact, I wanted to read this Mary Higgins Clark one—" The book was lying right there on the table. I grabbed it, resisting an urge to shake it in her face. "But I didn't even want to borrow it without asking you first."

"I would like my house key and the remote control for the gate returned now. You will no longer be needing them."

"You're firing me?"

"I see no way we can continue this arrangement under the present circumstances."

"But I didn't take your books! I don't know anything about them. This isn't fair!"

"I can hire whomever I want, and I can fire whomever I want," she stated. Which was obviously true. And grammatically correct. But it still wasn't fair! "My key, please."

I dug in my pocket for the key and handed it to her, resisting an urge to fling it across the room so she'd have to chase after it. Regrettably I have these impulses; fortunately I usually overcome them.

"I'll have to go out to my car and get the remote control."

"Please do that. I'll have the wages due you ready when you return."

I brought the remote control in and held it out to her. She held the envelope out to me. We exchanged them like two distrustful spies swapping secrets.

I went back to my car. The gate was already open when I reached it. It swung shut behind me. I drove away feeling a bit dazed. At the edge of the city park I was so shaky that I pulled over to the curb and wiped my damp hands on my pants.

So, my days of gainful employment were over. I tried to put a lighthearted spin on the situation, maybe even make a funny story out of it to tell DeeAnn. But nothing amusing came, and all I could think of was that I could, at least, be glad I hadn't traded the old Thunderbird in on a new Camry on some overly optimistic idea of projected earnings.

I put it all to the Lord as I sat there. My disappointment. The hurt and frustration and sense of injustice at being fired for something I hadn't done. In all my years, I'd never before been fired from a job. *Why, Lord? What's going on here?*

Now was one of those times I'd like a booming voice, or at least a whisper, of advice or explanation in my ear. Maybe a reassurance that Leslie would discover how wrong she was and come rushing to me to beg forgiveness for her error.

No booming voice or whisper about Leslie seeing the light arrived. But a memory of Harley saying, back when we were unfairly sued over a minor incident at his pharmacy, "People may be unjust, but God isn't. So, no matter how this turns out, we don't have to worry about it. He's in charge."

I took a deep breath and let the words wash through me. Okay, I was hurt and disappointed, and I had been treated unjustly. But the Lord was in charge. And, peering around the edges of my disappointment, I could see several things to be cheerful about.

The job had been nice while it lasted. I had the satisfaction of having done it well. I'd seen Tara of the Ozarks from the inside, which few had. I had a few extra dollars in my pocket. And I'd taken what was surely one of the all-time grandest banister slides ever.

It was only when I got home and checked the money in the envelope that I discovered that Leslie had shorted me by ten dollars. I was indignant for a moment; then it struck me as funny, in a sad sort of way. She had, according to the ex-husband, a couple million dollars from the sale of some company they'd been involved in together. But she'd chosen to take petty satisfaction in cheating a fired housekeeper out of a few insignificant dollars.

*She's the one who needs the prayers, isn't she, Lord? And I do pray for her. Come into her heart, Lord. Open her mind and eyes and spirit to you.* I couldn't help adding one small afterthought. *And you might warm up her personality a bit too, if it isn't too much bother.*

Then that seemed a bit self-serving, and I apologized.

I thought that was the end of it. I was wrong.

# 12

The next day two things happened.

When I was leaving Bible study, I automatically reached up to finger the whistle that always hung at my throat, then remembered it was still in that kitchen drawer over at Tara of the Ozarks. (Leslie's ex-husband's name for the place had stuck with me.) I felt uncomfortably naked without my whistle. I'd never yet had to make emergency use of it, but I liked having it available.

The second happening was that Sgt. Yates showed up.

I was standing in the front yard after lunch, looking at a scalped shrub that I'm certain was cowering under my gaze. I stepped out to the flagstone walkway to meet him.

"I understand you've been working as housekeeper for Leslie Marcone," he said without the bother of how-are-you preliminaries. He tilted his head toward the house across the lake.

"Yes, that's right. Unfortunately, it was a rather short-lived employment. She fired me yesterday."

"So I understand."

I was surprised. I'd told Sandy, and her loyal reaction had been, "She didn't deserve you anyway." Skye had spent the night at our place because her dad was in Little Rock on some political thing, and Sandy may have passed the information along to Skye as reinforcement to support her dislike of Leslie. Skye could have told her stepmother, Tammi. Perhaps Tammi had mentioned it at the health club. Even with that chain of possibilities, I didn't see how the gossip could have blanketed the town already.

So, Sgt. Yates's information must have come directly from Leslie. It seemed doubtful Leslie had contacted the sheriff's office simply to give them a news flash about firing a housekeeper.

"Let me guess. Leslie has filed charges against me over the books missing from her library."

"The report said she has a valuable collection of books inherited from her father, and eight of them—"

"Eight!" I echoed. Yesterday it was five. How long before she was accusing me of carting them off by the carload?

"Eight, yes, that's what she says. Anyway, she claims these books are missing, and no one but you had access to them. She says you worked alone in the house while she was away overnight."

"Yes, I was alone there one day. Which gave me the perfect opportunity to make off with any number of items, I suppose. Is she missing a potato peeler? Or perhaps something larger? That leather furniture is quite nice. And I had time to call in my criminal cohorts, the Over-the-Hill Gang, and make off with a sofa or two. Although the bigger stuff is difficult to handle when you all have lumbago and rheumatism."

Sgt. Yates frowned disapprovingly. "Did anyone ever tell you, Mrs. Malone, that you have an attitude?"

Apparently he just had. I remained silent.

"She didn't go so far as to request that charges be filed against you—"

"How generous of her." I'm not, unfortunately, above a bit of snide sarcasm as well as facetious exaggerations.

"But she wants us to investigate." He frowned again, pulling that scar across his eyebrow into greater prominence. Did the criminals he interrogated find that scar intimidating? I did. It had an attitude of its own. "I'm with the Major Crimes Unit, and this isn't the type of case I usually handle, so I didn't talk to her personally. But when I saw your name on the report I became . . . concerned."

"I appreciate your concern, but I can tell you, as I told her, I don't know anything about any missing books. I may have been the only person with access to them at the moment she discovered they were missing, but who knows how long they've actually been gone?"

"An interesting point."

"As I pointed out to her, many people may have had access to the books before I came along." I ignored the echo of Leslie's accusation about my "ready list of 'someones'" and plowed through the possibilities.

"I'll suggest the officer check on what you've mentioned."

"Does Leslie indicate when that master list of books was made up? Was it before or after her father's death?"

"Why do you ask?"

"If it was an inventory made after his death, then yes, the books are missing now and someone must have taken them. But if the list was made while he was alive and the books still in his possession, perhaps he simply disposed of some of the more valuable ones but didn't take the names off the list. I believe the check marks on the list were made by an expert on the basis of titles and authors only, not a physical examination of the books."

107

Sgt. Yates folded his arms across his uniform. "Read a lot of mystery books, do you, Mrs. Malone?" he inquired.

I felt myself reddening. Okay, I'd been hitting Mike's library of mysteries rather hard lately. But that was surely irrelevant to this situation. I tossed his question back at him. "Why do you ask?"

"No particular reason."

Which we both knew was less than accurate. He was thinking that with my excursion into minute details I was trying to play clever amateur sleuth like some character in one of those mysteries. The one who comes up with that tiny but vital clue all the experienced officers and detectives have inexplicably missed.

He made no further comment along those lines, however. Instead he said, "Why don't you tell me a bit about your . . . ah . . . involvement with the books. Ms. Marcone indicated that you were organizing them, I believe. She requested that you do this?"

"No. I volunteered."

"I see."

A world of speculation in those two small words. Obviously, I should have stuck to the old army adage of never volunteering. I explained about my past as a librarian.

"There really wasn't all that much housekeeping to do with only one person in that big house, so I had extra time." Then, feeling as if I might only be digging myself in deeper, I stopped the explanations.

"Well, we'll see where we can go with this," Sgt. Yates said, not committing himself. I thought the interview was over. Because it had definitely been an interview. He may have been "concerned" about me because of his friendship with Mike and DeeAnn, but he was all cop, and this was business. Then he surprised me with another question.

"How do you feel about all this, being accused of something you say you didn't do, and getting fired?"

How did I feel? It seemed a non-cop type inquiry, too touchy-feely for a lawman, yet he was watching me with interest. Although at the moment I was undecided as to whether it was friendly interest or the kind of interest a scientist has in a wiggly new microbe he's peering at under a microscope.

"Well, I . . . uh . . . I'm certainly not happy about it. It seems unfair. And it's frustrating that I don't have any way to prove my innocence. Unless your department uncovers the real guilty party."

"Yes, it does seem an unfortunate circumstance. I hope you're not frustrated enough to retaliate in some . . . ah . . . physical way?"

I blinked at him. Physical way? "You're suggesting . . . what? That I might push Leslie down the stairs? Arrange for that dining room chandelier to fall on her? Whack her with an oar from the boathouse?"

"You're very imaginative, Mrs. Malone."

For a moment I thought he might actually be teasing me. There was a certain glint in those steely cop eyes. But it's difficult to discern teasing when a man is watching you from under an Al Capone–type scar on his eyebrow.

"According to official reports you did send a member of the Braxton clan up in Missouri to the hospital with a concussion."

I mentally rolled my eyes. *One little incident in my life, a purely accidental incident as I was trying to escape a dangerous criminal, and Sgt. Yates acts like I'm a major menace.* "This isn't the first time you've mentioned this," I pointed out. "I really don't think it has any connection with the current situation. My life was in danger then."

"Maybe I'm impressed with your . . . ah . . . unexpected

capabilities." Was there a smile behind that statement? I couldn't tell. Then he added, "My father has been a widower for a number of years now. He's somewhat older than you. But very active. Maybe you two should meet."

I was astonished at this apparent indication of approval. Was he suggesting that a woman capable of sending a Braxton to the hospital and jail would make a nice companion for his father? On second thought, it occurred to me that he could be saying that his father, who presumably did not go around attacking strangers, might be a good influence on me. I murmured a noncommittal, "That might be nice."

He appraised me a minute longer but didn't pursue this line of thought. Perhaps he decided he should check with his father before making any rash commitment to introductions. "In any case, you may be assured that we won't railroad you into a prison term," he added solemnly.

"Good. I'd hate to be known as the Blue-Haired Book Snatcher who got sent up for twenty years."

I felt restless after Sgt. Yates left. I thought about checking to see if there were any bookstores in Woodston or nearby towns where the thief could have sold the books. But the thought that I might encounter a deputy investigating at those same stores, a deputy who might report my sleuthing to Sgt. Yates, dampened that idea. So I went with a different one.

# 13

I looked up the name I'd scribbled on a scratch pad when I talked to DeeAnn. The only Diedrich in the phone book was an Alton. I dialed the number, and a woman answered on the fifth ring. Not a hello.

"Can you hold on a minute?" she asked on a frantic note. "Tricia threw a toothbrush in the toilet, and if she flushes it—"

So I held on, intrigued by the clunks and rattles and splashes associated with fishing in a toilet. Then the sound of the phone being picked up again.

"Okay, sorry, thanks for waiting. It's been one of those days. Kip got hold of my stamps and pasted them in a coloring book. Lisa ate a crayon and threw up. All I need now is for the toilet to plug up."

"Is this Cass Diedrich?"

"Unfortunately, yes. Who else would want to be me?"

"Uh . . . you don't know me, but my name is Ivy Malone. I've been working as a housekeeper for Leslie Marcone—"

"My sympathies."

"I understand you also used to work for her, and I was wondering . . . I hate to bother you, but do you suppose I could come over and talk to you for a few minutes?"

Given her bad day and a certain animosity in her tone about my connection with Leslie, I expected a rejection. I intended to add the persuasive point that Leslie had fired me, but I didn't have to. She said, "Sure. Come on over. I could use some grown-up conversation. But I think I should warn you about the Terminator."

"The Terminator?"

"The kids' pet rat." As if knowing what I must be wondering, she added, "The kids named her that. Don't ask me why. She got loose this morning. But don't worry. She's friendly. She just likes to crawl under your armpit."

I dug out a local map and looked up the address given in the phone book. Fifteen minutes later, arms protectively clamped to my body to deter armpit attackers, I was knocking on the door. I'd tried the doorbell, but it seemed to be out of order.

A frazzled-looking semi-blonde opened the door. She was wearing old black leggings and a sweatshirt, no shoes. Red polish decorated the toenails of one bare foot, but the pedicure had apparently been interrupted before it reached the other foot. A couple of angelic-looking little blonde girls peeked out from behind her. Which meant a third child—and a rat—were on the loose somewhere.

"Come on out to the kitchen. I'm washing dishes. The dishwasher is on the blink."

The stacked dishes suggested they'd been accumulating for some time, perhaps in hopes the dishwasher would heal itself. I've also been known to hope some mechanical breakdown would spontaneously heal.

"How about if I wash dishes, and you do . . . whatever

112

else needs doing?" Looking around the crumb-strewn floor, empty rat cage, and scattered toys, I figured that there was quite a lot that needed doing.

She looked at me in amazement. She didn't brush off the offer. "Would you? That would be wonderful. Al, that's my husband, he's a truck driver, has been gone since last Wednesday. He'll be getting in tomorrow, and I'd like to have the house at least halfway clean for him."

There was already water in one side of the double sink, but it looked a little thick to qualify as dishwater, so I pulled the stopper and started over. Cass disappeared into another room and came back with a load of dry laundry that she dumped on the table. She started folding and I started washing, keeping a wary eye out for anything furry interested in my armpits.

"How did you ever manage to work for Leslie Marcone when you have such a . . . busy schedule?" I asked.

"Al was out of work then, so he stayed with the kids. You wanted to talk to me about my working for her?" She suddenly sounded wary.

"Actually, I'm not working for Leslie anymore either. She fired me yesterday."

"Ah." Cass nodded knowingly, and the wariness went out of her voice. "Up to her old tricks, I see. What was her beef with you?"

"She accused me of stealing some valuable books."

"Oh, yeah, I remember those boxes of books. The only time I ever went in there was to vacuum and dust. I love to read, but . . ." She waved a hand in the direction of the kids, all three now playing on the floor and supplying sound effects for a trio of toys whose batteries had apparently long since worn out. "Maybe someday I'll get beyond *The Fish That Jumped over the Moon*. That's their current favorite."

"Were you happy working for Leslie?"

"I needed the job." (Honk of child imitating truck horn.)

"You quit because your husband found work?"

"Quit?" (Squeal of child doing skidding brakes.) "Oh, no. She fired me too."

Somehow this was no surprise. "If you don't mind my asking, for what reason?"

"There were usually leftovers from her meals. It was hard to figure exactly how much to cook, because you could never tell if she was going to eat like a pig or a hummingbird. And, as you undoubtedly know, she won't touch leftovers." (Rumble of toy tractor as interpreted by small girl.) "Anyway, it seemed a shame to throw out good food, and we could sure use it, so I started bringing the leftovers home."

"Leslie objected?"

"She threw a hissy fit when she found out. Acted like I'd made off with family heirlooms. I suppose I should have asked first, but it just didn't occur to me that she'd care. After all, as far as she was concerned, after she was done with it, it was garbage."

"I wonder why what you did with the leftovers mattered to her at all?" (Truck and toy tractor colliding. Crash sound effects.) It was a rather disconnected conversation, but I was getting a more complete, if still puzzling, picture of my former employer.

Cass shook her head. "I think maybe she thought I was cooking too much so there'd be leftovers to bring home. But I'm not really sure. There were lots of things I never could figure out about her. Like why doesn't she answer the telephone about half the time? Why is she such a fanatic about exercise?"

I thought I knew the answer to that last question. She'd been overweight when she was married, and the husband was running around with "bombshell redheads." She'd grimly decided to get rid of the excess weight, and she'd done it. And wasn't about to let it homestead her hips again.

I'd had to deal with leftovers too, of course. As carefully as I'd tried to calculate the proper amount of food to prepare for Leslie, it was impossible to figure it down to the last carrot. As Cass said, you could never tell if Leslie was going to eat like a pig or a hummingbird. I'd sometimes finished off a few bites of leftovers, but mostly I'd just tossed them. Leslie had never asked what I did with them. But maybe she checked the garbage can to be sure they were there.

"Did she call the police?" (Word *police* brings trio of child shrieks of sirens.)

"I don't think so. I mean, Leslie can get up in arms over most anything. She jumped all over one poor gardener for accidentally cutting down some ugly old bush she liked and made him replace it. But I guess even she drew the line at involving the police with leftovers."

"Were you working there when the neighbor rammed the gate with his pickup?" (Little boy on knees heads for bathroom, zoom-zooming toy truck with him.)

"Oh, yeah. We both heard this awful noise and ran out, and there he was, barreling right through the gate. I thought he was going to run us both down." Sounding reluctant, as if she hated to say anything even minimally nice about Leslie, she added, "Next to that weirdo creep, even Leslie seemed almost normal. He really scared me."

"Did he do anything else?"

"Before the gate incident he came to the house several times, haranguing her about using her boat landing and dock. Once we found red paint sprayed all over the boathouse door, and I was pretty sure he did it. But I don't think she called the police then. She just had a guy come and paint over it."

Thinking of the question Sgt. Yates had asked me, I asked it of Cass. "How did you feel about getting fired?"

115

"I wanted to shove her head in the toilet. And when I came home and told Al, he was ready to roar over there and do it. I think if I hadn't hung on to the car keys until he calmed down, he would have. We had a really hard time financially for a while there, when we were both out of work. We're still catching up on bills."

(Little boy returns, turns toy truck into attack plane, and crashes into small girl's head.)

"Are you?" I asked. "Still mad about it, I mean."

"Oh, a little, I guess. But I believe in the Lord, and forgiveness is part of believing, so I've tried to just let it go. But Al, he's not much on forgiveness. Especially when she only paid me half of what I had coming for my last week there. He's still mad about that. Every once in a while he mutters something about getting her to pay up." Hastily she added, as if she wanted to make sure I didn't get a wrong impression of her husband, "But Al's really the greatest, most generous guy in the world."

"She shorted me a few dollars too."

"In a way I feel sorry for her," Cass went on as she folded a raggedy towel. "I mean, she has that big house and all that money, but you have to wonder what's lacking in a person's life if she can get in such a tizzy about leftovers."

I was about done with the dishes, and I was thinking I'd thank Cass for the information and head on home. But just then one of the kids whopped the other on the jaw with the police car. A yowl exploded and then all three were bawling. Cass looked ready to cry too.

"How about you go relax in a hot bath, and I'll watch the kids for a while?" I said impulsively. I turned to the kids. "Hey, anyone want to read the story about the fish and the moon?"

The crying stopped, and Cass looked at me as if I'd just handed her a winning lottery ticket. Without a word of polite demurral she grabbed a freshly folded towel from the table and headed for the bathroom. The kids stared at me expectantly, and I wondered what I'd let myself in for. Maybe they had some predetermined attack-the-babysitter plan in readiness. Maybe Cass had no intention of coming out of the bathroom until husband Al got home.

The kids and I settled on the sofa. *The Fish That Jumped over the Moon* turned out to be a nice little story about a fish and the reflection of the moon in the water, and then I told them one about Jonah and the whale. They responded with a garbled version of Joseph's coat of many colors, which they'd heard in a Sunday school class. Cass did come out about an hour later, hair damp and fresh and toenails fully painted, and by that time the kids were sprawled on sofa and floor in peaceful naps.

And I had a rat, a big black and white one, snuggled under my left armpit. Which actually wasn't as bad as it sounds. I gently extracted the creature and nestled her beside a sleeping child.

I had no doubt the kids would soon be up to their live-wire tricks, but Cass looked relaxed and better able to cope now. And then I thought, *Hey, I enjoyed this. Why don't I volunteer at church to help out in the nursery?*

On the way home I waved at Hanson Watkins, out in the yard washing his mother's motor home. It looked like an older model, not nearly as large as Magnolia and Geoff's behemoth, smaller, actually, than Mac's modest home on wheels as well. And a different style, with a section for what must be the bed extending over the cab. Offhand, I wondered what one like that was worth.

By the time I got home, however, my thoughts were back

117

to my absent whistle. I could easily buy another one, probably for less than a dollar. But this one was special. Silver-plated. Although silver plating wasn't why it was valuable to me. I cherished it because it was a last gift from Thea, my longtime friend back on Madison Street. Thea was gone now, lying beside her husband back there in Parkdale Heights cemetery, but whenever I fingered the whistle, I felt the strength and warmth of our long, sisterly friendship.

I wanted my special whistle back.

I watched for Leslie on the trail, planning to intercept her and tell her firmly that I needed to come over and retrieve my whistle. I didn't see her, but it was late enough in the day that she may have already finished her run.

That evening I tried to call Leslie. Sandy had another gymnastics practice, but I had a few minutes before it was time to pick her up at the studio and could drive over and get the whistle during that time.

I felt unexpectedly jittery dialing the unlisted number. Leslie wasn't above throwing what Cass Diedrich had called a "hissy fit" over the phone. But I intended to persist. I let the phone ring five, six, seven times. No answer. Which meant . . . what? That she'd gone out of town again? Or, just as likely, that she simply wasn't answering the phone. She could glance at a ringing phone and then, either less curious or stronger willed than I am, just let it ring. Another of her peculiarities was that, although she must be a technological genius with that computer—I once saw her physically open it up and do something with its innards—she didn't even own an answering machine. She'd never explained any of this to me, of course, but I wondered now if her odd attitude about the phone was connected to the ex-husband and the failed company they'd been in together.

I took a walk the following afternoon at about the time Leslie usually jogged. Again she didn't show. I was puzzled.

Could she feel uncomfortable enough about encountering me on the trail that she'd change her jogging route? Unlikely. She was capable of running right by me—or over me—with never a glance. Yet, as I'd already observed, Leslie was a woman of odd contradictions.

Once more I tried calling her that evening. Again, no answer. I doubted she considered avoiding me important enough to stop answering the phone completely. So I was back to wondering if she was out of town.

On Saturday afternoon, when I still didn't see her on the trail, I debated about going into town and buying another whistle. I didn't like being without one. But I still wanted *my* whistle.

And I was, I decided, going after it.

I marched out to the Thunderbird, which, indifferent to my determined mind-set, refused to start. It had, in fact, been grumpy about starting several times lately. Battery or ignition problems? Nonspecific old-age debilities? Or just general stubbornness? I gave it a few minutes to pout, tried again, and this time it started cheerfully. I gave the dashboard an appreciative pat. "Good girl."

The gate at 2742 Vintage Road was closed when I reached it, of course, and I now had no remote control with which to open it. I parked the T-bird off to the side of the driveway and crawled through the board fence.

I started out walking briskly down the driveway, but I hadn't gone more than a dozen steps when my feet slowed. I wasn't certain why. Because I dreaded what might well be an unpleasant confrontation with Leslie? Or because the place felt . . . odd? I hesitated, trying to analyze that oddness. A feeling of emptiness? Yes. Spooky? Somewhat. Scary?

*Don't be ridiculous.* I'd had a similar feeling of oddness the morning I came to the house when Leslie was away overnight, and nothing was wrong then. Nothing was wrong now.

I resumed walking, deciding I'd go to the back door I'd always used.

That was when I saw the flash of movement. Something . . . no, *someone*, moving fast—ducking into the heavy underbrush that separated house and road. A thud and muffled grunt as the person apparently crashed into a tree or stump.

Then . . . silence.

I stood still, frozen in midstep. The person couldn't have continued through the wooded tangle without making noise of some kind. Which meant he was still in there.

Who? What was he doing? Or what had he already done? I took a step in the direction of the sounds, head cocked to listen for any rustle of movement.

Caution suddenly overcame curiosity. He could be hiding from me . . . or waiting to pounce on me. Whatever, his sneaky actions said plainer than words that whatever he was up to, it was no good.

In sudden panic I turned and ran, clambered through the fence so fast I clunked my funny bone. I was frantically trying to jam my key in the car door and massage my elbow at the same time I heard more thudding and crashing in the brush. Was he coming after me? I blessed the old T-bird when it started like a race car raring to go.

I thought I'd feel foolish for my panic in broad daylight. If I'd hung around, perhaps I'd have seen the intruder crash out of the brush and thus could have identified him.

But no feeling of foolishness materialized even when I was several miles away from Vintage Road. My heart was still in overdrive. The steering wheel felt slippery under my perspiring hands. I couldn't swallow past what felt like the Diedrich kids' toy truck caught in my throat.

All I could think was, *Thank you, Lord, thank you for getting me out of there.*

# 14

I drove on home slowly. So who was it, hiding there in the brush? A burglar checking to see if anyone was home? Or something more personal, perhaps the ex-husband or the man with binoculars whom Leslie seemed to think was someone named Michael? I hadn't seen a car, so maybe it was the "weird creep" neighbor. Or someone else Leslie had had a run-in with, since hostile clashes seemed a frequent occurrence in her life.

At home I again tried to call Leslie, now thinking I should warn her that someone was skulking around her place. Again, no answer.

Should I call Sgt. Yates to tell him what I'd seen? I had to admit a reluctance to do that, because the first thing he'd surely ask would be, "What are you doing skulking around Leslie's place?" And my answer, I wanted my whistle, sounded both petty and ridiculous.

Reluctantly, however, I decided it was my duty as a good citizen to report skulking. But when I called the county sheriff's office I learned Sgt. Yates was off duty for the weekend. I dug out the card he'd given me, which had his home and cell phone numbers, and debated with myself. Should I interrupt his time off? After a few minutes of indecision I concluded that wasn't necessary. All that crashing in the brush suggested the intruder was as anxious to get away as I was. He was no doubt long gone now. So calling Sgt. Yates could wait until Monday when he was back on duty.

A decision I'd later regret. Although it was probably too late even then.

Sandy and Skye arrived in Sandy's usual mini-tornado of excitement. "Is it okay if Skye stays overnight?"

"Of course. We're always glad to have you," I said to Skye. But, concerned, I added, "Are you sure your folks don't mind your staying over here so often?"

"Dad got home from Little Rock. He's definitely going to run for a seat in the House of Representatives. Tammi is fixing a candlelight and champagne dinner to celebrate."

Skye spoke with a hint of scorn, an implication that this was more of the Dumpling's silliness, but I suspected she was really feeling she'd be an outsider at the intimate celebration. Did bubbly Tammi realize Skye felt shut out? I doubted it. She might even be wondering why Skye didn't want to celebrate with them. Should I say something to Tammi? Or would either or both of them resent the interference?

"We're going to do our hair," Sandy interrupted. She held up a carton showing a woman with sunshiny streaks in what would surely qualify as chestnut tresses in some romance novel. "Skye's mom sent her this cool highlighting kit, and Tammi said it was okay—"

"Not without calling *your* mother, it isn't okay for you."

122

Sandy gave me one of those exasperated looks only a teen can produce, but she dashed off to make the call. Skye handed me a wrapped package.

"Tammi sent this over to you."

"Me? Why would Tammi send me something?"

"She wanted to thank you for staying with Baby. She said to tell you she's sorry it took so long, but she wanted to find something exactly right."

I wanted to rip into the surprise package instantly. I guess that's something we never outgrow. Although I had to admit to a certain apprehension. What would Tammi consider "exactly right"? Useless doo-dad? Something elderly . . . talcum powder, lavender cologne, uselessly dainty handkerchief?

"She didn't have to do this. I really enjoyed Baby. And I like Tammi too. She seems very friendly and sweet. And she shouldn't worry about a few extra pounds. She's very attractive."

"She's okay."

So, Skye's cool tone said, are cockroaches, if you like cockroaches. Especially overweight ones.

The gift was nicely wrapped in silvery paper, which I automatically started to fold and save before remembering I didn't do that anymore. Although it's a hard habit for a thrifty person to break, and I couldn't bring myself to toss the red bow. I set it aside and pulled out the gift. I was astonished. A book of inspirational Christian poems! I flipped through the pages—everything from John Donne and Gerard Manley Hopkins to Ruth Bell Graham and Laurence Dunbar. And some of Mary Sidney's wonderful work with the Psalms too. Yes, a gift that was indeed "exactly right." Bless you, Tammi.

Sandy returned to report that DeeAnn had okayed hair highlighting, and exclaimed, "Hey, awesome!" over the book.

The girls trooped off to commence hair makeovers, and I went to the phone to call Tammi immediately.

"Oh, I'm so glad you like it!" Tammi gushed when I'd expressed my thanks. "I know you're a believer, so I thought it would be right for you! I'm a believer myself, of course."

"You are?" I asked, surprised. I hadn't inferred that from anything Skye or Sandy had said about Tammi.

"Oh, my yes! I've meditated since last year, and I've found this marvelous mantra that clears my mind instantly! I can't tell you what it is, of course, because then it loses its power. But I can help you find your own!"

I sighed inwardly at Tammi's interpretation of a "believer." "No. Thanks anyway."

"I had a hard time deciding between that book and another one about all the paths that lead to God," Tammi went on. "It's about how God is like a rainbow because there are so many facets and colors to him. Sometimes when I'm meditating, I feel as if I'm climbing a rainbow right up to him!"

"Actually, there's only one true path to God. It's through Jesus," I said gently.

"You think so?" I heard a hint of challenge in her skepticism.

"Perhaps we could get together and talk about this—"

"Oh, yes, let's do! I've been thinking it would be nice to start a local spiritual group. Something that's *in*clusive, you know, not *ex*clusive? So we can share all viewpoints! I know a woman who's really into crystals, and she has a friend who channels . . . oh, who is it? I forget, but it's one of those old biblical names!"

Oh, dear. My first thought was, *Count me out of that.* But on second thought I said, "Be sure to let me know when you're meeting." Anything I could do to turn this misguided group around, yes!

"I heard from Skye about the . . . unpleasant incident with

Leslie Marcone. I'm so sorry." Tammi's tone, on what she obviously viewed as a Sensitive Subject, turned subdued now. No exclamation points. "I hope she isn't going to make trouble for you?"

"She talked to the police. Sgt. Yates came to see me."

"Oh, well, everything will be okay, then! He's such a sweetie, isn't he?"

"Sweetie?" It was not a word I'd associate with Sgt. Yates.

"He's trying to get a skateboard park built, you know. Where the kids can skateboard without getting in trouble like they do out on the sidewalks. And my Brad lent his name to the committee trying to raise money! He'll probably help dedicate it, when the time comes."

"Maybe it's the scar in Sgt. Yates's eyebrow that kind of puts me off."

"Oh, that!" Tammi scoffed. "Don't you know how he got that?"

"In a struggle with a desperate criminal, I assumed."

"No, he was playing backyard basketball with some kids, and the hoop crashed down on him. Like I said, he's just a big sweetie!"

*Okay, if you say so.* But I wasn't totally convinced.

Back to her subdued tone, Tammi added, "Sgt. Yates was the one who brought Skye home when she ran away right after her mother first sent her here. She was out on the highway, trying to hitchhike—"

"Hitchhike?" I repeated, appalled at the vision that brought to mind. Lovely, sultry, vulnerable Skye, out there with her belly button showing and her thumb lifted . . .

"He was so nice about it, really helpful, and just kept it all very quiet. We really appreciated that. Given Brad's position and all."

"I understand your husband may be going into politics."

"Oh yes! We're all so excited about it. He'll make an official announcement soon, and then we'll get a real campaign going."

"I'm sure he'll do well. He seems very personable on TV."

"Oh, he is! Thank you."

The girls highlighted their hair. The highlights didn't make much difference on Sandy's blonde, but after two heavy doses, Skye's dark hair definitely looked different. Not the sunshiny splashes of gold on the girl on the carton. Skye's highlights were more a muddy-river reddish. I'd have been inclined to hide under a paper bag, but the girls seemed delighted. "Really punk," Sandy said approvingly. "Maybe we should get some of those stick-on tattoos too!"

"Stick-ons?" Skye pooh-poohed. "How about we go for the real thing!"

Sandy looked at me. "I know. Not without asking Mom."

We all went to church together the following morning. I volunteered for the nursery, an offer that a harried-looking woman instantly snapped up. In two minutes I found myself surrounded by babies, toddlers, bottles, and diapers. It was wonderful!

Back at home after church, I fixed tacos. The girls decided to go pick up Baby and take him for a ride in Skye's car. I took a walk on the trail and on the way back spotted a gleam of metal near the bottom of the boat landing by the boathouse over at Tara of the Ozarks. On closer inspection, I realized the gleam was a car.

I stopped short. Leslie's Mercedes? But she never left it out of the garage. Why would it be down there? She could, I supposed, have had something to unload at the boathouse and parked down there for closer access. Although I couldn't think what.

At the house I got Mike's binoculars out of a drawer by the window, but from there the angle was wrong and I couldn't

126

see the car at all because the boathouse was in the way. I took the binoculars down to the little dock for a better view.

From that vantage point I saw no sign of movement, so if Leslie had something to unload she'd apparently already done so. But if she was finished, why hadn't she put the car away?

Another study through the binoculars raised a different question. *Was* it Leslie's car? Someone else's car parked on the property seemed unlikely, given Leslie's hostile "keep out" attitude. But I'm not good at car identification even up close, and, with the glint of sunshine and the distance across the lake, I couldn't even tell if the car was pale-colored, like Leslie's light blue Mercedes, or something different.

The car must have been put there just this morning, because I hadn't seen it before—

Not necessarily. From the house, with the boathouse blocking the view of the boat landing, I couldn't have seen a car if one had been there. Could the car have been there even when I made my ill-fated excursion to the house to claim my whistle? It was possible. The driveway dipped steeply downward just above where boats could be put into the water, and I hadn't ventured far onto the property that day. My attention had also been considerably distracted by the intruder in the brush. The car could have been there and I just hadn't seen it.

In any case, the presence of the car, assuming it was hers, indicated she was home, probably had been home all along and just wasn't answering the phone.

I marched into the house and dialed her number once more. I really did want my whistle. I let the phone ring eighteen times. Eighteen! Wouldn't that be enough to drive even Leslie crazy? But no answer.

I was just hanging up the phone when a motor home pulled into the driveway. My first thought was that it was

Magnolia and Geoff returning. But they wouldn't be on their way home this soon. *Oh, I hope nothing's wrong* . . . Then I realized the motor home wasn't as big as their behemoth. Also, when it turned around in the driveway, I saw that a rack on back held a bicycle, and there was no magnolia mural—

Mac! Mac MacPherson.

# 15

I felt unexpected fireworks of excitement as he stepped out of the motor home. (Yes, in spite of what Generation Xers may believe, even LOLs can have unexpected explosions of fireworks.) Mac looked trim in tan pants and blue polo shirt, silver-white hair still crisp and thick, stride still vigorous.

Just as quickly, the fireworks froze up like a computer program, and everything stopped dead.

Yes, this was Mac MacPherson. The man with "commitment issues." The man who thought I was a man-hungry spinster out to snare him like a dogcatcher after a stray dachshund.

A more disturbing thought suddenly overrode that indignation. How had he found me? Because if *he'd* been able to do it—

So that was the first question out of my mouth when I went out to meet him. "What are you doing here? How did you know where to find me?"

"I'm glad to see you too," he muttered.

"I'm sorry. I mean, I am glad to see you. It's just that I've been trying to keep my whereabouts secret—"

"I know. I ran into Magnolia and Geoff at a powwow over in Oklahoma that I was covering for a travel magazine . . . you can't miss that motor home with the magnolia on back, you know? Anyway, they told me you were temporarily hiding out away from home. But we talked it over, and none of us could see any problem with my knowing where you were. So I thought I'd stop in and say hello on my way up to Lake of the Ozarks. I have a travel magazine assignment to do a piece on fishing and camping there."

The long explanation sounded as if he felt he had to defend his presence here, and guilt hit me like a soggy dishrag. He was right, of course. Nothing to get in a tizzy about. Mac knowing my whereabouts surely couldn't hurt anything. He wasn't operating a hotline to the Braxtons. This was a nice gesture, stopping to see me, and I was being rude.

I considered giving him a hug to show him I really was glad he'd come. But I didn't want to encourage his skewed view of my matrimonial intentions. My next thought was, *Offer food*, which I figure takes care of most situations. Then the thought occurred to me that he might interpret that as the old the-way-to-a-man's-heart-is-through-his-stomach ploy, so I just stood there feeling awkward and uncomfortable. Up close, I could see a faint stubble of silvery beard on his tanned face. Stubble makes some men look old and unkempt; on Mac it was rakish and masculine.

"Seen any good meteors lately?" he inquired, cautiously referring to the Meteor Daze celebration we'd shared last year.

Then I thought, *Phooey on this!* I was glad to see him, and not showing it was petty and dishonest. I threw out my arms and gave him a big hug, which brought a surprised smile, as well as a return hug. "I haven't seen a good meteor in months," I declared, and then I invited him in for oatmeal cookies and coffee.

I thanked him for earlier sending me a copy of the article he'd written about the Meteor Daze, and he told me about his travels since last summer. We talked about the murder trial I'd been involved in and the ensuing threats on my life. About DeeAnn and Mike moving to Hawaii, and my short-lived job with the abrupt ending.

It was much like the way old-friend Thea and I used to talk, unrelated subjects segueing comfortably into each other. I was just starting a chicken and rice casserole for dinner when Skye dropped off Sandy. I introduced Sandy and Mac, and about five minutes later she edged me off to the side and whispered, "Aunt Ivy, I didn't know you had a boyfriend!"

I hastened to bury that line of thinking. "No, just an acquaintance," I whispered back. "He's a friend of Magnolia and Geoff's."

"Okay, whatever you say." It was the kind of cheerful agreement that isn't agreement at all. She even winked at me. "Great tattoo!" she added.

Mac has a tattoo of a blue motorcycle on his right forearm. We've never gotten around to discussing it. I have mixed feelings about it. Why does any man decorate an arm with a drawing, let alone one of a blue motorcycle? Yet it isn't truly unattractive . . .

Sandy and Mac got along fine. It never occurred to me they'd have anything in common, but they're both the kind of people who can find something to talk about with almost anyone. Turned out Mac has a granddaughter who is just getting into gymnastics, and he and Sandy had this whole lively conversation about balance beams and floor exercises and vaults.

It was well past dark by the time we finished dinner, but the night was clear and a half moon sailed grandly across the sky. I put on a jacket, and Mac got one from his motor home, and we strolled along the trail. On the way back I led him down to the little dock. Most of the houses across the lake were lit up, lights reflected in the water below, the reflections so clear that it looked as if another world existed down below the familiar houses. A silvery moon shone in that world too. We even saw a shooting star, which was a nice reminder of last summer.

Lights showed in the windows at Tara of the Ozarks, confirming that Leslie was home. Although, on second thought, I realized that wasn't necessarily true. Leslie had the lights set on a timer system so they came on automatically whether she was home or away. For what reason she'd never shared with me, although I sometimes suspected she was somewhat intimidated by her oversized house. In the dark I couldn't tell if the car was still down there by the boathouse.

Mac had taken my hand when we scrambled from the trail to the dock, but it was a purely practical gesture to keep me from slipping on the damp ground, of course. Definitely nothing personal or romantic. "How's the fishing here?" he asked. "I hear there's bass and catfish and crappie in these Arkansas lakes."

"I see boats out there sometimes, and once in a while someone fishes off the shore. I don't know if they're catching anything."

"Too bad I don't have any fishing gear with me. I broke my pole down in Baja and never got around to replacing it."

"Mike has equipment out in the garage. I'm sure he wouldn't mind if you used it. We could go out in the boat in the morning." I motioned to the skiff still tied to the dock.

"Hey, that'd be great!"

I told Mac he could park the motor home in the yard for the night, but he said he hadn't had hookups for several nights and needed a sewer connection so he could dump the holding tanks. The practical complications of on-the-road living that never occur to those of us whose homes stay attached to one spot of earth.

We looked up RV parks in the phone book, and he called the closest one to make sure they had a vacancy. After he left I dug out Mike's fishing equipment, much of which had once been my husband Harley's. Most of the fishing flies were ones I'd tied for Harley. I felt a moment of nostalgia, remembering fishing jaunts we'd shared and the special "Ugly Bug" I used to tie for him. Would Harley mind if Mac used his gear?

No, Harley had always loaned it generously. Always loaned everything generously, for that matter. A good man, my Harley.

When Mac showed up next morning, freshly shaved, he'd already acquired bait and a temporary out-of-state fishing license from a local sporting goods store. He wore a battered straw hat, khaki shorts, beat-up running shoes, no socks. His knees were as knobby as I remembered. Although I had to admit there was something mildly endearing about their knobbiness.

I'd packed a lunch so we could stay out as long as we wanted. Mac had information about a "hot" fishing hole up at the northern end of the lake, and we took turns rowing. We were well out on the water before I remembered I'd planned to call Sgt. Yates this morning about the prowler at Leslie's. But I could see now that the car was still there, and it was definitely light colored. So she must be home, and, knowing Leslie, the skulker was probably in more danger from her short-edged temper than she was at risk from him. *Better wear your steel-plated armor, fella.*

It was a great day. Sunshine, gentle breeze. Three bright, deep-bodied crappie quickly snapped up the bait, and Mac plunked them into the ice chest he'd optimistically brought along to hold his catch. We saw a long-legged bird majestically poised in shallow water looking for fish of his own, and a big-eyed doe watched us calmly from shore.

We rowed into shore to eat an early lunch of leftover chicken and baked beans. This was beyond the private land, a government-owned area where homes could not invade, and only a couple of ducks quacked their annoyance at our intrusion. Mac tied the boat to a bush, and we settled on a grassy slope that smelled of damp earth and lush green growing things. A tiny green frog jumped out of the way when I spread a plaid tablecloth. A stand of cattails grew nearby.

We ate and drank the coffee I'd brought in a thermos, and afterward Mac lay back against the grass, hands pillowed behind his head, hat shielding his face from the sun. I thought he was dozing, but unexpectedly he said, "Sometimes, when I'm out on the road driving in the middle of the night, I listen to one of those evangelist preachers on the radio."

I cautiously thought this could be good news. Mac's deceased wife had been a Christian, but I already knew from our conversations last year that he was a confirmed skeptic. So a new willingness to listen to a radio message might suggest a change of heart. On the other hand, I'd heard some late-night preachers who, if I weren't already a solid Christian, would have sent me skittering in the opposite direction. So what I said was a cautious, "Oh?"

"One night one of them was talking about God never abandoning his people. Always being there for them. He had some Bible verse, of course."

"Perhaps the one in Hebrews: 'Never will I leave you; never will I forsake you.'"

"Do you believe that?"

"Of course. Another one that comforts me is Psalm 46:1: 'God is our refuge and strength, an ever-present help in trouble.'"

"They're just words. I write words. Thousands of them."

"But these are inspired words from the Lord."

"Don't you feel abandoned?"

"Me? No. Why would I?"

"Why? You lost your husband and son. You have no grand-children. You have, for all practical purposes, been driven out of your home. You have a family of thugs after you. You were unfairly fired from your job—"

"My goodness, I didn't realize I was so bad off. And you don't even know about my bad hair days, the senior moment when I brushed my teeth with Ben-Gay, or the fact that I've come to the realization I'm never going to climb Mt. Everest, swim the English Channel, or wear a thong bikini."

He ignored my facetious list. "Seriously, don't you some-times feel as if God forgot about you?"

I sat up straighter. "No, I certainly don't. I might prefer that some parts of my life were different, but God isn't a vending machine where you put your prayer in one slot and an easy solution pops out of another."

Mac changed his argument. "Maybe he didn't forget you. Maybe the whole God thing is just a . . . crock. Wishful think-ing. A desire for an eternal justice to make up for all the injustice here on earth."

"I look outside me and see all God created. I read my Bible and understand that Jesus died for me. I peer inside me and see him alive and well in my heart. No, I don't think it's all a crock."

Silence. I wasn't certain if that meant he was thoughtfully digesting what I'd said, gathering arguing points, or had fallen asleep. Then I was curious about his jumping-off point into this conversation. "Why are you out there driving in the middle of the night?"

"Sometimes I get restless. It's only a few feet from the bed to the driver's seat, so I get up and head for wherever I'm going."

135

"Where are you going?"

"Well, you know, here and there. I've been from Montana to Baja to Florida this past year. There's always a festival or an odd museum or some kind of doings or just an interesting new place to see and write about. And my kids to visit, of course."

"Did it ever occur to you that maybe you're searching for something?"

"Like what?" He slid the straw hat aside, and I saw alarm in the exposed blue eye.

"Searching for God. You're wandering all over the countryside looking for him. You just don't know it yet."

I thought that interpretation might annoy him, but, oddly, he looked relieved, and I suddenly realized what he'd thought I meant. "You thought I was implying that you're subconsciously looking for a companion in your travels. A *wife*."

"A lot of women alone are eager to marry again." A wariness in his tone suggested he'd encountered a few of them.

"It's the statistics. What are there, ten of us for every one of you?"

"I don't think the odds are quite that bad," he protested.

"You were afraid I might suggest myself as a suitable candidate for the wife position?"

This time he sat up and studied me squarely. Finally, his expression a combination of miffed and surprised, he shook his head. "Ivy, I don't think you'd marry me if I pulled out a diamond ring right here on the spot."

"Hmmm."

"Hmmm, what?"

"Hmmm, what size diamond are we talking about?"

Mac laughed. "Would it matter?"

"No," I had to admit. I liked Mac. I enjoyed his company. We had good times together. But I wasn't in the market for a bridegroom. "It wouldn't."

He hadn't exactly offered marriage. I hadn't exactly declined. But we both knew where we stood. He momentarily looked undecided as to whether he should be relieved or disappointed. Relief won.

"Good. That's settled then."

About that time a gust of wind startled us both. I looked up, surprised to find that dark clouds were rapidly eating up the blue sky. We dumped everything into the boat and raced for home. At least as fast as two seniors in a rowboat can race.

We didn't beat the storm. It hit us a good fifteen minutes from the dock. We were soaked, hair flattened to our heads, clothes plastered to our skin, by the time we slipped and slid up the trail to the house. Soaked and muddy and laughing.

From then on, we laughed a lot; that awkwardness when Mac first arrived had vanished now. He elaborated on his travels: a Crawdad Festival, complete with Crawdad Queen. An encounter with an oversized and very grumpy lizard in Baja. A letter, which made its way through a magazine publisher to him, from a woman proposing marriage, after which she said she'd provide an introduction to aliens who had recently given her a ride in their UFO and might give him one too. He could write a book about it, she suggested.

Maybe the man had a right to be suspicious of female intentions, I had to concede. And I didn't even have alien friends to offer as inducement.

I cooked the fish, frying them up crisp and golden and adding oven-baked fries and coleslaw. Mac offered enthusiastic compliments. Sandy mentioned her upcoming gymnastics meet in Fayetteville and invited Mac to come. He said he was leaving in the morning, but he'd try to be back this way in time for it.

Which was more than I'd known about his plans before that moment.

Later, Sandy's Christian rock band friends came over for practice in the basement. Mac's initial reaction was like what mine had been: shock at all the noise and blue hair. He never did go so far as to express approval of the group, but I noticed his toe tapping to the beat.

Before I fell asleep I had a thought. Mac was leaving in the morning, but perhaps he'd have time to go over to Leslie's with me first. It seemed unlikely I'd encounter the skulker again, but I'd rather Mac was with me, just in case.

A plan that floundered before it ever got off the ground.

# 16

I found Mac's note on the door:

Dear Ivy,
I decided to get an early start. Thanks for your hospitality.
It was good seeing you again. You're a great person to be
caught with out in a storm! Maybe I'll be back this way in a
few days.
Your friend,
Mac

I stood there with the brief note in my hand, pricked
by disappointment that he was already gone and that the
possibility of his return was definitely on the vague side. It
was just as possible he wouldn't return, that he'd be off to
investigate anything from an Edsel rally to a dress-your-cat
contest.

Following hard on the heels of the disappointment was a different reaction. We'd settled our relationship. Friends. No hidden agendas. Yet now he'd run off as if he suddenly feared I was going to pull out a fishing net and drag him in. I felt . . . betrayed. And angry.

I stomped around preparing breakfast, the eggs for French toast frothing under the furious attack of my eggbeater, the toast itself whapped into flattened submission with my spatula. Insufferable, egotistical male!

Yet Sandy's reaction to Mac's sudden departure was an unmiffed, "Hey, wouldn't it be fun to be able to just pick up and go whenever you wanted? He's a really cool guy." It made me step back to reassess the situation, and by the time Sandy headed off to school, I was embarrassed by my petty internal outburst.

I was reading too much into Mac's departure, which probably had nothing to do with me. Mac was simply being Mac. A man who might get up in the middle of the night and drive a couple hundred miles. A man I was almost certain was really restlessly searching for God, even if he didn't know it yet.

But that was between Mac and God, not Mac and me.

And, who knows? Maybe God had an appointment with a late-night radio preacher scheduled for Mac last night, and he had to be on the road to meet it.

*Go with him, Lord. Help him to find you.*

Then a disconnected thought struck me. One that was much more disturbing than Mac's sudden departure. He'd driven his motor home right into the yard to leave the note on the door, and I hadn't even heard it! I could apparently be overrun by Braxtons arriving in cars, trucks, or tanks and never hear a squeak of warning. It was enough to make me want to set up warning barricades of tin cans in the driveway.

On careful consideration, however, the alarm slipped back

to the be-aware-but-don't-panic level. Sandy usually remembered to activate the security alarm system for the house, so
Braxtons wouldn't get inside without our knowing it. And
what I'd told Mac was true: God is my refuge and fortress
and in him I can safely place my trust. *So here it is, Lord. My
trust. Watch out for those Braxtons for me, will you?*

Okay, that was settled. But I still wanted that whistle Thea
had given me. Once more I tried to call Leslie. Once more
she didn't answer. Once more I went down to the dock with
the binoculars. The car was still there. She surely wouldn't
allow some outside car to remain on her property this long,
so it must be hers, which also meant she must be home.

Once more I drove around the lake and parked outside
the gate at 2742 Vintage Road, crawled through the fence,
and, keeping a wary eye out for skulkers, marched down the
driveway. I couldn't think why Leslie would object to my
retrieving such a trivial item, but if she felt possessive about
leftovers, who knew what attitude she might take toward a
whistle in her cabinet drawer?

A running dialogue with her in my head broke off. My feet
slowed, and I reluctantly acknowledged what I'd been trying
to ignore from the moment I crawled through the fence.

The eeriness.

"Vibes," my friend Magnolia would say ominously. Bad
vibes.

I reminded myself, as I had last time, that the house had
felt eerie the time Leslie was away overnight, and it hadn't
meant anything then. I couldn't convince myself it didn't
mean something now. The feeling was just too . . . dense.

I stopped, listening for any sound that might suggest I'd
blundered into a second encounter with the skulker. Rustle,
snap, thunk? No. Footsteps? Breathing? Scratching an itch?
No. Nothing.

A car passed by on the road, but somehow the sound

only emphasized the silence on this side of the gate. As if I'd stepped into another world here. Another dimension.

*Let's get this over with.* I hurried to the door and rang the bell. I knocked. I pounded. Nothing.

Leslie, the Queen of Cool, could, of course, be doing what she did so well with ringing phones. She was probably sitting in there with her usual aloof, superior expression. Maybe she was even laughing at me. I tried to feel amused or indignant at such pettiness, but I couldn't muster much of either.

The eerie feeling was, in fact, growing stronger by the second. The back of my neck felt as if some powerful magnet was pulling at it, raising minuscule hairs I hadn't known existed. I wanted to turn and run, dash back to my T-bird and burn rubber screeching out of the driveway. But . . .

*Something is not right here.*

Could Leslie be inside and ill or injured? Perhaps she'd fallen down the stairs or had an accident on one of those weird exercise machines? A couple of them looked as if they'd happily chomp down on an unwary human body and turn it into a trapped pretzel.

Reluctantly, conscience not allowing me to run and escape, I warily circled the house. The ragged grass looked as if it hadn't been tended since my employment ended, but I didn't know if Leslie had the gardener scheduled on a regular basis or if he came only when she called. Or maybe she was between gardeners as well as housekeepers.

I walked up the broad front steps and rang the doorbell. I'd never heard it before, because no one had ever come to the door during my term of employment, and I was surprised to hear a few incongruously cheerful tinkles of "Camptown Races." At the moment, even in broad daylight, they bore a disquieting resemblance to whistling in the dark. I peered through a window, hands cupped between face and glass so I could see inside, half afraid of what I would see. Leslie peering back at me, with a stun gun ready to blast me? Or maybe a Frankenstein-faced intruder who was hiding in there staring back at me? Or perhaps ex-husband with a bloody hatchet?

But the living room looked just as I'd left it, neat and impersonal as an expensive hotel room, and quite empty. From here I couldn't see if Leslie's office door was open or shut.

Turning, I could now see that the car down by the boathouse was definitely Leslie's light blue Mercedes. Cautiously I walked over to where the straight section of driveway led downward to the water, then on to the car. It was only a few feet from the water's edge.

I tiptoed up to the car. Why the tiptoe? It just seemed the proper way to approach. I reached for the door handle, wondering if the car was locked. But some subconscious buzzer made my hand jerk back without touching it. Instead I leaned over and peered through the window. The car keys were hanging in the ignition. A purse and the remote control for the gate lay on the passenger's seat.

Which meant . . . what?

Cautiously I circled around the rear of the car and onto the boat dock. Going in front of the car would have been the shorter route, but I didn't want to put myself between the car and the water. It was foolish, I knew. The car was obviously empty. But I couldn't escape the feeling that it might somehow plunge forward, gleefully malevolent as some Stephen King creation, and crush me under its wheels.

The dock creaked gently under my footsteps. I paused at the boathouse door. The brass padlock and chain were still in place. I didn't touch them, but I peered through the crack. The small boat looked the same as always, suspended above the water in its cradle.

I walked out to the end of the dock.

And then I knew why Leslie hadn't been answering her phone or doorbell.

## 17

Her face wasn't visible, but the long hair, floating like blonde seaweed in the greenish water, was unmistakable. A section of her blue velour sweatshirt was snagged on the ladder. Her arms floated out to the sides. Her body hung below, trailing down into the green depths, undulating gently in some unseen movement of the lake water.

Strangely, as I stood there frozen, the first thought that came to my mind was the memory of Leslie saying, "I don't believe in eternity."

*Oh, Leslie . . .*

Then a handful of tiny fish, hatchlings no more than an inch long, fluttered around her floating fingers, and suddenly the bile rose in my throat at the horror of it. This was Leslie, Leslie *dead*, and fish were nibbling at her flesh . . .

I stepped back, hand to my midsection, the world momentarily reeling dizzily around me as my throat worked in reverse. I clenched my fists and willed my stomach not to rebel and my knees not to collapse.

Then I realized what I was doing. More important, what I wasn't doing. I was simply standing there, helplessly clenching my hands, concentrating only on my own sick feelings. And maybe I was wrong. Maybe she wasn't dead! Maybe, even if her face was buried in water, she was just unconscious and still living. People had been underwater for minutes and still survived . . .

I knelt on the dock and frantically tried to get my hands under her arms. If I could pull her up on the dock, remember those CPR lessons Thea and I had taken a half dozen years ago . . .

*Help me, Lord!*

In the water her body felt almost buoyant. It bobbed gently as I struggled to lift her, almost as if it was trying to help me. Little wavelets raised by the movement splashed against the dock. Drops of water spattered my face. One hit my lip. I quashed a half-hysterical urge to drop the body and wipe those contaminated drops away.

I got her up a few inches, one wrist draped over the dock. I still couldn't see her face, but her fingers had an eerie, bluish look. And now, shoulders out of the water, she became sluggishly immovable, as if some malevolent force held her from below. Even straining until my muscles burned and my arms shook and my eyes lost focus, I could lift her no farther.

A dead weight.

No! She could be alive. Perhaps a state of suspended animation. Or a coma. Wasn't that possible?

I kept one hand under her arm and tried with the other to grab her hair and lift her head. If I could just get her nose and mouth out of the water . . .

Her hair slipped out of my grasp. Then I realized in horror that some of it had come loose in my fingers. I shook my hand frantically, trying to get rid of it, and she slipped back in the water with a splash that spattered my face again.

Her hair, once pale gold and glossy, now dull and lank, was only inches from my face as I knelt over her to reestablish my hold. I tried not to gag again as the scent of waterlogged flesh and clothing—and some other, uglier scent of death and decay—filled my nose. Bits of greenish lake stuff clung in her hair. Some of the hair I'd pulled out floated loose in the water.

CPR couldn't help her. I could feel the death in the body as surely as I felt the hard wooden deck under my knees. I knew it and yet I kept struggling. I had to get her out! I couldn't just let her dangle here in the water, caught like some dead fish on a line. With tiny fish nibbling at her flesh . . .

The velour sweatshirt bunched up under my hands, and I tried to get a better grip on the soggy material. My hands slipped, and the body drifted sideways. Frantically I yanked it back.

Only to feel it slipping even farther out of my grasp. Somehow in trying to lift her I'd loosened the shirt from where it was snagged on the ladder, and she was floating free.

I plunged forward, desperately grabbing to keep the body from sinking or floating away. My face pitched into the water, and then I was choking and spitting and frantically scrabbling and scrambling with hands and elbows and toes to keep from plunging over the edge of the dock myself.

But as the roiled water cleared I saw the body below me, out of reach, slowly bobbing and drifting away. It moved almost leisurely, rising and falling, twisting gracefully, hair disappearing last, like some golden wraith reaching for the surface.

I stared after it for a paralyzed moment. What had I done? Then I struggled to my feet and stumbled up the driveway. Telephone. Help!

Too late for help. The knowledge clanged in my mind like a doomsday bell. But I had to get someone here—the thought of her drifting down there below the surface, at the mercy of whatever might be down there, panicked me. I ran to the double doors at the house. Locked, of course. I tried every door I could find. A couple of side doors I'd never seen used, the rear door, even the garage doors. Everything locked. Irrationally, I ran back and pounded on the rear door. Strangely, I heard the phone inside ringing. But it was as inaccessible to me as if enclosed in a steel vault. Later, I was to think, *Why didn't I look in her purse in the car for house keys?* But that never occurred to me at this frantic moment.

I ran to the gate, then across the street. The gate-rammer's house? It didn't matter. Again I pounded until my fists numbed under the blows. No answer.

I ran back to the road. I flapped my arms frantically at an oncoming car. The lone woman in the car looked as if she was going to detour around me. I realized how I must look, like some dripping, deranged scarecrow.

*Lord, make her stop!* I pleaded. I brushed back the wet hair plastered to my forehead.

She did stop finally, a few feet past me, two wheels on the shoulder. She didn't open the window, just eyed me warily as I ran up.

"Do you have a cell phone?" I yelled. I pantomimed holding a phone to my ear. "Leslie Marcone is in the water. We need help!"

The window came down a few inches. "What do you mean?"

"The woman who lives here—" I motioned toward the house. "I found her at the end of the dock, in the water—"

"You mean she fell in?"

"I don't know what happened. I tried to get her up on the dock, but I lost hold of her—"

"She's *drowning*?"

"I don't know. I think . . . I think she's already drowned. Please—"

"I don't have a cell phone." The woman hesitated a moment, then apparently decided I was more panicky than dangerous. "But you can come to the house—"

"No, I have to go back down there. Call 911."

Logic told me I could do nothing for Leslie now. Emotion told me I couldn't leave her alone down there.

The woman hesitated a moment, as if wondering if this was real or some ghastly joke—or even if I was quite sane.

"Please," I said again, and she must have heard some desperation in the plea. She nodded and drove off, slowly at first, then with a squeal on pavement as she suddenly sped up.

I ran back, clambered through the fence, down the driveway. More logic told me I could do nothing to help her. But run, hurry, was something I *could* do.

I knelt and stared down into the water at the end of the dock when I reached it, eyes straining. Nothing. For a split second, I wondered if maybe I'd imagined all this. Maybe I'd taken a spectacular swan dive into the sea of senility.

Then I spotted a few blonde hairs floating in the water, a few blue threads clinging to the metal ladder. No, this was all too real. Leslie's blond hair. Leslie's blue sweatshirt.

I took a deep breath and tried to think logically while I waited for help. What had happened here? I turned to look at the car as I tried to piece things together.

She'd obviously driven the car down to the boathouse for some reason. (Why?) Then she'd walked out on the dock (why?), where she must have slipped or stumbled and tumbled into the water, and the sweatshirt had caught on the ladder as she fell.

An accident. Accidents happened all the time. Forget the unexplained whys. I remembered an elderly woman from Madison Street who'd gone on vacation with her family and drowned in a few feet of water in a creek.

But Leslie wasn't elderly. She was in excellent physical

condition and, from what Sandy had said, an excellent swimmer as well.

If she'd accidentally fallen into the water, she surely could have pulled herself out. So she must have hit her head on the dock when she fell. Knocked herself out and drowned before she regained consciousness. Yes, a logical explanation.

And why was I so frantically proposing these logical accident scenarios to myself?

I knew why. Because down beneath them, down in depths murkier than the water in which Leslie bobbed and drifted, lurked the ominous thought that this was no accident. That Leslie had been pushed into the water. Maybe knocked out by some malicious blow before she was pushed. Maybe held under to finish the job.

She had enemies, no doubt about that. She may, or may not, have been in hiding here at Little Tom Lake, but the ex-husband's surprise visit had made plain that she was at least avoiding people from her past. And she'd made new enemies here as well.

Another thought hit me. The skulker. Had I barely missed encountering a murderer the last time I was here? Had I scared him off, but he'd come back and killed Leslie later? Or had he already killed her, and I arrived just as he was escaping?

Surely not. Surely Leslie's body couldn't have been down here in the water, snagged on the ladder, since then! *You've got to stop reading those murder mysteries, stop letting imagination take you on a rocket ride.* Sgt. Yates would say this. This surely had to be exactly what it looked like—an accident. Ghastly, yes. But an accident, nothing more. To think otherwise was morbid imagination.

I hadn't looked at my watch when I asked the woman out on the road to call 911, so I had no idea how much time was passing as I leaned against the boathouse for support. It

149

felt like hours before I heard sirens in the distance, though logic, which I kept trying to summon, told me no more than ten minutes had elapsed.

The thought occurred to me as a siren wailed up to the gate that Sgt. Yates was not going to be pleased. Hadn't he warned me: no dead bodies?

And I definitely had a dead body for him.

# 18

Two uniformed officers were the first authorities on the scene. Sgt. Yates was not one of them. But he wouldn't be, I reminded myself. Because this was an accident, and he was in the Major Crimes Unit. The two men came running down the driveway, one of them yelling when he spotted me, "We got an emergency call. A woman drowning—"

I pointed to the end of the dock, and they ran by me. I followed, putting one foot carefully ahead of the other because I felt as if I might all too easily wobble over the edge of the dock myself. I pointed again. We all stared into the greenish depths.

It was a pleasant morning. Unseasonably warm. Almost hot. Calm and peaceful. Sunlight shafted into the water, highlighting specks like watery dust motes. The ladder, I now saw, ended three feet below the surface. It looked deceptively inviting. *C'mon in, have a swim.*

Yeah. Just you, me, and a dead body.

"You're sure?" The officer sounded doubtful.

"I'm sure. I saw her."

"You saw her fall in?"

"No, but I saw her drift away just a few minutes ago—"

He didn't give me a chance to finish before he jerked his head at the other officer and barked, "Get on the radio. We may need a diver."

This all seemed vaguely unreal, as if I were an actress in some bizarre play, and none of the parts were very well rehearsed.

"I don't think you need to—"

Another siren wailed to a stop at the gate, and the first officer turned to me. "How do we get the gate open? We're going to need equipment down here."

I started to answer that they'd have to get inside the house, where the gate controls were located, but now I finally remembered what I'd seen in the Mercedes. I pointed to the car. "Remote control for the gate. On the front seat."

The other officer headed for the car.

"Hey, wait!" I yelled. "You can't—"

Too late. He'd already grabbed the handle and yanked the door open, no doubt obliterating any fingerprints that might be there. *No matter*, I reminded myself. *This is only an accident.*

The first officer was stripping off his uniform. His shoes clunked to the deck, blue shirt flung atop them, belt with holstered gun, cell phone, and other police gear strapped to it placed more carefully atop the other items.

I admired his willingness to plunge instantly into the depths in a rescue attempt, and I was disturbed about Leslie being down there somewhere. But the sad fact was that this heroic gesture wasn't exactly necessary. "I don't think there's any big rush—"

"You said she's only been underwater a few minutes. We might be able to save her." He yanked a wallet out of his pants pocket and dropped it on the pile.

"That's right. But you didn't give me a chance to finish. She was already dead when she drifted away. Her body was caught on the ladder. I was trying to get her up on the dock, but she . . . got away from me." I ended on a lame note. Spoken aloud, my contribution to this situation sounded both careless and incompetent. "I tried to hold on to her, but she just . . . slipped away." It didn't sound any better on second telling.

The young officer stood there barechested and barefooted, a fine male specimen who looked as if he was ready to toss me over the edge. "She was already dead? Are you sure?"

"I think she'd been dead for . . . some time. Although I'm no expert," I added hastily.

"Why didn't you tell us this to begin with?"

"You didn't give me a chance."

He started putting his clothes back on. "Okay, how long had she been in the water before she, as you put it, 'got away' from you?"

"I don't know. Although I think it could have been . . . a while. I came to retrieve something I'd left in the house—"

"Retrieve?"

"I was Ms. Marcone's housekeeper up until a few days ago. I'd left a personal item in a kitchen drawer and wanted to get it back. No one answered my ring or knock. I was curious about her car being parked down here. So I came down to the dock and . . . there she was."

"In the water?"

"Caught on the ladder." I showed him where her velour sweatshirt had snagged. I pointed out the blonde hairs and blue threads caught on the ladder and other hairs still floating on the water.

"So you don't know what happened?"

"No. I suppose she must have stumbled or slipped or something, hit her head and drowned."

153

"You saw a head injury?"

"No. But something like that must have happened. She was a good swimmer . . . she could swim across the lake and back . . . so she wouldn't have drowned just falling in the water."

He gave me an up-and-down inspection, as if I'd only now registered as something more than an anonymous blip on his radar. "And you are . . . ?"

I gave him my name and pointed to the house across the lake. "I live over there—"

I didn't have time to explain further. With the gate apparently open now, the police car, which I saw was from the county sheriff's office, roared down the driveway, brakes screeching when it stopped behind the Mercedes. Behind it lumbered a red fire truck, then another car marked with the sheriff's emblem. The officer I'd talked to was still barefoot but tucking in his shirttail as he trotted over to meet them.

"Don't go away," he turned and called back to me. It sounded as much warning as command.

A few minutes later another car with a fire department emblem arrived. Two men slid out. One dragged out scuba gear—black rubber suit and yellow oxygen tanks—and put it on. He plunged off the end of the dock. By this time a small crowd had gathered, arriving from wherever it is crowds emerge from in catastrophes. A boat was stopped about a hundred feet offshore, sun glinting on binoculars as the occupants watched the activities.

A newly arrived officer herded me, along with everyone else, off the dock and away from the car. A few minutes later the diver surfaced about thirty feet from the dock. Something bobbed beside him. He dragged it with him back to the dock.

There, two officers took the body from him and laid it on the dock, water sloshing across the wooden boards. More water sloshed when the diver came up the ladder and stood on the dock, peering down at Leslie's body. A murmur like a passing wave rolled through the crowd.

An officer knelt by the body and pressed fingers to her throat. It was a formality only. I don't think anyone expected anything but his negative shake of head as he stood up.

In life Leslie had always appeared so lean and toned and healthy, like a racehorse ready to run. Regal and a bit disdainful of more ordinary human beings. Not stunningly beautiful but definitely attractive. Now, even from a distance, her body looked . . . odd. Bloated. It was probably fortunate, I realized with a sick churn of stomach, that I hadn't gotten a look at her face when I tried to lift her head. I knew she'd have hated having all those officers gathered around staring down on her now.

There seemed to be some sort of conference taking place among those officers. One of them was on a cell phone. I wondered if a coroner or medical examiner had to come before the body could be removed from the dock. That usually happened in the murder mysteries I read.

But this wasn't a murder, I reminded myself. Just a terrible, tragic accident. Why did my thoughts keep slipping in that other direction? Although another part of my mind instantly countered, *Why cling so stubbornly to the accident theory?*

I knew the answer to that. Because, even though I knew it happened over and over in this imperfect world, I didn't want to think about one person being capable of deliberately snuffing out another's life. It was too . . . horrific.

My stomach was feeling ever more unreliable, and there was a peculiar ringing in my ears. I approached the officer assigned to crowd control. I leaned across the imaginary line created by his outstretched arms.

"Please, may I go home now? I'm not feeling too well."

The officer's impatient glance flicked in my direction but didn't focus on me, a situation with which I am not unfamiliar, given my general tendency to fade into woodwork, landscape, or crowd. "Sure, no one needs to stick around. Stay back, everyone stay back."

"I was the one who found the body," I said. "The other officer told me not to leave."

That finally brought a direct focus on me. "I'll check."

He motioned the first officer on the scene over for a conference. A few minutes later, after taking down my name, address, and phone number, plus a warning that they'd want to talk to me again, they let me go.

My feet had at some time gotten wet, and my shoes squished as I plodded up the driveway.

From across the lake, after changing my clothes and shoes, I watched the activity through binoculars. As a number of other people were doing, I realized.

The fire truck was gone now, and another vehicle had arrived. People, apparently people official enough to be allowed on the dock, milled around. The thought occurred to me that they could very well be destroying evidence. A man in dark clothing knelt over the body. Medical examiner?

Eventually two men put the body in a bag and carried it on a stretcher to a van. The vehicle drove away. The crowd shuffled around for a few minutes, then, reluctantly it seemed to me, started to disperse.

Where were they taking her? Who would look after the arrangements? Who would mourn?

The whole situation suddenly seemed unbearably sad.

Leslie, from all I'd seen, was so alone in the world. Alone, unloved . . .

And still, lurking in the dark basement of my mind, there was the ugly thought that perhaps she'd been even less than unloved and uncared for than I realized; perhaps someone had hated her. Hated her enough to kill her.

I'd forgotten lunch, I realized when the place across the lake finally appeared deserted by late afternoon, but I definitely had no desire to eat. I wondered if anyone had collected those blonde hairs and blue threads on the ladder. My whistle seemed unimportant now. I mentally apologized to Thea as I decided I'd just let it go.

Sandy had an after-school meeting. I automatically put three plates on the table when I saw Skye's red car with both girls in it pull into the yard. I wondered if news of the accident had reached the school yet. Apparently not, because Sandy and Skye were giggling and chattering about some guy at school who'd caused an uproar when he showed up with a reverse mohawk—shaved strip on top his head, long frizzed strands on the sides. I was thinking I should tell them about Leslie when Skye suddenly looked at the clock, grabbed the remote, and turned on the TV. She always liked to watch her father on the local news.

Leslie wasn't the top story. That went to a car accident on the other side of Fayetteville that had killed three people. But she was in second place.

"The body of a woman was discovered in Little Tom Lake in the elite Vintage Estates area near Woodston about 10:30 this morning. The identity of the body has not yet been released pending notification of next of kin, but outside sources say it is that of the owner of the property on which the body was found. Details of the drowning are still sketchy, but we'll keep you up-to-date as further information is released."

Brad Ridenour's reporting of the incident was done with proper solemnity, but the announcement was so brief that I had the odd feeling Leslie had been cheated. Her death deserved more than this.

For a moment I thought the news had passed right on by Sandy and Skye, but then it registered with Sandy and she gasped, "Somebody drowned right here in the lake today?"

"Leslie Marcone," I said. I swallowed. "I—I was over at her place, and I found her body."

They both looked at me. Even blasé teenagers' mouths can drop open, I realized. I explained the day's events.

"How awful," Skye said. "Finding someone dead." She shuddered delicately, an expression of distaste wrinkling her petite nose. "I saw this movie once, about a body being discovered after it had been in the water for days, and—"

"Skye, shut up," Sandy said, the command so fierce and harsh, so totally unlike Sandy, that Skye and I both looked at her in astonishment.

"Well, *okay*," Skye said, an offended note in her voice.

Sandy swallowed. "I'm sorry. It's just that . . . I mean, she was always jogging on the trail . . . and now she's dead . . ."

"You didn't even like her."

"That doesn't make any difference."

Sandy turned and walked over to the window. Skye and I followed. Skye, more understanding than I expected after Sandy's sharp outburst, put her arm around Sandy and squeezed her shoulders. We all stared across the lake at the big white house. I wondered if the car was still down there by the boathouse.

"But how could she drown?" Sandy asked finally. "She could swim like a fish."

I wasn't about to offer the girls my dark speculations, so all I said was, "She could have slipped and hit her head before falling in. There's a ladder at the end of the dock, and her sweatshirt was snagged on it. It kept her from sinking right away. I tried to get her body up on the dock before the police got there, but I . . . couldn't."

"I wonder how long she'd been dead," Sandy said.

"I suppose they have tests or something to figure that out."

Sandy suddenly turned and hugged me. "I'm glad Leslie fired you," she said unexpectedly, her tone almost fierce again. "If you were still working for her, maybe you'd have been down there on the dock with her, and you'd have fallen in too."

*Or been attacked by the person who attacked Leslie.* But I didn't say that. Although the thought occurred to me that the dock was a difficult place to sneak up on someone. Did that mean she'd known her attacker, and it had been a surprise assault?

*Whoa! Remember, this was an accident.*

I put the stir-fry dinner on the table and we ate, our conversation a bit subdued but on the normal subjects of school and gymnastics and Skye's mother's magazine and the Dumpling's latest dietary kick, which was anything green. Green yuck du jour, as Skye put it. The girls studied together for a while, and then Skye went home about 9:30. Sandy and I watched the 11:00 local news together. Brad Ridenour had more information about the drowning to offer now, including that a former employee had found the body, but Leslie still wasn't identified by name.

"They must be having trouble figuring out who her next of kin is," Sandy said, and I agreed. I wondered if an ex-husband was considered next of kin. Would it be helpful to

159

the authorities if someone told them about him? Although I didn't even know his name, of course.

I did, however, know the name of that dot-com company about which he and Leslie had exchanged hostile words. Which gave me an idea.

# 19

Sandy had always been the one in the family who made most use of the computer, but it was in the den next to the living room, not in her bedroom. I waited until she went to bed right after the news, then turned it on.

I connected to the Internet and typed the company name plus the usual dot-com into the address line on the browser. If CyberPowerAds had a web page, that should bring it up. But all I got was one of those frustrating this-page-cannot-be-displayed notices. I've snagged on this before, but my computer expertise is too limited to know exactly what it signifies. That there is a page, but people like me can't access it? That there had once been a website under that name, but it doesn't exist now? That computers were purposely designed for maximum user frustration?

I tried a different tactic, a fishing expedition. I put the company name into a search engine and clicked "go." Jackpot! All kinds of URLs popped up. What I wanted was a site that gave a simple, straightforward explanation of what this company was, who was involved, and what became of it.

It wasn't that simple. What I got were sites where the company was briefly mentioned, often with something along the lines of "the surprising demise of dot-com powerhouse CyberPowerAds." Also mentioned were "heretofore unrevealed capitalization problems" and "unrealized expectations." A little later I found what appeared to be one of the earliest references to the company and finally identified what the company actually did. In terms glowing enough to herald a discovery that simultaneously cured baldness, cancer, and absentmindedness, an online business magazine article announced the launch of this new business, CyberPowerAds, dedicated to capturing the market in Internet ads.

Internet ads. Did that mean those annoying things that were always popping up on the computer, interrupting whatever I was doing? Or spam? Maybe both?

Another, less formal, reference called the company "hot," the partners "hip," and the results "dazzling." Projected sales of 7.3 million dollars the first year, one item said, and destined to rise like a rocket taking off. No one site named all the partners in the company, but I scribbled names on a scratch pad as I found them here and there: Michael Flattery, apparently the head honcho. Also Shane Wagner, Leslie Wagner, Dirk Carson, and Lissa Rambough.

Leslie Wagner. Leslie's married name, of course. Which meant the ex-husband was Shane Wagner. One site even showed a photo of him, his grin confident and cocky as he slouched in jeans and baseball cap in front of a computer. Part of the new generation that scorned suit and tie while they racked up their millions.

I found nothing publicly accusing Leslie of pulling a sneaky, unethical scam on her partners in selling out before the company collapsed, but another article was headed with the speculative question, "Did the Brains of CyberPowerAds Leave When Leslie Wagner Sold Out?" Finally, one article gave a brief but telling recapitulation: "CyberPowerAds: hype high, partners young and brash, profits nonexistent. Prognosis: painful corporate death."

About that time Sandy appeared in the doorway, yawning. "Aunt Ivy, what are you doing? You're going to run into weirdos if you surf the Net at this time of night."

"I was just checking some business articles. No weirdos," I assured her. I quickly broke the Internet connection and put the computer into shut-off mode. I couldn't say exactly why I didn't want her to know what I was doing. Maybe because I was afraid she'd ask questions, and I was reluctant to voice my concerns. If Leslie had to be dead, I wanted it to be an accident, not some vicious murder.

But I couldn't stop thinking about the hostilities and angers in that company. A man named Michael who had furtively watched Leslie's home through binoculars. An ex-husband whom I'd personally heard make a veiled threat. An unseen skulker crashing around in the brush.

And now, Leslie Wagner Marcone was dead.

"Is something wrong, hon?" I asked as Sandy just stood there in her shorty pajamas and bare feet.

"No, I just couldn't sleep." She yawned, but she wiggled her toes restlessly in the carpet. "Things feel, you know, creepy with Leslie Marcone dying right out there in the lake. I think I had a bad dream."

"C'mon." I put an arm around her shoulders. "We'll go have a cup of warm milk and I'll take you back up to bed."

The hope that Sgt. Yates and I would not cross orbits fizzled when his police car showed up in the driveway the following afternoon. I was on the computer again, reading an online article about a dozen dot-com companies that had started, like CyberPowerAds, in a blaze of glory and then flamed out during the general dot-com bust, leaving onetime paper millionaires with nothing but scraps useful only for starting bonfires.

But not Leslie. She'd known when to get out, and had done so. With cash. To the original glee but later anger and resentment of her partners.

I opened the door when Sgt. Yates rang the bell. He was in uniform. This looked official.

"Got a minute?" he asked with what I thought was deceptive casualness. "I'm just checking on a few details from yesterday."

"'Yesterday' meaning Leslie Marcone's drowning, I assume?" I stood back to let him in and motioned toward a seat on the sofa.

"Right." He sat on the edge of the cushion and pulled out a small green notebook.

We went through the whole situation, from when I'd last seen Leslie to why I was at her house and why I went down to the dock. From description of the position of the body when I found it to what I knew about the remote control for the gate. He went into one subject that hadn't occurred to me, although, under the circumstances, I supposed it could be relevant.

"Do you have any personal knowledge of whether Ms. Marcone used alcohol or drugs?"

Either might have been a logical explanation for her tumble into the lake. Except for the fact that I'd never seen Leslie take so much as a glass of wine with a meal. Neither had I ever seen any sign of alcohol or drugs anywhere in the house. I told Sgt. Yates all that. "And I cleaned thoroughly," I emphasized. "I was into every nook and cranny."

"Drug users can be very adept at hiding their caches."

"Well, I didn't pull up floorboards or look behind electrical outlets or check the undersides of every drawer," I said. I didn't bother to *not* sound facetious. Actually, I felt a bit indignant on Leslie's behalf. Contaminate that buff body with drugs? No way. "And I never checked to see if all her perfume and talcum containers were real or phonies holding something else."

"You're very imaginative, Mrs. Malone," Sgt. Yates observed, as he had on another occasion. "How about sleeping pills? Did she ever take those?"

"You're thinking she took a sleeping pill, wandered outside, and was so drowsy she walked right off the end of the dock?"

"You think that might be possible?" He managed to sound interested in my opinion, even though I knew he was really just dodging my question by asking another of his own.

"I left about 2:00 every day, so I don't know what she may have taken at bedtime. But I never saw any sleeping pills in the medicine cabinet or anywhere else. But you'll have a toxicology report, I'm sure, to tell you for certain what was in her body."

An uncommunicative "Hmmm" was all I got in response.

"I didn't expect you to be involved in this, Sgt. Yates. I thought major crimes were your area of police work, not accidents."

I was fishing, of course, wondering if someone besides me was speculating that this might not be an accident. I was suddenly almost certain Sgt. Yates was suspicious. Not taking anything at face value was, in my own suspicions, as much a part of Sgt. Yates as that scar across his eyebrow. I just couldn't see him as "sweet," no matter what Tammi Ridenour said. This was the kind of man who might risk his life to save you but who would also look for ulterior meaning in a morning hello.

Though all he said at the moment was a mild, "Our manpower is limited."

That apparently closed the subject. However, my curiosity knows few bounds, so I jumped to a different subject. "Has Leslie's next of kin been located yet?"

"Yes, an uncle in Toledo. However, he has Alzheimer's, so it's his wife who will be coming here. Arriving tomorrow, I believe. And, since the next of kin has now been contacted, Ms. Marcone's name has been released to the news media."

I didn't expect Sgt. Yates to let me in on how they'd acquired this information about an uncle, but I asked anyway, and, to my surprise, he told me.

"We lucked out. His name turned up on an admissions form Ms. Marcone filled out at the local hospital when she went to the emergency room for a minor accident a few weeks ago. Their forms always require the name of a next of kin."

"How in the world did you discover she'd filled out such a form?"

"We have very few cases that require autopsies here in Woodston, so the few we do have are conducted at the hospital. The form, with the information about the uncle, turned up when we made arrangements for an autopsy."

"Autopsy?" I repeated with a little shiver. It's a word that invariably brings up ugly images.

"Standard procedure in a death of this kind."

Of this kind. What did that mean? That they discovered a lot of stray bodies in the lake?

I squelched that mental remark. Sgt. Yates would undoubtedly identify it as an "attitude."

"Will you be attending the autopsy?"

"Why do you ask?"

Okay, I asked because in detective books the detective on

the case always has to attend the autopsy of the victim. But nothing, I decided, required me to tell Sgt. Yates that. He'd already politely implied on another occasion that I read too many mysteries.

"Just curious, I guess." Which was true enough. My mutant curiosity gene never blinks.

"Yes, as a matter of fact, I will be attending the autopsy. It's scheduled for tomorrow morning."

Okay, I'm just going to leap into it, I decided. "Does anyone think this might not have been an accident?"

"It would seem an unlikely way to commit suicide."

Suicide! That thought had never entered my head, and it slammed around in there now like a ricocheting ping-pong ball while I stared at him. After the initial shock of the suggestion, no, I didn't think it was likely. I suspected Leslie may have felt murderous toward the ex but never suicidal about herself. Was suicide even possible, given the circumstances?

Then, spotting a twitch around Sgt. Yates's stern mouth, I had the unexpected feeling that he might, with some macabre sense of humor, be teasing me again about my tendency to amateur sleuthing.

I kept my dignity. "As you say, suicide seems highly un-likely. So everyone accepts that this was an accident?"

Sgt. Yates gave the smooth, fits-all-occasions response that he'd used before. "Why do you ask?"

"The situation does seem a little odd. Leslie was an expert swimmer."

"So others have mentioned. But I believe you suggested to an officer on the scene that she may have slipped and hit her head, rendering her unconscious before she fell in."

"Isn't that a possibility?"

"These are your speculations, Mrs. Malone, not mine," he countered, his tone gently reproving.

"Okay, then, I'm also wondering why her car was down at the boathouse. With keys in the ignition and purse on the front seat."

"You inspected the car?"

"I didn't *inspect* it, but I looked in the window." I felt defensive, as I often seemed to with Sgt. Yates. "At that time I didn't know her body was in the lake. But I didn't open the door, if that's what you mean. So I didn't disturb any fingerprints that may have been there. Although one of the officers did touch the door handle."

"I see."

At this point, I reluctantly realized, I couldn't *not* mention the skulker. As much as I'd prefer Leslie's death to be a simple accident, if there was a murderer out there I couldn't let my silence help him escape justice. "There's something else," I began. "Yesterday wasn't the first time I'd been over to Leslie's place trying to retrieve my whistle."

Sgt. Yates's eyebrows, scar and all, lifted, but he listened attentively while I told him what I could about the person I'd encountered crashing through the brush at Leslie's that day.

"You're sure this wasn't an animal? A deer? Maybe even someone's big dog? The Martinsens down the road have a big German shepherd."

"No, it was a person. I saw enough to tell that. But for only an instant, so I can't give you a description," I added hastily before he tried to pin me down. "I tried to call you shortly afterwards, but you were off duty and it didn't seem important enough to disturb you at home. Then some things came up, and I just forgot to do it later." Guilt still gnawed on me about that. Would it have changed anything if I'd called him at home immediately?

He didn't chastise me, but he said, "If anything else happens, you get in touch right away, okay?"

168

"Like what would happen?" I asked, puzzled. I certainly wasn't going to be over there prowling around Leslie's property again.

"Do you think this person you saw could identify you or your car?"

For a moment the question seemed irrelevant. I hadn't seen the skulker for more than a split second, couldn't say if he was tall or short, white or black or green. Then I got the ominous connection.

The skulker, if he'd had something to do with Leslie's death, might think I'd gotten a better look at him than I had, that I knew more than I did. And it was possible he'd gotten a much better look at me and the T-bird than I had at him. A man who'd murdered once probably wouldn't be reluctant to do it again.

But I didn't say any of that. I just tossed Sgt. Yates's all-purpose question back at him. "Why do you ask?"

"Just trying to cover all bases." He stood up and closed the notebook. "Probably no need for concern. We'll see what the autopsy shows."

Actually, Sgt. Yates didn't inform me what the autopsy showed. It was on the local news, Brad Ridenour reporting.

# 20

It was the top story on his early news program a day later. I'd already seen considerable activity over at Tara of the Ozarks that day, with two cars in the driveway identifiable through binoculars as police vehicles, one of them possibly state police. It looked as if a couple of officers were working around the perimeters of the property, although from this distance I couldn't tell what they were doing. Two other men crawled around on their hands and knees on the dock for a long time. It appeared they were making an inch-by-inch examination of every board. Another officer took dozens of photographs. I also saw people coming and going in the house, although I couldn't tell how many or what they were doing.

I might be an amateur, but I could tell what this was: a crime scene investigation.

Sandy and I were eating dinner when Brad Ridenour's smooth voice came on the local news. We stopped eating and turned to look at his husky shoulders and blond-haired, square face filling the TV screen. His voice and expression always matched the tone of the news story he was covering, and now both were grave.

"After an autopsy this morning, authorities have released new information regarding the body recovered two days ago near a dock in Little Tom Lake. The body was earlier identified as that of Leslie Marcone, owner of the lakeside property in the exclusive Vintage Estates area where the body was found. First indications were that the victim had drowned, but this morning's autopsy revealed that she was already dead before her body entered the water. At this time, local authorities have changed classification of the death from accidental to probable homicide, although actual cause of death has not been released.

"This news has hit this small, closely knit community hard—"

Sandy suddenly jumped up and flicked the remote control to turn off the set, cutting off any further details. She sat down again and picked up her fork.

"I'm sorry," she muttered. She stabbed a slice of cucumber as if she had a grudge against it. "I just didn't want to hear any more."

"That's okay."

"How do they know she didn't drown and was already dead?" Sandy asked in a tone that suggested she wanted to challenge this decision.

"I think it has to do with whether or not there was water in her lungs. No water means she wasn't breathing, so she didn't inhale any water when she was in the lake. Which she would have done if she were alive." Another of the charming facts I'd gleaned in my many hours immersed in mystery books. "Although there may be more to it than that."

"Homicide means somebody killed her. And then dumped her body in the water," Sandy said.

"I'm afraid so."

"I've never known anyone before who . . . got murdered."
Sandy suddenly sounded even younger than her fourteen
years, like a small, wounded child who's made a discovery that
alters her view of the world. Now it was a new and frightening
place where people we actually knew could be murdered.

I'd known another young woman back on Madison Street
who was murdered. That didn't make this any easier. Maybe
it was a reason I'd so strongly wanted to keep this in the
"accident" category.

"But who could have done it?" Sandy asked.

A number of possibilities instantly crowded my mind, but
all I said was, "The authorities will find out. They're already
working on it. I saw a whole herd of police officers over at
Leslie's place today."

Sandy now battered the slice of cucumber into mushy
slivers. "She wasn't a very nice person," she said. "She was
rude and snobbish and bad-tempered and stingy and mean.
Look how she fired you."

I knew what Sandy was trying to do: make this not quite
so awful by reminding us both that this wasn't a kind and
good and loving person who had died. It wasn't working, I
could tell from her scrunched-up eyes and compressed lips.
Sandy was too good and sweet a person herself not to be
stricken about this no matter what kind of person Leslie had
been. I patted her hand sympathetically.

She pushed her plate back. "I guess I'm not hungry."

I didn't try to encourage her to eat. I wasn't particularly
hungry myself.

I wasn't surprised when I got a call from a crisp-voiced
woman at the county sheriff's office the following morning. She said Sgt. Yates would like to talk to me about the

Marcone case. Could I come in at 2:00? I said yes, and she gave me directions to the station on the other side of town. I knew this would be a more formal, official interrogation than the relatively casual interviews Sgt. Yates had conducted with me before. We weren't into missing books or accidental drowning now; this was murder.

At 2:03 Sgt. Yates came out to usher me through a side door after the woman at the barred front window used an intercom system to announce my presence. He led me to a room where the only window was a small square in the door with metal mesh crisscrossing the glass.

"This room will be quieter, with less chance for interruptions, than my office," he said as he stepped aside to let me enter.

"Am I a suspect?" I gasped when I saw the room's sparse furnishings. A scuffed table, two wooden chairs, and a tape recorder. This was obviously where they interrogated suspects or prisoners. "Do I need a lawyer?"

"You can have one present, of course, if you'd prefer. But no, you're not a suspect."

"Thank you."

"At least not at this time," he amended smoothly. "Until we have the perpetrator, no one is ruled out."

Fair enough. Although it didn't exactly raise my self-confidence or calm the nerves that felt like ants playing hockey under my skin. There was something about the stark room that brought up unfocused shivers of guilt, a feeling that I had surely done something reprehensible and Sgt. Yates was going to pry it out of me. I was still feeling guilty for not contacting him immediately about the skulker.

It's also difficult to exude a no-fear confidence when a chair is man-sized and your feet don't quite reach the floor. I tried scooching down in the chair until they did touch, but that left my chin uncomfortably close to the top of the table. I scooched back up. The feet would just have to dangle.

Sgt. Yates checked the tape recorder to make sure it was working. He also had a pad for notes.

"I'm . . . uh . . . sorry about the body," I said, recalling his earlier admonition about "no dead bodies."

"Someone had to find it."

A noncommittal comment, but I couldn't help wondering if beneath it he was thinking, *But isn't it strange that it was you?* I was reminded that even though I was not an official suspect, I could become one.

The interview started with mundane questions about my identification—name, address, date of birth, occupation, my relationship to the deceased, etc.—and then went into more detailed questions on everything we'd talked about before Leslie's death turned into a homicide. He asked minuscule specifics about my finding the body and why I was on the property. He even asked how I'd broken the cord attached to my whistle, a question he hadn't asked before.

I was tempted to give a dignified explanation. *I was dusting the banister, you see, and the whistle accidentally snagged on the newel post, and the cord broke.* That would sound logical and sensible, wouldn't it? But my squeamishness with not-quite-truths got in the way, as it usually does, and so I wound up telling a considerably less dignified story about scooting down the banister on my bottom.

"Did Ms. Marcone make any comments about such un-orthodox dusting methods?" Sgt. Yates inquired.

"I don't believe she was aware of this particular incident. At least she didn't mention it when she fired me."

"I see."

From the seriousness of his expression, I thought perhaps he was accustomed to murder cases involving LOLs breezing down banisters.

Today there were also questions about the gate-ramming neighbor, and I suggested Cass Diedrich's name for further information about him. I didn't want to tell Sgt. Yates that Cass's husband still had a grudge against Leslie. For Cass and the kids' sakes I deeply hoped Al Diedrich hadn't had anything to do with Leslie's death.

Yet, even though I didn't know him, I could uneasily picture an unpleasant scenario. Al (I saw him as big and burly) goes to confront Leslie about Cass's unpaid wages. Leslie happens to be down on the dock. They argue. He gives her an angry shove. She hits her head when she falls. He is horrified but scared when he realizes she is dead. He shoves her body into the water and leaves town on his next truck run.

I blinked. It was, momentarily, so real . . .

As it turned out, however, I didn't have to mention Al Diedrich after all. Without any help from me, Sgt. Yates wrote the name Al in parentheses after Cass's name. He apparently was not unfamiliar with Leslie's former housekeeper and her husband.

I did, however, volunteer information about the man with binoculars down on the dock, whom Leslie had identified as "Michael" and whom I now thought was probably the CyberPowerAds's head man, Michael Flattery. I detailed the ex-husband's appearance at the house, his hostile attitude about Leslie selling out her share of the company, and his veiled threat. I also offered what I'd gleaned about CyberPowerAds from the Internet. I handed him a page I'd prepared listing some of the more informative websites.

"Well, you've been busy, haven't you, Mrs. Malone?" Sgt. Yates raised the scarred eyebrow as he glanced at the page. I tried to tell myself that in spite of the deprecating tone, *busy* could be a compliment. "We'll be doing a complete background check, of course, on all the persons involved." He set the paper on the table and continued with the questions.

Did I know if ex-husband Shane Wagner had stayed at a motel here in town? (I had no idea.)

Did any other guests come to the house while I was employed there? (Nary a guest that I ever saw.)

Did Leslie have any pets? (Not unless she acquired one after she fired me.)

Did I know the name of the man who took care of the mowing and yard work? (Sorry, no.)

Did I ever overhear phone conversations suggesting conflict between Leslie and any of her former partners in the company or anyone else? (I never overheard phone conversations on any subject. Leslie was a fanatic about that. Although I did mention her peculiarity about often letting the phone ring.)

I couldn't tell from his unrevealing demeanor if Sgt. Yates thought I was supplying valuable information or babbling irrelevant nonsense. I also didn't know if interviewees were allowed questions of their own, but I tossed some into the mix anyway.

"Do they know yet how long Leslie had been dead when I found her?"

"The fact that the body was in the water makes precise determination difficult. The estimate is from five to seven days."

"But that would make her dead since before I went over there the first time! Before I almost ran into that guy skulking around."

He gave me a speculative look. "Actually, although we're still in the preliminary stages of investigation, we've talked to a number of people. So far we haven't been able to locate anyone who saw her after the morning you were fired."

I was the last one to see her alive? My spine prickled. I looked at Sgt. Yates out of the corner of my eye. Did he attach any significance to that timing?

"Did the autopsy show a head injury?"

Sgt. Yates riffled his notebook papers, apparently using the time to consider whether or not I was entitled to that information. Finally he said, "No. No apparent head injury."

176

"I don't understand. What caused her death, then, if she didn't drown and wasn't hit on the head?"

"The medical examiner says cause of death was asphyxia."

"Asphyxia?" I paused to run that through my mystery-novel expertise, remembering that there was a differentiation between cause of death and manner of death. They'd already established that manner of death was homicide, now we were into what actually caused her death. "You mean as in strangled, with a rope?"

Another of Sgt. Yates's considered pauses. "No. Suffocated. Smothered."

"Like with a pillow held over her face?" It was the only means of suffocation I could think of. Yet this didn't really sound logical. "I can't imagine Leslie just letting someone hold a pillow over her face until she suffocated."

"Information about a possible murder weapon is not being released at this point in time."

"Perhaps you should be looking for someone with scratches or bruises. Because she'd surely have fought back."

"If you see anyone who meets that description, be sure to let us know right away." It was too politely spoken to qualify as outright sarcasm, so I was also polite when I said, "I'll do that."

Then another appalling thought occurred to me. "Is there any indication that this crime was of a sexual nature?"

"No."

I thought back to Brad Ridenour's TV report about the changed status of Leslie's death from accidental drowning to homicide. "The information about suffocation wasn't on the news."

"We don't tell the media everything, Mrs. Malone," he said smoothly, with what I thought was a controlled satisfaction. "Although they'll have that particular bit of information shortly." Which was why he'd so readily given it to me, of course. I saw annoyance or frustration here, as if he'd prefer the media got freeze-dried crumbs.

Which made me wonder. Was there something more the authorities weren't telling the media? I went fishing again. "I suppose there are various laboratory tests on tissue and fluid samples that take time to process?"

Sgt. Yates's smile held a glimmer of frosty satisfaction that made me suspect I was right. The authorities were holding something back. But all he said was, "Nothing gets by you, does it, Mrs. Malone?" Unspoken were the words, *Deliver me from little old ladies who read mystery novels.*

He stood up. Interview, and my questions, over. I also noted that today there were no hints about me and the older-but-still-active Pa Yates getting to know each other better.

Not one to give up easily, however, I said, "Has the uncle's wife made arrangements concerning the body?"

"Cremation, I believe. No formal services. At least not here."

"I wonder if the uncle inherits everything?"

A tap of notebook on table and a speculative look. "Why do you ask?"

I murmured, "Just wondering," but I'm sure he knew what I was thinking. I also suspected he may have given this question some thought himself.

Because murder has been done for considerably less than a plantation-style estate, a portfolio of stocks, and who-knew-how-much cash and other assets. And even if the uncle wasn't capable of this, maybe his wife was.

Sgt. Yates glanced at his watch, which might mean he had an important conference with his superiors. Or maybe it was time for his coffee break. However, considering that the glance came at mention of the uncle's wife, I wondered if it meant something else.

# 21

Three people were in the reception area when I came out of the hallway leading to the interrogation room. An older man with gold-rimmed glasses sitting with his ankles crossed. A blue-suited businessman pacing the floor and eying his watch. A young guy in baggy camouflage pants and combat boots, a staple in his ear, and a smoldering mess-with-me-and-you'll-be-sorry attitude.

Camouflage Guy didn't look at me, but I uneasily wondered if I'd encountered him before. Maybe skulking in that wooded jungle on Leslie's place, before or after murdering her? The outfit looked appropriate, and he was muscular enough to toss her in the lake with one hand. Was he here for questioning by Sgt. Yates?

Yet I was almost certain Sgt. Yates was expecting the aunt-in-law, or meeting her somewhere. Maybe I'd just hang around for a few minutes and see what happened.

Because the more I thought about the uncle's wife, the more she struck me as a potent possibility in Leslie's death.

The ex-husband and other partners in CyberPowerAds had anger and vengeance driving them. As did the gate-ramming neighbor and maybe even Al Diedrich. Camouflage Guy here may have thought she was into drugs, as Sgt. Yates had apparently speculated, and Leslie had the misfortune of getting in his way when he searched for them. But the motive of the uncle's wife might trump them all. Good ol' greed, the powerhouse behind many a vicious crime.

While I was pretending to search for something in my purse, just in case anyone was watching and wondering why I was loitering, the outer door opened, and a tall, fiftyish blonde in spike heels strode in. A handful of heavy gold chains were draped on her leathery neck, and two more hung around her ankle. Her muscles were long and lean and competent looking. Muscles capable of skulking through a jungle of brush and woods. Or wielding a murderous pillow. I waited expectantly for her to march up to the window and identify herself as the uncle's wife.

Instead she marched straight to Camouflage Guy, grabbed him by the scruffy T-shirt, and shoved him toward the door. He didn't look nearly so tough now when he whined "But, Mom!" as she harangued him about . . . what? Skateboarding on the sidewalk.

I sighed. I know better than to judge by appearances, but, with both mother and son, I'd done it. In the meantime, a refined-looking LOL had slipped in without my noticing. She was now at the reception window, stretching up on her toes to speak through the bars.

I dodged around Camouflage Guy to get closer. I was afraid my intention to eavesdrop might be all too obvious, but no one seemed to notice my hasty move. I was too late to catch her name, but I heard the last of what she was saying in a cultured voice to the woman at the window.

". . . appointment with Sgt. Yates concerning the death of my husband's niece?"

It came out more question than statement, as if she were uncertain about the validity of the appointment. I felt an instant flood of foolishness. This was my greedy murderess? Here she was, practically a clone of me. A bit younger and not as gray and considerably more stylishly coiffed, but the same height and weight and small-boned structure. I'd fit into her powder-blue, polyester pantsuit, probably the blue pumps as well, and she could jump right in to my purple pants and orchid blouse. Even the shade of discreetly applied blush on our cheeks matched. She didn't look around, as if afraid she might meet some criminal's eyes, and I felt safe in guessing that this was her first time in a police station. I wanted to rush up and squeeze her shoulders and assure her everything would be okay.

"He'll be right out," the woman behind the barred window said. "Just have a seat."

I didn't have time for a reassuring squeeze, however. I spotted the side door opening, and I scurried toward the outside door before Sgt. Yates could catch me. He would not, I knew, appreciate my show of interest in Leslie's next of kin. Though at the moment that interest was overridden by guilt for letting my imagination again operate at warp speed. I didn't know that the uncle and his wife were inheriting so much as a nickel, let alone getting all Leslie's assets dumped in their laps, and the idea of this delicate little lady smothering Leslie and tossing her body in the lake was as preposterous as the prospect of her suddenly whipping out a 9mm Glock and taking everyone in the sheriff's office hostage.

Back in the T-bird, I started to turn the key, then hesitated. Here the woman was, not young, alone in a strange town, struggling to cope with the niece's murder, surely worried about her husband with Alzheimer's back in Toledo. I should be helping her, not waltzing with unfair suspicions.

She came out about forty-five minutes later, during which time I'd observed an interesting parade of people coming in and out of the police station. I slid out of the car and hurried to intercept her on the sidewalk.

"Hi. You're Leslie Marcone's aunt, I believe? From Toledo?"

She gave me a puzzled but not unfriendly look. She had a delicately boned face and blue-gray eyes, and, at the moment, lines of stress bracketed her mouth and grooved her forehead. Had Sgt. Yates, I wondered with a surge of indignation, been giving her a bad time?

"Yes, Leslie was my husband's niece." She eyed me warily, as if I might be selling cemetery plots.

I held out my hand. "I'm Ivy Malone. I was Leslie's housekeeper until shortly before her death." I figured this was no time to go into the unpleasant aspects of our parting. "I'm so very sorry about what happened to Leslie."

"Thank you. Everyone has been very kind." Her tone and handshake were less wary but still short of enthusiastic.

"You mustn't let Sgt. Yates intimidate you," I said impulsively.

She blinked. Nicely made-up eyes, I realized, with a delicate palette of pastel eye shadow well beyond my makeup skills.

"Thank you. He can be rather intimidating, can't he?"

"Makes you feel as if he might slap handcuffs on you at any moment."

"I feel so bad about Leslie's death, and then to have him act as if . . ." She shook her head and laughed shakily, as if she wanted to find some humor in the situation and couldn't.

So I was right. Sgt. Yates was suspicious of her. Which was ridiculous, I thought with another rush of indignation.

Okay, I'd been suspicious too, considering the inheritance angle. But that was before I got a good look at her. Surely even Sgt. Yates couldn't think this small, genteel lady had managed to smother strong, athletic Leslie, haul her body down to the dock—

No way. Impossible.

She glanced at her watch, but something apparently clicked in her head, and she looked at me again. Her reserved expression changed. "Housekeeper . . . Oh, you must be the person who found Leslie's body?"

"Yes. I hadn't been able to reach her by phone, so I went over that day. Again, I'm so very sorry. It's so difficult to believe someone deliberately killed her. It must be a terrible shock."

"Yes, a terrible shock." She looked me over with a dry-eyed interest that I found both surprising and mildly disconcerting. I also expected more in the way of outrage about the murder. Still, shock affects us in unlikely ways.

"I was wondering . . . Are you staying there at the house?" I asked.

"No. The whole place is surrounded by that yellow crime-scene tape, and they won't even let me into the house yet. Which does seem so inconsiderate, under the circumstances. That big house sitting there empty, and I'm stuck in a motel."

Her fretful dissatisfaction was obvious. I'd been about to suggest she stay at the house with Sandy and me, but now I hesitated. I wasn't certain why. Even if we were almost clones, something in this proprietary attitude toward the house put me off. People were passing by on the sidewalk, and I stepped over to the edge of the grass to get out of the way.

"I'm sorry, I don't seem to know your name," I said.

"Astrid Gallagher. Leslie's mother was my husband's sister, Willow. She's been dead for some years now."

"Is there other family?"

"No, just the three of us. Walter, Leslie, and me."

She strung the names together as if they were a loving family with lives entwined. Sharing a Thanksgiving turkey. Trimming a Christmas tree. Filling a family photo album. I was doubtful about that coziness, given Leslie's lone-wolf lifestyle, but it sounded as if the uncle might well be the only heir. Unless Leslie had left a will naming someone else. But from what I knew of Leslie, I also suspected she'd never written a will. She wouldn't have wanted to think about having to give up her assets to anyone even if she was dead. She was also young enough that death probably still looked dim and distant, not something of current concern.

"You must have been very close." Fishing, I admit it.

"Well, not close in terms of keeping in touch frequently," she admitted, eying me as if she wondered if I already knew that. "Leslie was raised out in California, you know, and only recently moved here to the Midwest. But she was very dear to us, of course. Although my husband's condition—he has Alzheimer's, as you may know—precludes true awareness of the loss. How long were you her housekeeper?"

"Only a short time."

"But you're familiar with the interior of the house?"

"Yes, of course."

"Could you tell me how many rooms there are? I drove out there, but you can't see much from the road."

I was startled by the unexpected eagerness of her interest in the house. "You've never been in it?"

"My husband is no longer able to travel, so we were unable to respond to Leslie's invitations."

I was doubtful about the invitations, and I didn't know the exact number of rooms, but I named some of those I remembered. Living room, family room, the den Leslie used as an office, dining room, library, game room, exercise room, four bedrooms . . . or was it five?

"Is there a private bath with each bedroom?"

"Yes. Plus . . . ummm. . . a couple of other bathrooms."

She nodded, pleased, it appeared. Perhaps she'd had a bathroom-deprived childhood.

"A garage, of course?"

"Yes. A four-car garage, I think it is, attached to the house. Very roomy."

"But there's only the one car?"

I found all these questions about the house and car and nothing about Leslie or her murder a bit off-putting. And the way Astrid Gallagher said "one car" sounded as if she'd hoped for more. "One car was all I ever saw."

"But it is a Mercedes. Fairly new," she said, and I suddenly suspected that Auntie Astrid here knew down to the buck how much a year-old Mercedes was worth. "Which the police have latched on to, of course," she added, again sounding vexed.

"I imagine they have to look for fingerprints or other evidence." I suddenly thought of a roundabout way to approach the key question without bluntly asking it. I smiled warmly. "I'm sure you'll be very comfortable in the house."

"Yes, I'm looking forward—" She broke off, nicely made-up eyes narrowing as if she realized she'd stepped in something. But she was too late. I'd found out what I wanted to know. Auntie Astrid fully expected the house to be hers.

She glanced at her watch. "I'm sorry to rush off, but I have another appointment this afternoon. I didn't think talking to Sgt. Yates would take so long. Perhaps we can talk again."

Until then I was still thinking I should offer her a place to stay, but the don't-call-us, we'll-call-you attitude took care of that. "It's been nice meeting you," I said instead. "And, again, I'm so sorry about Leslie."

I watched her walk down the street and unlock the door

on a dark green sedan. Her own or a rental? I couldn't tell, of course. Neither could I tell the make or year of the car. My vehicle identification skills don't go much beyond color and size. But I was fairly certain this was no more than an economy-priced model. Which, whether it was hers or a rental, suggested that Astrid Gallagher had to watch her pennies. Caring for a husband with Alzheimer's could be a strain both financially and emotionally. A strain that might be eased with a hefty inheritance?

She pulled into the street. A pickup came up behind her. Impulsively I slid the T-bird in behind it and, keeping a discreet distance, followed the green sedan. I may be semi-invisible, but sometimes the classic old 'bird is uncomfortably noticeable.

She seemed to know where she was going. She parked on a side street. I slid to the curb several cars behind her. She got out and headed toward a one-story brick building with Samuels & Lightower, Attorneys-at-Law, written in heavy wrought iron across the front.

Was Astrid Gallagher wasting no time getting Uncle Walter's claim to the estate in order? Or getting her legal ducks lined up in case Sgt. Yates made an outright accusation about her involvement in Leslie's death?

I drove away thinking hard. The fact that Astrid Gallagher appeared to be a bit on the avaricious side, more interested in the size and details of an inheritance than in the niece's murder, might say something uncomplimentary about her character. But it certainly didn't mean she'd had anything to do with Leslie's death. The idea was surely preposterous, I reminded myself. Even if she desperately needed the money and was willing to dispose of a niece whom I suspected she barely knew, it was, basically, a physical impossibility. I couldn't have overpowered Leslie, and neither could Astrid.

At worst, she was surely nothing more than a genteel opportunist eager to latch on to an unexpected windfall.

Or was I again letting appearances deceive me?

Because even a sweet LOL in a polyester pantsuit might find a way to hire a hit man.

# 22

I was still pondering that thought when Hanson Watkins waved to me and motioned me into the driveway. He had the awning attached to his mother's motor home open, apparently checking for holes in the canvas. I rolled down the window, and he walked over and leaned against the car door.

"That must have been quite a shock, discovering that dead woman over there across the lake," he said. "I went back home for a few days and just heard about it."

"It definitely turned off any desire to go swimming in the lake in the near future."

We talked for a few minutes about Leslie and the murder, and then he gave the window frame of my car a little tap with his fist.

"This is one great old T-bird." He glanced inside at the odometer and whistled. "Is that original miles?"

"Original miles" has always struck me as a peculiar phrase. There are, perhaps, old used miles? But I just nodded.

"Hey, why don't you trade me for the motor home here? Straight-across deal. T-Bird for the motor home."

"The motor home is surely worth more than this old car!"

"The motor home's in great shape, all right. I've had everything checked out. Appliances, engine, generator. Good tires. And the awning's solid too, as you can see. But I've discovered that there's not a whole lot of demand for fifteen-year-old motor homes. At least not by anyone with cash." He grimaced and stood back to admire the T-bird. "And this really is a fantastic old 'bird. It's sure worth as much as the motor home. To me, anyway."

An odd sales talk, I thought. I'm telling him his motor home is worth more than my T-bird; he's telling me how great the 'bird is. Finally I just laughed.

"What would I do with a motor home?"

"What would I do with a T-bird?" he countered. "Drive around. Enjoy!"

"A motor home isn't exactly a practical vehicle for trips to the supermarket."

"True," he agreed ruefully.

I waved as I backed out and pulled on down to the next driveway, which was ours. I stopped at the mailbox to pick up the usual junk. Bills, ads . . . postcard with a picture of a place called "The Mothball Museum of America." *Mothball Museum? Who would visit a place like that?*

Only one person . . .

With a small tingle of anticipation I turned the card over and read the message in Mac MacPherson's blocky printing only to be disappointed to find he wouldn't be coming back this way after all. His daughter's husband out in Montana had just broken his leg, and Mac was headed there to help out. He said he was sorry to miss Sandy's gymnastics meet and was rooting for her.

I thought Sandy might be even more disappointed than I was. She'd enjoyed Mac and had made a special point of inviting him to the gymnastics meet. But it was like him, of course, to jump in and help with a family problem.

Sandy didn't show much reaction when I handed her the postcard at the house, however. Not disappointment with the message, not even a smile at the museum with its oversized replica of a mothball on a pedestal outside a building that appeared to be constructed of mothball-shaped lumps.

"I'm sure he really wanted to come," I said.

She shrugged. "It's no big deal."

Sandy, I realized, had been acting rather odd the past few days. Her mind didn't seem to be on the food she was eating—or, more often, not eating—or the program she was looking at on TV. I had the feeling even her studies might be suffering. Skye also hadn't been around much.

"Is something wrong, Sandy?"

"What could be wrong?" A question answered with a question. Not good.

"Did you and Skye have an argument or something?"

She looked unexpectedly alarmed. "No! Why do you ask that?"

"You've just seemed . . . oh, kind of preoccupied. And Skye hasn't been around lately."

"Umm. Yeah, well, you know. Finals coming up before long. And Skye is getting involved in more school activities and some stuff with her dad's politics too."

"Nervous about the gymnastics meet?"

"I told you. It's no big deal."

"C'mon, Sandy, this is Aunt Ivy," I said reproachfully. The gymnastics meet had certainly been a "big deal" for some time now. "We're roomies, remember?"

She gave me an unexpectedly wobbly smile. "I know. I'm sorry. It's just . . . Leslie Marcone was almost a neighbor, you know? And to think someone deliberately killed her and threw her body in the lake as if she were a . . . a piece of garbage or something. It makes something like a gymnastics meet seem . . . trivial."

I put my arms around her. "Oh, sweetie, I know. It's a terrible thing. But the police will catch him." Or her, as the case may be.

"Then sometimes I think about those awful Braxtons who want to kill you, and that's terrible too. Killing on TV isn't like people you know getting killed. Or might get killed."

I rubbed her back. "Are you scared? Don't be scared. Whoever killed Leslie has nothing to do with us. And the Braxtons don't even know where I am. They've probably given up the idea of doing anything to me by now." I hesitated. "Would you rather go live with your folks in Hawaii right away instead of waiting till school is out?"

"Oh no, I want to finish the year here. And I don't want you to be here all alone."

"I will be later on anyway. I don't mind."

"You can come to Hawaii with me!"

"We'll see."

"It isn't that I'm really scared," she said, frowning now, as if she were trying to sort through her feelings. "It's just that things . . . and people . . . don't seem the same anymore. You don't know who to trust."

"God is still in control, just as he's always been."

"I know. But . . ." She stepped back and looked at me. Looked *down* at me, I realized with a small shock at how she was growing. Her face was troubled. "Do they have any idea who killed Leslie?"

"I think there are a number of 'persons of interest,' as they're sometimes called. People she used to work with, maybe some local people she had run-ins with. Maybe even an ex-husband and some out-of-state relatives." Although

I had to admit those were my suspects, not necessarily Sgt. Yates's. "I know they're working hard on the case."

The phone started ringing then, but I looked at Sandy anxiously before I went to answer it. I had the feeling she was still keeping something to herself. "Is there anything more than Leslie's murder and the Braxtons coming after me that worries you? Talk to me if there is."

She looked a little better now. She tilted her head to study me and then laughed. "Oh, Aunt Ivy, you're one of a kind. You find a murdered body in a lake, and you have this gang of psychos after you, and it doesn't even faze you. You worry about *me*."

I was relieved to see her old spirit bubbling up again. "I don't know that I'm exactly blasé about the murder or the Braxtons. But I don't want you worrying."

"I'll try to be more like you."

She kissed me on the cheek and ran up to her room then, taking the stairs two at a time, and I thought everything was okay. Which just shows how wrong I can be, I suppose.

I picked up the ringing phone. "Hello?"

"I'm trying to locate Ivy Malone. Is she available at this number?" An authoritative male voice, one that sounded vaguely familiar but I couldn't quite identify. But *good* familiar or *bad* familiar? I wasn't certain.

Warily, since Sandy had just brought the ongoing Braxton threat to my attention again, I said, "This is the Harrington residence. Who's calling, please?"

"This is Jordan Kaine. Ivy and I worked together on a cemetery vandalism situation up in Missouri." His tone was brisk and formal, in keeping with his before-retirement occupation. "I'm anxious to get in touch with her again."

"Jordan!" I said, relieved.

"Ivy, is that you? Do you remember me?"

"Of course I remember you!" He'd taken me to a lovely

dinner and had been very helpful with the cemetery vandalism problem. But then the same uneasy question that always came to mind here in Woodston instantly surfaced. "How did you know where to locate me?"

"I read a news story about a murder near Woodston, and an Ivy Malone was mentioned as the former employee who found the body."

"You read this where?" I asked, alarmed at the thought that my name was being served up to the Braxtons with their morning coffee.

"The Little Rock newspaper. One of my daughters lives there, and I've been visiting for the past couple weeks. I'd earlier tried several times to get in touch with you on Madison Street, but you were never around. Which I eventually concluded had to do with that trial you were involved in."

"There were threats before the trial. Making myself scarce seemed advisable."

"Anyway, when I saw this, I decided I was going to check and see if that's the Ivy I knew."

I was flattered but still uneasy. The Braxtons probably didn't read the Little Rock newspaper, but if my name was gracing its pages, where else had my name appeared? Another disturbing question: "How did you get my niece's phone number?"

"I was on my way home to Missouri, and I decided it wouldn't be much out of the way to come around by Woodston—"

"You're right here in Woodston?"

"I drove in a couple of hours ago. I just started asking around town if anyone knew the lady who found the murdered woman's body. They all knew of you in a general way, and in the third place where I asked there was a woman clerk who knew you through church and right away came up with the information that you were related to the Harringtons and living in their house. I hope you don't mind."

"Of course not." I was uneasy with the level of local notoriety, and "The Lady Who Found the Body" was not the way I wanted to have my fifteen minutes of fame, but at least information about my whereabouts wasn't necessarily floating cross-country. "I'm delighted to hear from you," I assured him.

"I realize it's a bit spur of the moment to ask, but would you be free to have dinner with me tonight?"

"I'd like that." Jordan Kaine was a retired lawyer. Given an unhappy experience long ago, this was not my preferred choice of occupation, present or former, in a man, but Jordan transcended the genre. A very nice man.

I gave him directions to the house, and he said he'd check on a good place for dinner and be by around 7:00.

I went upstairs to tell Sandy and ask if she wanted me to fix something for her dinner before I left. I found her sitting at her desk, just staring into space. I was momentarily alarmed at the troubled look on her face, but as soon as I told her about Jordan, she came to bubbly life again.

"Aunt Ivy, another guy? I had no idea you had such a string of . . . what did they used to call them? Beaus?"

"I have two male acquaintances, not a 'string' of anything."

She grinned. "Okay, whatever you say. But won't Mac be ticked?"

"At my going to dinner with Jordan? I can't imagine why. Or what business it would be of his."

"Especially if he doesn't know," Sandy suggested. I rolled my eyes, and Sandy jumped up and gave me a hug. "That's okay, Aunt Ivy. Play the field. Keep 'em guessing."

I started back down the hallway, and she called after me,

"Don't worry about my dinner. I'll fix a grilled cheese or something."

Again I thought everything was fine with Sandy. Just a bit of teenage angst, perhaps. Nothing to be concerned about.

Back on Madison Street, Magnolia had advised me to wear something "enchanting" the first time I went out with Jordan. Since my wardrobe has a low enchantment level, I wore the same dress I'd worn that time, a pale pink with matching jacket. Jordan had seemed to like it then.

Sandy, apparently blessed with a curiosity gene of her own, rushed to the door when Jordan rang the bell. She introduced herself and looked him over like a critical parent sizing up an offspring's date. After a few nosy questions, she gave me a surreptitious thumbs-up, but she also whispered an aside. "Nice going, Aunt Ivy. Though he might be a little on the stuffy side."

"He is not stuffy," I whispered back indignantly.

Jordan's gray suit, blue tie, and polished black shoes were a bit formal compared to Mac's usual attire of khaki shorts and knobby knees, but they were not stuffy. Besides, we were going someplace nice for dinner.

"What was that all about?" Jordan asked with a bewildered look in Sandy's direction as she ran up the stairs after quizzing him.

"My niece tends to be a bit overly protective. It's a wonder she didn't make you fill out a questionnaire and put up a bond."

Jordan laughed. "Okay, I get it. My daughters have some of that attitude too. Though I'm sure they'd approve of you. Are you living here in Woodston permanently now?"

"No, it's just a temporary situation." I didn't go into a complete explanation. "How was your visit in Little Rock?"

"Great. My grandson ran me ragged. I have to go home to rest up. But I'm curious about this local murder."

"I just stumbled into it by accident, of course."

I filled him in with details as we drove away in his Lincoln. He didn't seem to find it shocking that I was involved with another murder. Perhaps because, in his legal career, shocking crimes were all too familiar to him.

"I remember that whistle," he said unexpectedly when I was explaining why I'd gone to Leslie's. "You were wearing it that night we went out. I wondered about it then." He gave me a sideways glance. "There's something intriguing about a woman who wears a whistle instead of pearls."

Intriguing? Me? Again I had to admit to being flattered.

I was surprised when we drove right on through Woodston. I looked at him questioningly, but he just smiled. We small-talked about his family and mine and the goings-on back at Tri-Corners Community Church until twenty minutes later he pulled in to the parking lot of a rustic-looking lodge with a lake behind it. A sign hung between two posts, letters branded into wood: The Inn at Lost Lake. Evening shadows hung over the lake, but a lingering glow of sunlight gilded a wooded hill beyond the water.

"I asked the man at the motel where I'm staying where would be a nice place for a special occasion, and he said a local businessmen's group he belongs to meets and eats here every month. He said everyone liked the food."

"I've never been here. It looks great."

The restaurant was busy on this Friday evening, and we followed several other couples inside. The interior was also rustic, dimly lit by tiny bulbs on wagon wheel chandeliers overhead and candles in old-fashioned lamps on the tables. Everything was oversized. The chimney of an enormous fireplace led up to a cavernous ceiling lost in shadows. The wooden tables looked hefty enough to hold entire carcasses. I was puzzled by odd, shiny pairs of dots gleaming high up on the walls. Then, with a jolt as my eyes adjusted, I realized what they were. The glassy eyes of an assortment of mounted animal heads hanging high on the walls. And in a far corner the full-size figure of a bear standing upright.

I swallowed, suddenly feeling not so hungry under the glare of all those dead animals. And uneasily thinking that in a Stephen King world there might come a day of reckoning when all these glassy-eyed creatures took revenge on the meat-eaters below.

Jordan had made reservations, and the hostess seated us at a table beside a window overlooking the lake. I felt uncomfortable even looking out on the beautiful lawn dotted with tall pines sloping to the lake. When I looked up, I knew why. An enormous buffalo head loomed over the window. And us. I wondered how securely it was anchored to the wall.

"Are you a . . . uh . . . hunter?" I asked.

He peered apprehensively at an antlered deer head beyond the buffalo. "I'm not sure I even want to be a meat-eater, with all these creatures staring at us." He hesitated. "Maybe I should have inquired about what kind of businessmen's group this was."

My gaze followed his. Carnivores-R-Us, perhaps?

"Perhaps we should go somewhere else," he added.

Jordan Kaine, for whom I already had a strong liking and respect, took another enormous leap upward in my estimation. A man not afraid to admit he'd made a mistake. "Would you mind?" I said.

"Don't look back," he cautioned as we stood up. "I think the bear may be gaining on us."

I was glad to be going, but we hadn't taken more than a half dozen steps when I stopped short, startled by the sight

197

of a man sitting a few tables away. I'd seen him only the one time, but I recognized him instantly. That blond hair and husky body . . .

Then, when he turned his head, I was less certain. Maybe not. The curly blond hair was right, but he appeared older than I remembered. And not as good looking.

Was it him, or wasn't it?

# 23

A woman was with him, but definitely not a bombshell red-head. Her shape was on the dumpy side, and her long hair was brown, center-parted and flat on top but frizzed to a startling width on the sides. She wore a pseudo-cowgirl fringed vest, but a pair of undersized glasses perched low on her nose gave her an intellectual air.

"Is something wrong?" Jordan asked.

I looked at the guy again. In the dim light, I still couldn't decide if he was Leslie's ex. And it would take an extremely odd detour to get closer to his table for a better look.

"I've . . . uh . . . changed my mind. I'd like to stay after all. Would you mind?"

"Whatever you'd like." Jordan sounded puzzled, but he didn't hesitate about putting a hand on the small of my back and steering me back to the table.

"The food must be excellent, if the man you talked to liked to come here," I said brightly. Although I didn't feel any more comfortable sitting below that monstrosity of a buffalo head.

I've heard of buffalo jumps, where Indians ran a whole herd of buffalo over the edge of a cliff for their winter's food. I felt as if I were at the bottom of the cliff with a herd of at least one oversized creature poised to plunge down on me.

The waiter came. I asked for the vegetarian meal. Jordan, after a moment of hesitation, ordered chicken cordon bleu, perhaps influenced by the fact that we hadn't spotted any glassy-eyed chicken heads decorating the walls.

"So, what do you do there in Woodston?" Jordan asked conversationally.

I managed to carry on a reasonably coherent dialogue. I think. I told him about church and Sandy's gymnastic activities and my short-lived housekeeping position. Jordan had amusing anecdotes to tell about his grandson. I managed to laugh at the right places. I think. Our salads arrived, and Jordan offered the blessing. Mine, crispy greens and crunchy croutons, was delicious. I think.

But I'm not certain, because my attention was more focused on that guy than on food or conversation. I didn't want to outright stare, of course, but I kept shifting in the chair, trying to get a better look. Jordan looked at me as if wondering if I had an itch in some unmentionable place, but he was too polite to ask, of course.

If it was Shane Wagner, what was he doing here? Had he been hanging around here all along, ever since that confrontation at Leslie's house? Had it been him skulking in the bushes that day? Were we here in the same room with a murderer?

Did he have any idea I was watching him? I didn't think so. His gaze roamed the other diners a couple of times but never settled on me.

Yet maybe it wasn't him. I'd have to get closer to be certain. I also wanted to see if his face showed scratches or other marks of an encounter with a woman who surely objected to being smothered.

Their dinners had already been served. Ours were just arriving. They'd be leaving well before we did. I didn't have much time.

I took a few bites of my stuffed eggplant, murmured, "Delicious," and then interrupted Jordan's story about a trip to the zoo to say hastily, "Would you excuse me for a moment?" I couldn't think of any truthful excuse for my exit, so I just waved in the general direction of the ladies' room.

I had to make an odd zigzag detour to go by the table. I was afraid the guy would notice, but I needn't have worried. My LOL shield of invisibility was operating at full power, perhaps aided by the fact that a knockout redhead two tables over suddenly stood up, and his attention riveted on her. I got a good look at him, full face, full on.

Yes! Shane Wagner in the flesh. No doubt about it.

I was so keyed up, however, that I was by him before I realized I'd forgotten to check for scratches. I made a hurried scoot through the ladies' room and boldly strolled by the table again. Even without the redhead's help, my invisibility held. In fact, I probably could have tromped on his toes and never been noticed. Such inconspicuousness may not be flattering, but it's useful. I got another good look.

No big scratches, but definitely one small one along his cheek just in front of his ear. There could be other incriminating scratches on his arms, of course, but he was wearing long sleeves, so I couldn't tell.

"Is everything all right?" Jordan asked when I slid into my chair again.

"Yes, fine."

"You seem a bit . . . distracted."

I hesitated, feeling momentarily foolish about my elderly Nancy Drew moves, and inexcusably rude to Jordan as well. But I was stuck with my straitlaced stance toward fibs, of course. I couldn't make up something just to keep from look-ing foolish.

"I'm sorry. I thought I spotted the ex-husband of the woman who was murdered. I wanted to be certain. Don't look," I cautioned when Jordan started to turn in the direction of the table I'd been watching. "I don't want him to know I saw him."

"Is he a suspect?"

"I'm not sure. Maybe. He has a motive. He was furious with her over some business matters and made an indirect threat when he came to the house."

Jordan looked troubled. He rearranged his silverware. "Ivy, should you be getting involved in this? Your last dabble in murder apparently had some unpleasant consequences."

True. It was why I was hiding out in Woodston. But I couldn't just ignore this. "All I'm going to do is tell Sgt. Yates I saw the man here."

That wasn't all I wanted to do, I realized a few minutes later when Shane Wagner and the woman picked up their checks and left. Separate checks, I noted. What did that mean? I wanted to know if they were staying here at the inn. I thought of a clever little ruse in which I'd inquire at the desk if my nephew was registered here. Whatever their privacy policy, they'd surely give such information to an innocent-looking LOL like me.

But, while I often think of clever ruses, I don't do them, so I devoted myself to focusing on relaxing and eating and Jordan. The stuffed eggplant really was delicious.

When we got back to the house I invited Jordan for break-fast. Partly to make up for my poor showing as a dinner companion, partly because I really did like him. He readily agreed, and we settled on 7:15, since he planned to drive on home and wanted to get an early start.

Sandy wasn't home. She'd left a note saying she and Skye

had gone to a movie. I was pleased. I'd still been worried there might be friction of some kind between Sandy and Skye, but, if there was anything, they must have smoothed it out.

Jordan arrived right on time the next morning. I figured he would and had bacon already sizzling. Since it was Saturday morning, Sandy was sleeping late. Jordan was less formally dressed this morning, dark slacks and an open-throated blue sports shirt, but I doubted he was capable of ever looking as scruffy as Mac could. He held out a small sack.

"I wanted to get something nicer, but the only place open this early was the convenience store at the gas station."

I peered in the sack. "A whistle! Jordan, this is so nice of you. And so thoughtful! Exactly what I need most."

I pulled the pale blue plastic whistle out of the sack and draped the cord around my neck. I was truly impressed. Not candy or some other useless trinket that might have been suitable for anyone, but *this*, just for me. Because he'd been paying attention and cared about my losing that old whistle.

He smiled, and I impulsively gave him a thank-you kiss on the cheek. Which was exactly when Sandy chose to saunter down the stairs, of course.

# 24

Jordan didn't seem in a big hurry to get on the road after all. He hung around for an hour and a half drinking coffee and talking, so it was after 9:00 before I called Sgt. Yates. He had someone in his office at the moment, the woman said, so I left a message asking him to call me. Then I phoned the Inn at Lost Lake (forever to be known in my mind as Dead Critters Inn) and asked for Shane Wagner. I was told they had no one by that name registered there.

I answered the phone a few minutes later, thinking it was Sgt. Yates returning my call, but it was Skye asking for Sandy. I chatted with her a minute and then called Sandy down from where she was upstairs doing something gymnastic on the hallway mattress. I couldn't hear Skye's end of the conversation, of course, but I heard Sandy make some lame excuse about having things to do. Not untrue, of course. We always have things to do if we want to do them. But I couldn't help thinking there was more to it than that. I was trying to decide how to ask about the call without being too nosy, but I didn't have to ask.

"Skye wanted me to go over to Fayetteville with her and her dad this afternoon. He has a meeting at the college, and Skye said we could wander around the campus." Sandy still had her hand on the phone, as if she were perhaps uncertain about the answer she'd given Skye.

"That sounds like fun. It isn't too early to be thinking about college, you know. And it's a beautiful day for campus exploring."

Which it was. Sunshine sparkling on the lake, daffodils blooming in the yard, cotton-candy puffs of cloud dotting the sky. The kind of day that gave even me some college-girl zing.

"I'll probably go to college in Hawaii or out in California where Rick and Rory are, not here."

Which had nothing to do with today, of course. "Sandy, are you avoiding Skye?" I asked bluntly.

Her gaze twitched to the side. "No . . . Well, kind of, I guess. Today, anyway. It's just that her dad thinks he's . . . so important, and he gets on my nerves. I didn't want to ride all the way into Fayetteville in the same car with him. And Skye thinks he's so perfect."

She sounded so resentful that I was puzzled, but I just said, "Okay, if you don't want to do that, how about a row on the lake with me? It's a perfect day for that too."

I thought she'd turn that down, since she seemed in such a negative mood, but she jumped on it. "Yeah, I'd like that. Let's go."

I packed a lunch, we got the life preservers out of the garage, and within twenty minutes we were out on the water. Sandy immediately grabbed the oars, and she whipped the little boat across the water as if pirates were after us. She headed straight north, not crossing over to the Vintage Estates side where we'd rowed before. I finally became concerned about all the energy she was throwing into this.

"Don't row so hard you injure a muscle or something. You want to be in top shape for the gymnastics meet next weekend."

"I'm okay," she said and kept rowing as if the pirates were gaining.

She kept at it full blast for close to an hour, and it was obvious she was using the physical exertion to work off some kind of frustration or anger. Just as obvious it wasn't something she intended to share with me. Eventually she had to rest, and I took over the oars. I let the boat drift for several minutes, thinking this was a good lull in which to talk, and suddenly she did become very chatty. Mostly to keep me from asking questions, I suspected.

Animated talk about school, a letter from Rick and Rory, a gig the Christian rock band had with a teen group over in Morrisville, and lots of teasing about my innocent little peck on Jordan's cheek. She gulped lunch when we pulled into the shore where Mac and I had stopped, took off on a hike while I recuperated from rowing, and then rowed most of the way home herself.

Carefully leaving no open time for nosy LOL questions.

I drove into town to pick up groceries, and then, curious about whether Astrid Gallagher had gotten into the house yet, I drove over to the far side of the lake. I had no intention of going in, of course. I'd just drive by and see if the crime tape had been removed.

As usual, my timing was impeccable. Just as I reached the driveway to 2742, Sgt. Yates stepped up to his sheriff's department car parked in the driveway, crime tape looped around his arm like a yellow lariat. I wanted to drive on by. Sgt. Yates already thought I was much too snoopy. Maybe he wouldn't notice me.

Fat chance. Sometimes I think I really should get rid of this big, in-your-face T-bird. He waved me down, and I turned into the driveway. He walked over and peered in the car, observant gaze immediately covering everything from dashboard to backseat.

"I tried to return your call, but no one was home."

"Sandy and I went out on the lake. Beautiful day for rowing. Lots of people out fishing."

If I thought I could distract him with fishing chatter, I was mistaken. "And now you are . . . ?" he pointedly inquired of my presence here.

"Fortunate to run into you," I said blandly. I told him about seeing Shane Wagner at Dead Critters Inn but that my phone call had turned up the information that he wasn't registered there. "Unless he's using an assumed name, of course."

"Why would he do that?"

"I doubt he'd want it known he was in the area when Leslie was murdered."

"Actually, Mrs. Malone, Shane Wagner is registered right here in town at the Shady Lane Motel, under his own name." His smile was superior, as if he'd put something over on me.

Which he had. He'd known about Shane Wagner all along and let me make an idiot of myself rattling on about Shane and an assumed name.

"Mr. Wagner arrived in town yesterday afternoon," Sgt. Yates added.

My immediate thought was, *Oh yeah? How do you know he just arrived?* But I kept my mouth clamped shut since my foot was already wedged in it.

"He's been back East on a business trip," Sgt. Yates went

on, "and he stopped here planning to spend more time with Leslie before going back to California—"

"Spend more time with her? She threw him off the place!"

Sgt. Yates went on as if I hadn't interrupted. "He immediately encountered the crime scene tape when he drove out here, of course. Then he learned Leslie had been killed, and he came to see me first thing this morning. He's eager to assist in any way he can. I was talking to him when you called, I believe."

"So he does admit he was here before, and there was that unpleasant scene with Leslie at the house—"

"He says he stopped to see Leslie on his way back East. He also says it was a cordial meeting, that they were even talking about getting back together."

"But that isn't true! I heard them argue. I heard him threaten her!"

"He says none of that happened. He seemed quite bewildered about your version of the meeting. He says no one else was even present when he and Leslie talked."

Shane Wagner's flat-out lies flabbergasted me. Although I had to grant that it was possible he'd simply missed seeing me. I'd been standing inside the doorway, somewhat behind Leslie, and maybe he actually hadn't seen me. And then, of course, there was always the invisibility factor. But that didn't change the fact that he was lying about the content of the meeting. Why?

"Why would I tell some big phony story about their arguing?"

"As I said, Mr. Wagner seemed bewildered by that. He suggested perhaps you'd witnessed an unpleasant scene between Leslie and someone else and mistook that person for him."

"In other words, he classified me as a DOB."

"DOB?"

"Ditzy Old Broad."

Sgt. Yates made a noncommittal murmur. Not a denying murmur, I noted.

"So how does he explain my recognizing him at dinner last night?" I asked.

"He didn't know you saw him at dinner, and neither did I at the time I talked to him, so we didn't discuss that." Sgt. Yates paused reflectively. "I believe you earlier mentioned seeing a photograph Ms. Marcone had of Mr. Wagner? Sometimes it's difficult to identify a person from an old photograph."

He was politely giving me a way out. Having seen Shane Wagner only in a photo, I'd been mistaken when I saw this person arguing with Leslie.

"What about the scratch on his face? Did you ask him about that?"

"The woman who accompanied him, a Lissa Rambough, who was also a partner in the dot-com company, said her cat scratched him before they left California."

Lissa Rambough. Apparently the frumpy woman I'd seen with Shane at dinner. "Did they volunteer this information about the scratch?" Meaning they knew it had to be explained.

"No, I asked."

I reflected on the timing. "The cat must have had tiger-sized claws for the scratch to stay visible for so long."

"Mr. Wagner said it had become infected, as cat scratches often do."

"Did you ask to see his arms?"

Heavy sigh, as if he carried some big burden. Me, no doubt. "No, Mrs. Malone, I can't say that I did."

"Was there material under Leslie's fingernails that could be used for DNA identification?"

"Actually, no. No DNA material under her fingernails."

Which meant the scratches on Shane Wagner's face were irrelevant, and Sgt. Yates had just let me blather on again.

Another pause until he added, "Although there were a few fibers under her fingernails."

"What kind of fibers?"

"Synthetic fibers."

"From her home or car?"

"So far we haven't been able to determine their origin." He looked at me as if expecting me to produce some wild theory about fibers, but I was fresh out of theories.

"Were there fingerprints in the car or on the door handle?"

"The handle appeared to have been wiped clean. Inside, all that were found were Ms. Marcone's prints. Although it seems probable that someone else drove the car there, because the steering wheel had also been wiped clean."

Why, I wondered, was he telling me any of this? Probably none of it was truly confidential, but I hadn't any particular right to know. Still, if he'd keep answering, I'd keep asking.

"What is Lissa Rambough doing here?"

"She and Shane Wagner are working together on this business deal back East."

"They drove all the way across country and back on this business deal rather than flying?" I asked skeptically.

"I believe so. They were here in a car with California license plates."

"Doesn't driving all the way across country strike you as odd?"

"Lots of people strike me as odd, Mrs. Malone," Sgt. Yates said with what I thought was unnecessary meaningfulness, although he wasn't so blatant as to say, "And I'm looking at one right now."

"Can you check and see if their story holds up, that they were definitely somewhere else when Leslie was killed?"

"We'll look into that, of course."

I had an "ah-ha!" moment. "Except you haven't been able to pin down exactly what day she died because of the body being in the water. Which leaves the time element up in the air. They could have killed her and left town. And come back."

"They? Now you figure the murder was a conspiracy? All the disgruntled ex-partners got together, invested in a pillow, and mapped out a plot to do Leslie in?"

The part about pillow buying was a bit snide, but I ignored it. "A conspiracy isn't out of the question. Rambough alibies Wagner, he alibies her."

"We'll do our best with the investigation, Mrs. Malone," he said. He sounded resigned, as if he figured I was going to be his burden until the case was solved. One hundred and two pounds of LOL on his back.

"But you don't think either of them had anything to do with Leslie's death," I said.

"As I told you before, until we have the perpetrator, we don't rule out anyone."

"So who are your front-runner suspects?"

"Now, Mrs. Malone, you know I can't discuss that with you," he chided.

"Are Shane Wagner and Lissa Rambough going to stick around for a while?"

"I have no reason to hold them here. They volunteered their fingerprints, which will be compared with those found in the house and car. They left phone numbers and email addresses where I can get in touch with them."

"Such helpful folks," I muttered.

"I also want to thank you for your helpfulness in calling to keep us informed of your observations, Mrs. Malone. The police always appreciate citizen involvement."

He spoke blandly, but I challenged him with the question

I'd been wondering about for several minutes now. "Why do you discuss any of this with me, Sgt. Yates?"

"You did find the body." He tilted his head and studied me. "And I usually find your questions and observations . . . interesting."

Interesting as in amusing? Was I Sgt. Yates's comic relief in a mostly unamusing job? He tossed the crime scene tape into the police car and slid in himself, leaving me with more questions than answers.

Shane Wagner's contact with the authorities probably looked good to Sgt. Yates. Conscientious citizen trying to find out what's going on and be helpful.

Or, less innocently in my mind, it could be a preemptive strike. Shane Wagner surely knew that sooner or later he'd be considered a suspect, so he figured he'd make himself look good by going to them first. It was also possible that Shane and Lissa hadn't originally intended to go to the authorities, had intended to slip away unnoticed and perhaps contact the police from California, but maybe Shane *had* spotted me at the restaurant and figured he'd better do it now. It was just my word against his about the content of his meeting with Leslie, of course.

But the fact that I knew he was lying, even if Sgt. Yates didn't, was surely important. Very important.

## 25

The week dragged by. Sandy was at the gymnastics studio every evening preparing for the upcoming meet. The Fayetteville newspaper sent someone to interview me, probably because the authorities were being so closemouthed. I politely declined. The last thing I wanted was my name hanging out there for curious eyes to see. I received another card from Mac "the Postcard Man" MacPherson, this time one of the standard scenic variety showing a lot of Montana sky. He said his son-in-law's broken leg was healing, but he'd be staying with them for several weeks yet. I called the Shady Lane Motel and learned that Shane Wagner and Lissa Rambough were not registered there now. I could see lights in Leslie's house at night, but I didn't know if that meant Astrid Gallagher was in residence, dripping bubbles as she merrily dashed from bathroom to bathroom, or if Leslie's light-timing system was still operating.

I assumed Sgt. Yates and other members of the county sheriff's department were working diligently, but lack of visible progress frustrated me even though I knew there were undoubtedly details the police were withholding from the public.

Shane Wagner's big lie about his meeting with Leslie put him high on my list of suspects, maybe with Lissa Rambough as an accomplice. Although Astrid Gallagher's greedy grab for the house also kept me thinking. She, too, would have had an accomplice, the actual killer, who was surely long gone by now. How to run him down? And I kept wondering about binoculars-man Michael, who seemed to have surfaced only the one time and then dropped out of sight. Neither could I eliminate the gate-ramming neighbor or Cass Diedrich's angry husband.

I spent a considerable amount of time on the Internet but didn't dig up anything new on CyberPowerAds. Dead dot-coms fade quickly. Individual searches on the partners' names turned up Lissa Rambough's personal website about her cat, some rare, naked-looking breed that the good Lord must have created when he was in a joking mood. The website proved she did have a cat, I had to admit. Which might have scratched Shane Wagner. So what? I wasn't convinced those weren't Leslie's fingernail scratches on his face, even though the experts hadn't found anything under her fingernails to test for DNA. Maybe whatever DNA material had been there had washed off in the lake water. Although the fibers hadn't washed away . . . Well, perhaps synthetic fibers cling more persistently than skin off a human face.

But I couldn't do anything but speculate, so Sandy's big gymnastics meet in Fayetteville the following Saturday was an especially welcome distraction. The meet was scheduled to start at 10:30. After a light breakfast, we planned to leave the house at 7:45. Sandy came downstairs in baggy blue sweats but with her hair pulled into an elegant knot at the back of her head and wearing a bit more makeup than usual. She seemed more somber than excited. Skye was coming over to go with us. She arrived with news.

"Dad and Tammi are coming to the meet this afternoon! Isn't that great?"

Sandy, just coming down the stairs with her gear bag, dropped it with a clunk. "They're coming to my gymnastics meet?" She sounded as horrified as if she'd looked in the mirror and discovered a zit the size of a cherry on her nose. "Why?"

"Because they like you, of course. And Dad's interested in all kinds of youth activities and wants to—"

"He wants publicity for his election campaign, that's what he wants! But I don't want him there."

Sandy's statement sounded so hostile that I was taken aback. Skye looked startled, and I threw in a question to defuse what felt like a peculiarly explosive situation.

"What about Baby?" I asked. "Who'll be staying with Baby?"

"A neighbor down the street," Skye said with a distracted air. To Sandy she snapped, "It isn't up to you to decide who comes to the meet and who doesn't. Anybody who wants to can come. I think I'd better go back to the house and ride with them. Or maybe not come at all."

Sandy suddenly seemed to deflate. Her shoulders slumped. "No, don't do that. I'm sorry. Just nerves, I guess." She leaned over and picked up the gear bag holding her leotard, chalk, bottles of water, and other necessities.

Skye had looked ready to storm out but instead, with an understanding and bigheartedness I had to admire, reached into the funky patchwork bag hanging from her shoulder and tossed Sandy a stick of gum. "Here. Chew this. It'll relax you."

Sandy managed a smile. "Thanks."

The gymnastics studio in Fayetteville was several times as large as the little one in Woodston. Kids, preschool up to mid-teenage, many more girls than boys, were already on the floor warming up in a miniature circus of activity. We got Sandy registered, and she went to change into her leotard. Skye and I found places to sit on the tiers of benches lining two sides of the big room.

It was hard to keep track of everything going on. Children flipping and spinning and tumbling. Parents milling around. A heavy thud punctuated the hum of voices and shuffling feet, and a coach ran out to check on a girl who'd crashed from the parallel bars. Excitement bristled like static electricity. Music blared from a far corner where a girl about Sandy's age was practicing her floor exercise. She was good, especially on the aerial cartwheel, but with auntie pride, I decided Sandy was better.

"Have you been to one of these meets before?" I asked Skye.

"A couple, but not here." Skye hesitated, as if uncertain of my reaction, before she said, "Dad and Tammi have never been to one. They're really looking forward to it."

"That's nice. I'm looking forward to meeting your father."

She leaned toward me, obviously relieved with my attitude. "He really does *care*, you know. About kids and the environment and the economy and everything."

Sandy came out dressed in her blue leotard spangled with silver stars. She carried her gear bag over to where Miss Cassidy, the coach, had a space set up for the Woodston group. Sandy found a spot on the floor and started warm-up exercises. Stretches and bends, skips, splits, bridges and rolls. She touched her head to her knees both sitting and standing and worked up to forward and backward flips.

"I hope Sandy does well. She's practiced so hard," I said.

"She's really good. She might even take all-around in her age group."

A statement unfortunately not borne out as the day progressed. And it was a fairly slow progression, even though more than one competition was held at a time, as there were separate age-group competitions for each event. Sandy did okay on the vault, no major falls or errors, although she didn't nail the landing the way I'd seen her do it before.

Brad Ridenour and Tammi arrived just before 12:00, earlier than Skye expected them. Sandy was right about one thing, I decided as I spotted the photographer trailing along with them. Brad Ridenour definitely intended to use this as a photo op. Skye ran over to meet them and bring them to where we were sitting. Brad's face was familiar to TV viewers, and he smiled and glad-handed everyone along the way. I saw Sandy glance his way once, but she turned her back and pretended to be absorbed in rubbing her ankle.

"You've already met Tammi, of course," Skye said to me, although she did it with a hand on Tammi's arm, not as if she were bypassing the stepmother or downgrading her importance. I was pleased. Perhaps their relationship was improving.

"I'm so excited about being here!" Tammi gushed. "All these children with so much talent and energy!" She obviously hadn't run out of exclamation points. She was in buttercup-yellow today, a sleeveless linen dress that some saleswoman should have received at least forty lashes with a feather boa for selling her. Even in matching yellow and white high-heeled sandals, she barely came up to her husband's shoulder.

Then Skye introduced her father, her pride in him big enough to crown him king rather than merely elect him to some political office. We shook hands, his firm and personal, his eyes targeting mine with an expert politician intensity that said, "See? I'm noticing you personally. You're important to me."

"I'm pleased to meet you, Mrs. Malone. We've heard so much about you."

I wondered if that meant they'd heard of me from Skye or if I was simply notorious as "The Lady Who Found the Body." In person, Brad Ridenour was even bigger and blonder and broader shouldered than he looked on TV. Not overweight but substantial. His smile dazzled, and the cleft in his chin blended masculinity with boyish charm. He had a definite presence, even a charisma, that would certainly serve him well in the political arena. The Big Brad, as Skye had once said he was called. Yes, indeed. The Big Brad wants your vote. You can trust the Big Brad.

"It's nice of both of you to come today," I said.

"Oh, we wouldn't have missed it!" Tammi turned to the photographer. "Dick, we should get photos of Brad with some of the contestants! Skye, why don't you get Sandy to come over?"

"I don't think—" I began. I knew Sandy was already upset and nervous, totally opposed to Brad and Tammi's presence here, and being dragged into photographs wouldn't help.

But Skye was already running over to where Sandy was comforting one of the smaller girls who hadn't done well on her floor exercise. Even from this distance I could see Sandy's vehement shake of head. Skye captured a couple of other girls and brought them back with a mumbled explanation to Tammi about Sandy being too busy. The photographer posed Brad with the girls doing handstands together, feet touching.

I thought that Sandy, in spite of her negative feelings about Brad, would surely do the polite thing and eventually come over to say hi, but she never did. The announcer kept talking about "amplitude" and "rotation" in relation to the contestants' performances, which meant nothing to me, but it didn't take an expert to tell how poorly Sandy was doing. Her performance went from bad to worse.

She slipped and almost fell off the beam during the balance beam competition and bungled the landing as well. Her timing was off during the floor exercises, and she stepped out of bounds once. And her scores, of course, reflected the errors.

I watched her chalk her hands before her turn at the uneven parallel bars. By that time Brad and Tammi had gone, and I hoped this would help Sandy do better. She was so strong and graceful that the bars were usually her best event. Not today. She actually missed her first jump to grab the bar to begin her routine, something I'd never seen her do. From there on, even this proud auntie had to admit her performance was mediocre. She did nail the landing, but by then it was too late.

"I don't understand," Skye said as Sandy headed back toward the locker room, her head down. "She did just awful. She's so much better than that."

I didn't say anything, but I was determined to find out what was going on. Not while Skye was around, however, because it was as obvious as the cleft in Brad Ridenour's chin that whatever was affecting Sandy had something to do with the Ridenour family.

The ride home was silent, Skye's and my attempts to console Sandy shrugged off with a "It's no big deal" response from her. I'd planned that we'd all go out for celebration pizza after the meet, but I didn't even suggest it. Skye didn't hang around after we got to the house. Sandy went upstairs as if she wanted to be alone, but I wasn't going to let her get away with that. She hadn't eaten anything but a couple of high-nutrition bars and sports drinks all day, so I made grilled tuna sandwiches and hot chocolate and marched upstairs with them.

Her door was closed, and I braced the tray on one hip and knocked. Her answer was muffled. I decided to interpret it as "come in," even though I was almost certain that wasn't what she'd said.

She was lying stomach-down on the bed, still in the sweats she'd worn home, her hair sticking out of the once-sleek knot like blonde porcupine quills.

I thought maybe she'd been crying over the results of today's competition, but her eyes were dry, her face unblotched. Even so, her face had a haggard look, as if she'd just received failing scores not only on a gymnastic performance but on life.

"I thought we'd have something to eat together," I said. I looked for a clear place to set the tray. Every surface was covered with teenage stuff: clothes, books, CDs, her collection of teddy bears, old gymnastics awards, stray taco chips, old soft drink cans. I scooped a clear spot on the cedar chest at the foot of her bed for the tray.

I could have predicted her response to the food, of course.

"I'm not hungry."

"Okay, we can talk then. I know you were nervous, but something a whole lot more than nerves was wrong today. You performed like you'd never seen a set of parallel bars before. You had three left feet on the balance beam."

My honest assessment brought an unexpected smile from Sandy. "I was pretty awful, huh?"

"I couldn't have done much worse myself."

Sandy turned and sat cross-legged on the bed. I sat on the edge of it. We looked at each other.

"It was nerves, I guess," she said. After a long hesitation she added, "But not just about the gymnastics meet."

"So what is it, Sandy? I don't understand."

220

She swallowed, but I could see something in her face that said that this time she was going to tell me. In all honesty, I expected to hear anything from a revelation of teenage pregnancy to a confession of drug use. I braced myself. *Show me what to say, Lord. Show me how to help her.*

"I—I think I may know something," she said.

Not what I anticipated. "About what?" I returned blankly.

"About Leslie Marcone's murder."

# 26

"Leslie's murder?" I repeated, astonished. I cast around for some logical explanation. I remembered Camouflage Guy at the police station. Was he a student? "You heard something at school or from a friend?"

"No. I—I saw something." She twisted a loose thread on the teddy bear bedspread, her eyes turned downward.

"You saw something," I repeated, because the words seemed so disconnected from reality.

"And then today when I saw Skye's father at the meet, shaking hands and laughing like everything was just wonderful . . ."

Sandy looked up, and I saw anger in the taut set of her jaw but bewilderment in her blue eyes. I moved closer to her on the quilt and took her hand, wanting to reassure her even though I was bewildered too. "What did you see, sweetie?"

"It was last winter. Miss Cassidy and another woman from the studio took six of us to a gymnastics meet in Little Rock.

222

We had two rooms at a motel, and we stayed there two nights, Friday and Saturday."

"I see," I said, although I felt as if I were peering through a pea-soup fog and not really seeing anything at all.

"Friday night was fine. Saturday I had the high score of the meet on the parallel bars." Sandy motioned to a trophy on a chest of drawers in the corner, but it was an absentminded gesture, without pride in the success. But a powerful reminder of how differently she'd performed today.

"And then . . . ?"

"Saturday night after the meet we were all feeling hyper, giggling and acting silly. Our room was on the second floor of the motel, and I went downstairs to the machine in the hallway to get a 7Up. But the 7Up slot was empty and I re-membered seeing a little store down the street, about a block away. I should have gone back and asked Miss Cassidy if I could run down there—" She stopped and swallowed. "But I thought it would take just a minute, so I didn't."

Yes, she should have asked Miss Cassidy first. Not a smart move for a girl to be out alone on the street in a strange town. But I knew this wasn't the time to chastise her. I was still puzzled about where she was going with this, but apprehen-sion curdled in my stomach. Because somehow I knew it was going somewhere I didn't want it to go.

"Actually, the store turned out to be two blocks away. And I had to go by another motel before I got to it. I saw a light blue car stopped under a kind of carport thing by the registration office. Leslie Marcone came out of the office, and I was so surprised that I almost spoke to her. Even though she didn't know me from a crack in the sidewalk, of course. But I was glad I didn't, because she got in the car, and then I saw who else was in the car."

"Which was?"

Sandy twisted the thread so tightly around her finger that

the thread snapped. "Mr. Ridenour. Brad Ridenour. Skye's father."

For a moment, even with the triple identification, I was blank. Skye's father in Leslie Marcone's car outside a motel in Little Rock? That didn't make sense. And then it made too much sense. Ugly sense. Sandy spelled out the details as I sat there stunned.

"I ducked behind a hedge by the entryway so I could watch. I suppose I shouldn't have . . . but I did. Leslie parked the car in front of one of the motel rooms. She and Mr. Ridenour got out. She was wearing jeans and high-heeled boots and a black turtleneck, with her hair all swirly and loose around her shoulders. Very . . . sexy looking. He was wearing a dark suit and tie, just like he always does on TV. The Big Brad, you know." She snarled the nickname with bitter contempt, as if she'd like to strangle him with the tie. "He opened the trunk and got out a couple of small suitcases. One gray, one green. She unlocked the door to the motel room and went inside. I could see him lean over and kiss her when he followed her in with the suitcases."

The details about clothing and suitcases told me how deeply the incriminating scene was branded into Sandy's memory.

"Then I . . . I forgot all about my 7Up and ran back to our motel."

Sandy may be only fourteen, but she is considerably more mature and knowledgeable than I was at fourteen, and she didn't need diagrams to know what was going on. Brad Ridenour and Leslie Marcone at a motel in Little Rock. A clandestine affair.

The curdling in my stomach expanded to an industrial-strength churning. With the churning came a sudden spotlight on past events. Leslie's overnight absence from the house while I was working for her. Another out-of-town rendezvous with Brad? Her ill temper the next day. A lovers' quarrel? Her

224

stiff command that I never answer the phone. So I wouldn't hear Brad's distinctive voice? Even her peculiar system of sometimes answering the ring of the phone, sometimes not. Now I wished I'd paid more attention to those rings. Did they have some code worked out so she'd know when it was Brad calling and would pick up?

Now I understood Sandy's antagonism toward both Leslie Marcone and Brad Ridenour, and her recent avoidance of Skye as well. My heart ached for her as I realized how desperately she'd tried to figure out what to do with the unwanted knowledge of that clandestine relationship.

"You didn't tell Miss Cassidy or any of the girls what you'd seen?"

"No."

"And you never said anything about it to Skye?"

"No! I was afraid if she knew, if anyone knew, everything would just . . . fall apart for her."

I appreciated Sandy's caring concern for her friend. Skye's life had been unstable enough without the added disillusionment of finding out what a sleazeball her father was. Or having the marriage to Tammi explode and take Skye with it.

"Although I almost said something a couple of times, when she was going on and on about how wonderful her dad is, and I know he isn't wonderful at all. It . . . it just makes me so mad that he cons everyone about what a great guy he is, and Skye just swallows every bit of it."

I remembered Sandy and Skye's sharp exchange about Leslie too, Skye calling her beautiful and mysterious, Sandy countering that Leslie was a stuck-up snob. Knowing what she did, she'd undoubtedly wanted to say more, but for Skye's sake she'd held back. I admired her willpower.

I also felt a grim appreciation for her clear sense of right and wrong. She hadn't put blame on one of them and excused

225

the other. Both Leslie and Brad Ridenour were deeply in the wrong, and Sandy knew it.

"It was awful enough when I just knew about Mr. Ridenour and Leslie and their affair," Sandy went on. "But then after Leslie was murdered, and I realized he might have done it . . ."

For a few moments I'd been so wrapped up in thoughts of Brad and Leslie's relationship and its possible effect on Skye that I'd forgotten the connection with murder. A connection that sent snaky chills slithering along my spine.

This implicated Brad Ridenour right up to that cleft in his chin. I could feel it as surely as if I'd seen him toss Leslie's body in the lake. No wonder Sandy had seemed so strangely preoccupied and distracted ever since the murder. She'd had *this* slamming around inside her. No wonder she'd avoided any contact with Brad. And no wonder his presence at the gymnastics meet today had sent her into a tailspin.

I realized she was watching me now, her expression unexpectedly hopeful, as if she thought perhaps I'd pat her hand and tell her she was imagining things or somehow make everything right. I tried.

"An affair like this is . . . is unethical and immoral and awful, but it doesn't necessarily mean Skye's father killed Leslie."

I tried to think of all the reasons that could be true. After all, a man is innocent until proven guilty.

For one thing, Brad Ridenour had apparently always been an upright, law-abiding citizen. He was respected and well thought of in the community. A bit egotistical and self-centered, perhaps, but wasn't that practically a requisite to get anywhere in TV or politics?

Another possibility was that the affair may have been over for weeks or months. Maybe Brad had had an attack of conscience and ended it. Maybe Leslie had decided that sneaking around with a married man was a dead end. (*No pun intended*, I thought guiltily.)

Leslie's later overnight trips may have been with some new man. Yet it occurred to me now that there was a distinct physical resemblance between Brad Ridenour and Leslie's ex, Shane Wagner. Both men were big, blond, and husky. Was this her preferred type of man? Or was she working on some deeper psychological agenda? Shane had been unfaithful to her, so after her makeover she deliberately sought out another guy who resembled him?

No, I didn't think Leslie had acquired a different man. She was after the Big Brad. And Leslie was a woman of powerful determination.

But maybe Brad had a stainless-steel alibi. Maybe Tammi could vouch for every minute of his time. Or maybe he'd been so far out of town he couldn't possibly have killed Leslie. Hadn't he made a trip to Little Rock about that time?

Yet both those potential alibis were riddled with holes big enough to drain Little Tom Lake. Leslie's time of death couldn't be pinned down to a window of a few hours, and Tammi surely couldn't account for Brad's whereabouts every minute over a period of two or three days. As for being out of town . . . I hadn't heard it suggested anywhere, but who's to say Leslie hadn't been killed elsewhere and brought back here to be dumped in the lake? A motel pillow suffocating a scream of surprise and terror . . .

And motive. Brad Ridenour had it big time. Some well-known politicians have survived scandals, true, but Brad was just starting out in politics. News of an illicit affair could crash and burn his political career before it ever got off the ground. Even his position as a local TV anchor might be in jeopardy. Had Brad felt he had to kill Leslie before the relationship was somehow exposed?

Yet, on the other side of the motive equation, wasn't murder just a little extreme in this situation? If Brad got worried that the affair with Leslie could jeopardize either his political or TV career, couldn't he have simply said "It's over" and be done with it?

Or maybe he'd tried to do that, and Leslie was having none of it. I thought again about that day after Leslie's overnight absence, when she must have been with him. She'd been in a foul mood, angry and critical. Had he tried to break it off with her then? And she'd retaliated by telling him that if he did she'd blast him sky high with public revelation of their relationship? That it was leave Tammi and marry her *or else*?

I realized that I'd been silent for a long time as things whirled round and round in my head, like some video game spinning out of control. Sandy was still looking at me expectantly. "Well, uh, this, uh . . . puts a different perspective on things, doesn't it?" I mumbled.

I thought that was pretty lame, but she sounded relieved when she said, "I'm glad I shared it with you, Aunt Ivy. It's such a relief! I've been worrying and worrying. It was awful keeping it all to myself. Like carrying around a weight as big as your old Thunderbird."

She scooted down the bed and grabbed a sandwich and cup of hot chocolate from the tray I'd set on the cedar chest.

"I'm glad you shared it with me too."

And I was. This was too big a burden for a fourteen-year-old. The question was, what was I going to do with this revelation about Brad Ridenour and Leslie?

I struggled with the question all the next day. Should I go to Sgt. Yates with this? I took that question to the Lord, of course, both at church and on a long walk on the lake trail that afternoon.

Sandy had gone skateboarding with some friends from church, and I strolled alone, though I exchanged pleasantries with a young couple holding hands and Hanson Watkins taking a fishing break from remodeling work on his mother's house.

"Sure you don't want to trade me that old T-bird for the motor home?" he called from his stance on an old log sticking out in the water. "Think how handy it'd be. You get tired while you're out shopping, so you just climb in back and settle down for a nap."

"Think how handy it could be for you and your wife. You're off seeing the wonders of the world, and when you get tired you just climb in back for a nap," I called back.

"If we travel, we like big hot tubs and room service, not searching for dump stations, showering in a space the size of a shoe box, and repairing frozen water lines." The fishing line sang as Hanson whipped a lure far out in the water. The sound momentarily brought back nostalgic memories of Harley and his love of fishing. Hanson looked at me and grinned. "I guess if I want to sell the thing I need a better sales pitch than that, don't I?"

I waved at him and strolled on. A light spring rain had fallen earlier, leaving jeweled droplets shimmering on the green leaves. The sky was still overcast where I walked, but breaks in the clouds cast golden islands of sunshine on the gray waters of the lake. The damp ground squished under my purple tennies, and a doe peeked out of the bushes.

A lovely day for walking. A day for thinking about spring flowers and spring rainbows and maybe even spring love. But my thoughts were trapped in the dark corridors of murder.

One side of me shouted a vehement "yes!" to the question of going to Sgt. Yates immediately. Brad and Leslie were having an affair. He'd killed her to keep it quiet. Nail 'im!

The other side repeated in more explicit terms what I'd said to Sandy. The fact that Brad was a sleazy adulterer, a liar, and a cheat still didn't make him a killer. Maybe the affair was long over, or maybe Leslie's death at unknown hands had shocked him into a complete turnaround, and he really was a changed man, eager to help kids, save the environment, and grow the economy. The affair, sleazy as it was, was obviously over now, and unwarranted accusations of murder could do Brad, Tammi, and Skye all irreparable harm.

A third side (never let it be said that Ivy Malone is not many-sided) reasoned that Sgt. Yates was neither dumb nor incompetent. His investigation would surely uncover the affair between Brad and Leslie. Brad Ridenour might already be riding high on the suspect list, with evidence of his guilt piling up daily. Or he may have already been investigated and exonerated.

Sgt. Yates surely did not need or want any further busybody interference from me.

There. That took care of that. Sandy had it off her back. I had it off mine.

Almost.

Because I would feel a whole lot better if I knew the affair was over long before Leslie's death. Or if I knew there was some proof that said Brad couldn't have done it. Or if I was certain Sgt. Yates wouldn't somehow miss the affair and thus miss Brad's possible involvement in the murder.

I didn't get any emails from the Lord on the subject, but I did get a phone call that suggested the Lord might not be averse to my delving deeper into this.

The phone call came as I was eating a French dip sandwich of leftover roast beef for supper and watching the local news on TV. Brad was in top form, exchanging breezy comments with the woman coanchor but going properly serious with a story about a family losing their home in a fire. I snidely wondered if he'd be so breezy and confident with a big "CL" for "Cheating Liar" tattooed on his forehead. Sandy had already called to say she was going for pizza with her friends then to a movie at another church. If it was okay with me, of course. I was relieved that she sounded more like her old bouncy self. Now I flicked the remote to mute the sound on the TV and said hello into the phone.

# 27

"Aunt Ivy, is that you? It's me, Tammi Ridenour!"

"Hi, Tammi. How are you?" I glanced at the TV again. *And isn't that cheating husband of yours looking great?*

"Wasn't yesterday at the gymnastics meet fun?" she bubbled. Then, apparently realizing that might not be the proper attitude, considering everything, she added, "Except that it's too bad Sandy had such an off day. I hope she isn't ill or anything?"

"No, she's fine."

"Oh, good! I called because I'm wondering if she could come sit with Baby for a couple of hours?"

My first thought was that this was too much. Sure, Baby was an adorable sweetheart, and sitting with him was no chore. But maybe it was time they invested in some behavior modification training from an expert. A grown dog, especially a 260-pound one, shouldn't be allowed to demand constant company to keep him from destroying *his* environment. My second thought was that Tammi had obviously missed what was going on yesterday, that Sandy had deliberately avoided her and Brad. My third thought eclipsed both of the first two. *Hey, this is opportunity calling!*

"Skye is going to a movie with a date," Tammi bubbled on. "We're so pleased that her social life is expanding, and I don't want to interfere by asking her to stay with Baby."

Well, well. Skye on a date. Did that mean she was finally accepting Woodston guys as something other than hayseed hillbillies?

"But Brad doesn't have to do the late news tonight, so he wants me to meet him for dinner at a place called the Inn at Lost Lake! He says it's so rustic and romantic. Can I tell you a secret?"

"Please do."

"I doubt most people realize it, and Brad would surely be embarrassed if anyone knew, but he's such a sentimental man. And this is the anniversary of our first date! Isn't that romantic?"

I might argue with Brad's judgment of Dead Critters Inn as romantic, but I had to agree that remembering this little anniversary was impressive. Maybe Brad really was trying to make up for past bad behavior.

Which didn't mean, however, that he hadn't killed Leslie before this change of heart, real or pretended.

"Sandy isn't home," I said quickly, "but I'd be happy to sit with Baby. Would that be okay?"

"That would be wonderful! Baby will be delighted! Baby, Aunt Ivy is coming! Oh, he's smiling already." Small pause as Tammi apparently bared her teeth in a return smile. "Can you come over in, oh, say an hour and a half?"

"I'll be there."

Actually, I was there in just over an hour. I wanted to be early so I'd have time to make conversation with Tammi. On the drive over I'd experimented with various conversational forays, but in the end, as I rang the doorbell, I just asked the Lord to open the way. I needed to find out how much Tammi knew. And if Brad had an alibi.

"You're early! Oh, good!" Tammi said when she opened the door. "The most awful thing has just happened!"

My ready imagination tossed up disastrous possibilities ranging from Baby's demise under the wheels of a truck, to Skye calling to say she was eloping with her date, to Tammi's sudden discovery of her husband's infidelity and subsequent murder of his paramour.

Baby pushed around her, eliminating the first possibility. He sat down and offered me a paw. We shook. Tammi craned her head around to peer over her ample rear and lifted a high-heeled clad foot behind her. "Look!" she wailed.

What I saw was a drooping hem on her skirt, at which point I realized her classification of "awful" came at a lower level on the disaster scale than mine. She pulled me inside. "What should I do? I don't want to change dresses, because I've already done my hair and it'll get mussed. But I'm just all thumbs at fixing anything, and I can't be late! If there's anything Brad can't stand, it's late."

In the living room I saw that huge diet and exercise book sitting open on the coffee table. Tammi had apparently been studying it. I could see sentences she'd underlined. "What happened?" I asked.

"I was putting on my sandals, and I don't know how it happened, but a heel caught in the hem, and it just ripped!"

The seller of this black dress with a swishy skirt and long sleeves deserved a big bonus, I decided. It did everything a dress was supposed to do. Tammi, except for the scowl on her face, looked terrific. Sophisticated, sexy in an understated way, even a bit trimmer than usual, especially with those arm-slimming sleeves.

I leaned over and inspected the hem. "If you have a needle and black thread, it won't take but a minute to fix it."

"Really? Oh, Aunt Ivy, you're a miracle worker!"

Again, a different rating scale than mine. One of these days I intended to sit her down with a Bible and point out some real miracles.

Tammi bustled off. Baby, unasked, scrunched down on his stomach and did his caterpillar crawl. He also gave me one of his toothy grins. Tammi, obviously not a sewing person, returned with an undersized needle and oversized thread, but I thought I could make them work. Though I intended to take my time and use this opportunity to best advantage.

"It's so nice that you and your husband can go out to dinner on this first-date anniversary," I said in my best chatty manner as I poked the thread at the eye of the needle. "Not many men remember things like that."

"Oh, I know! I feel so fortunate."

I squinted as I tried again with the thread. Maybe I wouldn't need to use delaying tactics. They're making these holes smaller and harder to hit all the time. "He usually stays in Fayetteville between the early and late news shows, doesn't he?"

With the thread finally caught in the needle, I knelt behind her where I could access the ripped hem. Baby snuggled up beside me. He smelled fresh and clean, as if he'd just had a shampoo.

"Yes, he's such a busy man. So dedicated to his work and his service to the community! But sometimes he also likes to just relax at the library for some quiet reading between shows."

And sometimes he liked a little hanky-panky with Leslie Marcone. Which I didn't say, of course. Though it was the big question in my mind. Had Tammi known about the relationship when Leslie was alive? Did she know about it now? Did she have any fears her husband might be a killer as well as a cheater?

"That's a long drive coming home from Fayetteville after the late news every night. If the weather were especially bad, I think I'd be inclined to spend the night there."

I turned up the hem and started making tiny loops in that invisible stitch my mother had taught me long ago, congratulating myself on my cleverness in fishing for information without actually asking a question. Baby draped a big paw over my foot as he watched me work, as if he might be considering taking up sewing in his spare time.

"Yes, Brad does stay in town occasionally. But, as you said, only if the weather is really bad, or sometimes when he's exceptionally tired. He says he never really sleeps well unless he's right here at home in his own bed."

I didn't let myself even think a snide comment on that remark. Instead I asked, "He has to go out of town occasionally too, doesn't he?"

"Yes, now and then. He'll probably have to do more of that as his political campaign progresses. But I've always believed it's the quality of time a husband and wife spend together, not the quantity!"

Inspiration for a smooth segue here. "Are you a little uneasy, you and Skye here alone so much, since that woman out by the lake was murdered?"

"Oh, I was terrified when that happened! Brad had been out of town overnight. He'd flown to Memphis for a meeting with the station owners and got back to Fayetteville just that afternoon. I didn't know anything about the body being found in the lake until he told about it on the news, and then I couldn't help thinking, with him gone it might easily have been me or Skye who was murdered!"

"They didn't think it was murder at first. They thought she'd accidentally drowned."

"I know. But I had a bad feeling right from the start that it was more than that. Didn't you?"

Well, yes, I did. But maybe Tammi had more reason to be suspicious about the circumstances of Leslie's death than I did.

Okay, Brad was out of town, and he'd gone by plane. It was stretching even my fertile imagination to think he could have stuffed Leslie's dead body into his luggage and brought her home on the plane for disposal in the lake. It was also doubtful he could have pretended a trip to Memphis and stayed here in Woodston to murder Leslie instead; the flight and meeting could be verified. So here was what I was looking for. The alibi. Brad Ridenour was still a sleazy, cheating husband, but he was off the hook for murder.

The flaw in that conclusion shot up instantly, like a rotten egg in a pot of simmering water.

Yes, Brad was in Memphis when I found the body. But that was no alibi, because Leslie had been killed several days earlier. Where was he then?

"I was the one who found her body, I suppose you know. I'd worked for Leslie for a short time," I tossed out casually.

"Oh yes, I know! I've wanted to ask you about that, but then I thought, oh, it was probably such a traumatic experience that you wouldn't want to talk about it. I know finding a dead person would give me nightmares for days!" She patted my shoulder.

"Yes, it was quite a shock. They thought she'd been dead several days when I found her."

"Oh, how *ghastly*! I suppose you had to talk to Sgt. Yates about it?"

"He questioned me a couple of times, first when it looked like a drowning accident, and then again when they decided it was murder. I don't know if anything I told him was helpful. The police have talked to a lot of people, of course."

I left that hanging, wondering if she'd fill in that Brad had been questioned, but no comment was forthcoming. Which left me with the uneasy feeling that it was possible the affair was still unknown to Sgt. Yates.

"But you were closer to her than anyone else," Tammi said. "Surely you must have seen or heard something to suggest who killed her."

I detected a wheedling note, and a thought occurred to me: who was trying to ferret information out of whom here? Was Tammi trying to find out if I knew anything about a relationship between Leslie and her husband? Or just fishing for juicy gossip about the murdered woman to share with some diet club?

"There seems to be any number of suspects," I offered. "An ex-husband, irate partners from a company she used to be connected with, a man she was currently involved with, an angry neighbor, former employees, etc."

I'd buried the bit about involvement with a man in the middle of the list, but Tammi instantly latched on to it. "I hadn't heard she had a boyfriend! There are all kinds of rumors going around, of course. You know what a gossip mill Woodston is! But I haven't heard that one."

"She was a very private person," I murmured. That said nothing, of course, which was exactly what I intended. I shifted my weight from one knee to the other, grateful for the deep carpet.

"Did Sgt. Yates tell you about the boyfriend?"

"No, I just happened to know through my association with Leslie."

"But Sgt. Yates does know about the boyfriend?"

"I have no idea. Sgt. Yates isn't inclined to discuss his cases with outsiders."

"That's exactly what Brad says! He says they've had a terrible time getting information from the authorities about the murder. And people have a right to know these things!"

"I suppose it's helpful in some cases not to let the public know too much. The police can sometimes use unpublicized details to help pin down the murderer."

"Actually, I'm surprised to hear she had a boyfriend," Tammi added in a reflective tone. "Not that she wasn't very attractive, of course. But so aloof and unfriendly! Everyone had the impression she thought she was a cut above Woodston. I can't imagine who she thought was good enough for boyfriend status around here!"

"She was a bit standoffish."

"But you discovered a different side to her when you were working for her?"

"No, not really," I had to admit. "She fired me over a rather minor incident."

"Do you know who the boyfriend was?"

I felt as if we'd been dancing a verbal two-step and she'd suddenly cornered me with the direct question. I wasn't about to be the one to reveal her husband's extracurricular activities if she didn't already know, but I'm also the one who's stuck with this aversion to untruths, even if telling one would be easier and to my advantage.

"Leslie never confided in me about anything." Absolute truth. "Except that she hated the capers I put on her veal chops one time." More truth. The thread tangled, and I leaned back on my heels while I worked the knot loose.

"You never saw the man?"

"No. If he ever came to the house it was after my working hours. But I think she usually met him somewhere."

"How peculiar. And so mysterious! It almost makes you wonder . . . ?" She let the words trail off as she peered down at me, but there was a definite question mark at the end.

"Wonder?" I repeated in a puzzled tone that suggested I hadn't a clue what she was talking about. Naïve LOL who knows nothing about such worldly situations as an affair with a married man.

"Well, in any case, Sgt. Yates is very competent," she declared. "I'm sure he'll figure it all out and uncover the killer in no time."

"Yes, I'm sure he will."

I thought that ended the subject of the mysterious boyfriend, but Tammi wasn't finished yet. "I wonder if this man Leslie was seeing was local or from out of town?"

Definitely fishing now. I knew because I'd done it enough times myself. The thing was, I still had no idea if she was fishing from a vantage point of suspicion or even knowledge of the affair, or if she had a curiosity gene of her own. I tossed out Sgt. Yates's all-purpose question. "Why do you ask?"

"It's scary to think he might be from around here, don't you think? Maybe even someone we pass on the street every day! You know, the butcher, the baker, the candlestick maker? Although I don't really see Leslie Marcone with any of *those* men, do you? Anyway, I guess I'd rather he was someone from far away."

"Because the boyfriend might be the killer?"

"Well, these things happen, don't they, when a woman gets involved in some smarmy relationship?"

The word leaped out at me. *Smarmy.* General cattiness on her part? Or personal knowledge? Because *smarmy* certainly fit the level of Brad and Leslie's sneaky affair.

I tightened the last stitch, knotted the thread, and bit off the excess, still guiltily remembering my mother's long-ago warning that I was going to ruin my teeth doing that, but still doing it anyway.

Tammi moved over to a mirror in the hallway beyond the living room. She twirled in the dress. "Oh, that's perfect! Thank you so much!"

I got off the carpet and sat on the sofa, glad to be off my

knees. I nudged the big diet and exercise book to a more solid position on the coffee table. The thing was heavy enough to break toes if it fell off. I hadn't seen or heard anything of Skye, so now I asked, "Skye's already left on her date?"

"I think they were going for burgers before the movie."

"Did you meet him?"

"No, she was meeting him somewhere."

I looked at my watch. "She'll be home before you get back, I suppose?"

"Umm, I don't know." I could see Tammi smoothing a dark eyebrow with a fingertip, then checking for lipstick smears on her teeth. She turned to look at her backside and frowned slightly. The black dress was indeed flattering, but she still needed more exercise than underlining sentences in that big book.

"What time is her curfew?"

"We believe in letting Skye make her own decisions about such matters. We think it fosters a greater sense of responsibility than our making all the decisions for her."

While I was still absorbing *that* rather shocking system of child raising, Tammi moved on to the bathroom.

"You know, talking with you about Leslie Marcone's killer has made me feel better!" she called.

"It has? In what way?"

She came to the hall doorway, spritz bottle of Eternity perfume in one hand. I realized then that Baby's nice scent wasn't just doggie shampoo; he'd received a complimentary dash of Eternity.

"All along I've been afraid this murder could be the beginning of something awful. You know, a crazed serial killer running around killing at random, someone who might sneak in and attack any of us! But now I'm sure he was after Leslie specifically, and the rest of us are in no danger, don't you think? I mean, quarreling with business partners and neighbors, being involved in this *relationship* . . . Obviously she lived a totally different lifestyle than the rest of us."

"Some people who look upstanding and honorable have some rather dark secrets." Not a total non sequitur, but not exactly a conclusion to be deduced from what she'd said. Tammi did not seem puzzled, however.

"Yes, I suppose that's true," she murmured.

I'm not sure just what did it—maybe the lack of exclamation point on the thoughtful comment. But at that moment I made up my mind. The last thing I wanted was to cause embarrassment or anguish for Tammi and Skye, but I couldn't delay going to Sgt. Yates about both the illicit relationship and my suspicions of Brad Ridenour's involvement in the murder.

A decision reinforced by a discovery I made later, after Tammi was gone, when Baby and I went out to the kitchen to see what snacks were available this evening. I wasn't truly *snooping* when I made the discovery. If I'd really wanted to snoop I'd have prowled through the desk in Brad's small office off the living room and peeked at charge-card and phone bills. And searched for a cache of mementos and photos that "sentimental man" Brad might have stashed away.

Yes, those sneaky thoughts occurred to me, but I didn't turn thoughts into action, because I consider people's private belongings private. Or maybe, I had to admit, because I was also reasonably certain Brad wasn't dim-witted enough to let incriminating details show up where Tammi could find them. Although I also have to admit I did peek into the bathroom medicine cabinet. But doesn't everyone do that? Nothing to do with murder, just general inquisitiveness.

I found an out-of-date antibiotic prescription, Band-Aids, and first-aid creams. Plus four kinds of upset-stomach and heartburn remedies, and laxatives in liquid, pill, and chocolate-ype varieties. Someone in the Ridenour family had big stomach problems. Perhaps someone with a cleft chin and a guilty conscience?

I gave Baby some meaty snacks from a bag in the refrigerator and found a chocolate-covered Dilly bar for myself in the freezer. There were three boxes of them tucked under packages of Asian vegetables and Healthy Choice dinners. Then I noticed the calendar taped to the side of the refrigerator. No snooping involved here; it was right out there in plain sight.

Although I did have to lean over to focus my bifocals on the fine scribbles in Tammi's backhand. She apparently used the calendar mostly for herself and Skye. A few notes concerned Brad's activities, but he must have a more detailed calendar elsewhere. There were notations about appointments, things to do, things that had been done. A lunch meeting for Tammi with some committee at that chuck wagon restaurant, appointment for Brad with a Dr. Wertleman, Baby's date with the dog groomer yesterday. Reminder of joint hair appointments for Skye and Tammi with Carla for next week. (Skye was surely going to love *that* little duet.) A note that Tammi had ordered a new book, *Eat and Get Thin,* and another note that she'd sent twenty dollars with a birthday card to someone named Lisa.

Okay, I did have to move the page a smidgen to see farther back. Sure enough, there was a notation about Brad's overnight trip to Memphis for the meeting with the station owners, just as Tammi had said.

But that wasn't the date that interested me . . .

I peered farther back on the calendar, into the window of time when Leslie's death had occurred. Baby had been to the vet for worm medicine. Skye had seen a school counselor.

And Brad had been in Little Rock. An alibi?

Not necessarily. At least not a steel-clad one.

Because he could have had another secret tryst with Leslie,

a tryst that somehow escalated into suffocation and death. Or had he ruthlessly planned her murder and executed it with efficient precision, right down to getting both her body and car back to Vintage Estates?

Sgt. Yates hadn't been able to locate anyone who'd seen Leslie after she fired me. This could be the reason. She'd been killed that very night. Sgt. Yates would have some tough questions for Brad Ridenour after I told him all this.

Except that a few minutes later I was wondering if I'd ever have a chance to tell Sgt. Yates or anybody else anything. Or if I was about to wind up with my own face-down view of Little Tom Lake.

# 28

I had no warning of danger. No dum-de-dum-dum music or creaking floors or ominous shadows on the walls. Baby and I were just sitting there on the sofa, watching an old Humphrey Bogart movie on TV. I was licking the last dribbles of ice cream off the Dilly bar stick, Baby watching hopefully. My shoes were off and my feet resting on that oversized diet book. I heard a car outside and assumed it was Tammi, so I was surprised when Brad Ridenour strode alone through the front door.

He looked just like he had earlier on the TV news. Expensive, well-fitting dark suit, blond hair tousled to the proper degree of casualness, patterned tie a little flashy—his coanchor liked to tease him about his ties—but not overdone. Although, knowing what I now did about his relationship with Leslie, I knew I could never look at him with an unjaundiced eye again.

Baby slid off the flowered sofa and ambled over to him, brushy tail waving gently. With the release of Baby's weight, the sofa cushions and I bounced upward a couple of inches.

"Hey, this was great of you to come sit with Baby on such short notice." Brad gave Baby a pat, but he didn't make over the big dog like Tammi did. "We must be the only people in Woodston who can't go anywhere without a sitter for the dog."

An amused observation? Or an unhappy complaint?

"That's okay," I said. "It's always fun to sit with Baby."

"That your old Thunderbird out front? It's a beauty. A restoration?"

"No, all original. My husband and I bought it new in '75."

"Friend of mine at the station is into restorations in his spare time. I did some part-time work for a mechanic when I was a kid, so I give him a hand once in a while. But nothing beats an original. You've taken great care of the old 'bird."

All very nice and friendly. The Big Brad working his charisma. The kind of guy who automatically practiced on everyone, I suspected. Or was I getting special treatment to lull me into inattention? Because—

A jolt of wariness straightened my spine on the sofa. "Where's Tammi?"

"I asked her to run over to the Quickie-Mart and pick up some Pepto-Bismol." He rubbed his broad but solidly muscled stomach and grimaced. "I'm afraid I may have overindulged on the Cajun ribs."

Pepto-Bismol. A nice big bottle of the pink stuff sat in the medicine cabinet already, but he'd sent Tammi on a crosstown, late-night errand for more.

It was possible, of course, that neither of them remembered the Pepto-Bismol and other stomach medications in the medicine cabinet. It was also possible that Brad needed Tammi out of the way for a few minutes. So he could . . . do what?

Their dinner may have had romantic origins, but I doubted the evening's entire conversation had centered around starry-eyed reminiscences. Married couples tend to run dry on such subjects fairly quickly. Had chatterbox Tammi unknowingly alerted him to the fact that their Baby-sitter knew something no one else did, that the murdered woman had a mysterious boyfriend? Had she revealed that I'd been asking nosy questions about Brad himself? Had he put two and two together and decided he had to do something to eliminate this unanticipated danger before everything blew wide open?

*Like how is he going to do that within the next few minutes?* I scoffed. *Strangle me with his flashy tie and hide my body in the closet? Conk me on the head with that oversized diet book and throw me in his car for a quick disposal jaunt to the lake?*

No. Not practical. He'd have the Thunderbird to consider. All kinds of awkward explanations to make to Tammi and the police. No, if he wanted to do me in he'd surely have to pick a more appropriate time and place than this. A scary thought, one to be given further consideration. Yet much more scary was the way he was now looking at me with an oddly speculative expression. It occurred to me that Brad may have far more imaginative ideas than I did about committing quickie murder.

I slid into my shoes and stood up. "Well, I'd better be going," I said brightly. "It was nice of you to remember your and Tammi's first-date anniversary."

"Actually, I lucked out. I'd forgotten until she mentioned it. I just happened to have the time free for dinner together tonight. But don't tell Tammi."

He smiled and spoke in a rueful, just-between-you-and-me tone, but he was still looking at me with that odd expression. I considered what to do if he should make a move. My only weapon at the moment appeared to be one well-licked Dilly bar stick. Not a reassuring thought. Neither were Brad's next words reassuring.

"Tammi reminded me that you're the person who found Leslie Marcone's body," he said. "You must know something about her personal life?"

"Not all that much," I assured him. Baby was gently trying to extract my Dilly bar weapon from my hand. I yanked it away and edged toward the door. I'd heard about jabbing a key in an attacker's eye. Would a Dilly bar stick work?

"Mrs. Malone, I think we should talk."

About what I was going to tell Sgt. Yates? About what he was going to do to me if I did talk to Sgt. Yates? Or was "talk" a euphemism for something considerably more deadly? In any case, I wasn't about to ask for a detailed explanation. "Yes, we'll have to do that sometime," I said. I tried to muddy the waters by adding brightly, "Your venture into politics is a fascinating subject."

"I think you know what we should talk about, Mrs. Malone." He sounded reproachful, as if I were playing unfair. "And it isn't politics."

"Well, uh—"

The door opened and Skye walked in, belly button peeking between low-slung jeans and skimpy pink top. I'd never been more grateful for an interruption.

Brad looked at his watch. "You're just getting home from the movie *now*?"

A time-conscious attitude rather less liberal than Tammi's, I suspected. But I suppose even an adulterer/murderer can be a conscientious father.

"Well, I'll be going," I repeated with the same brightness, phony as a set of cheap false teeth. I reached for the doorknob.

"Did Tammi pay you earlier for sitting tonight?" Brad asked.

"No need. I enjoy sitting with Baby." I waved my stick. "And I ate a Dilly bar."

"I'll walk you out to the car. And follow you home, if you're uneasy driving alone at night," Brad offered.

And give him a second chance to employ some creative method of eradicating me?

"No, I'm fine," I said hastily. I gave Skye a fingertip wave.

Outside, I jumped into the Thunderbird, intending to get away from the Ridenour residence with all possible speed, only to have the engine sit there like a pet rock while I frantically pumped the pedal and twisted the key. But just when Brad opened the door and peered out, the engine suddenly roared to life and I was off like a skittish squirrel. *Thank you, Lord.*

Sandy was waiting up for me, all chattery about her day and curious about mine. I wiped my perspiring hands on my pants and tried to appear calm and normal.

She was astonished when I told her Skye had gone out on a movie date. "I wonder who with? She never told me anything about a date."

"You've been avoiding Skye just a bit lately, haven't you?"

"Yeah, I guess I have," she admitted. "I'm always afraid I'll slip and say something about . . . well, you know. Especially when she's going on and on about how important her dad is and his big political campaign and everything."

Silence while we both contemplated what she knew and what it might mean. She gave me a sideways glance.

"Have you told anyone about Mr. Ridenour and Leslie Marcone?"

"I'm planning to discuss it with Sgt. Yates very soon."

"Does Mr. Ridenour give you the creeps?"

I nodded. Oh, yeah. Oddly, however, by now I felt less apprehensive, even a little foolish about my melodramatic reaction to Brad Ridenour. I reminded myself that many people had been adulterers without turning into killers. Brad may truly have been concerned about my welfare when he offered to follow me home tonight.

But I was careful to set the security system before we went to bed.

# 29

I got up early the next morning and tiptoed around, inspecting both inside and outside the house before Sandy was up. I didn't really think Brad Ridenour was lurking out there somewhere. Surely it would take him time to customize a deadly scheme for me. But if he *was* lurking, or had booby-trapped the door or porch, I didn't want Sandy caught in the ambush.

As soon as she walked down the driveway to catch the school bus, I dialed the sheriff's department and asked for Sgt. Yates. Frustration. The woman answering the phone said he was out of town.

"Could you tell me where he's gone?"

"I'm afraid not." The woman sounded slightly indignant that I'd dared ask.

So, did this mean Sgt. Yates had zipped off to California to further investigate ex-husband Shane Wagner and/or the other discontented partners in the company? Or perhaps he'd gone to truck company headquarters to check into details about Al Diedrich's truck runs? Or to Toledo to pry into Astrid Gallagher's private life?

Those people, once high on my suspect list, had slipped away, like Leslie's body drifting away at the lake that morning. But Sgt. Yates apparently didn't know what I did about Brad Ridenour's involvement with Leslie, so these other suspects were undoubtedly still uppermost in his mind.

"Will he be back soon?"

"I couldn't say." Whether that meant she didn't know or wasn't about to tell me was not discernible. "Would you like to speak with someone else?"

I hesitated only momentarily before saying, "No, I'll wait for Sgt. Yates, thank you."

Sgt. Yates might raise his scarred eyebrow at my involvement in this murder case. He might tell me I read too many mystery novels. He may have reevaluated my eligibility as a companion for Pa Yates. But I was reasonably certain he'd investigate my information and suspicions about a popular TV anchorman, whereas some other officer might pass me off as a dotty LOL. I left my phone number and asked the woman to have Sgt. Yates call me as soon as possible.

So, no big deal, I told myself. All I had to do was stay out of Brad Ridenour's reach until Sgt. Yates was back in town. The best way to do that today, I decided, was to get out of town. Take a long, leisurely drive somewhere. Do my nerves good too.

I grabbed a map on my way out of the house. No way could Brad Ridenour ambush me when not even I knew where I was going.

Which, I realized about two minutes later, was nowhere. The old Thunderbird, which had been balky last night and several times previously, had no more spark than a magic coach morphed into a pumpkin. When I turned the key in the ignition, there was only the silence of one hand clapping. I remembered my father telling about how his father had gone out to plow one morning and found his mule dead. I now knew the feeling. Although, hopefully, my situation was only a temporary one.

So, now what? Call a tow truck and have the 'bird hauled in to a repair shop? Try to get someone to come out here and work on it? Expensive options. Then a disturbing thought occurred to me, and I peered around uneasily. Could Brad have disabled my car with the idea of trapping me here where I'd be easily accessible for some devious plot he had in mind? For a while I'd parked the car over by the garage, where it was not visible from the road, but I'd gotten out of the habit lately, and now it was right out in front of the house. Brad could have sneaked in during the night . . .

Although, more likely, I reminded myself, trying to re- press that tendency toward paranoia, the old 'bird was just feeling its age. Sometimes I didn't feel like revving up in the morning either.

Then I spotted Hanson Watkins on top of the roof of his mother's house, can of roof tar in hand. He'd once offered to take a look at the Thunderbird. Maybe he could at least get it running enough to stagger into a repair shop under its own power.

The shortest route to his house was on the lake trail. I set off briskly. Night rain had left the trailside bushes wet, so I was thoroughly sprinkled by the time I got to the yard and waved up at him.

"I hate to bother you," I called, "but do you suppose you could come over after you're done up there and take a look at the T-bird? It's gone balky again."

"Sure. I'm finished here anyway. Bedroom started leaking last night, but I think I've got it fixed."

He disappeared around to the other side of the roof, where

he apparently had a ladder. A minute later he came around the house, wiping his tar-stained hands on a rag.

"What seems to be the problem?"

"It just won't start. It doesn't even make that awful grinding noise like it has a few other times."

"Sounds like a dead battery. Let me get this stuff cleaned off my hands, and I'll bring my pickup over and we'll give it a jump start."

I walked back to the Thunderbird, and Hanson drove over a few minutes later. He parked with the nose of his pickup about a foot from the front end of the T-bird and popped the hood of the pickup. He then began a search through the back of it, which was filled with an assortment of tools, pieces of plastic pipe, and other house repair supplies.

"Would you believe I don't seem to have jumper cables in this mess?" he finally said, sounding disgruntled. "They must be in my wife's car back home."

"That's okay. I'll just call a repair shop." For which my checkbook would undoubtedly go into shock.

"Let me take a look anyway. If it is the battery, we can run into town and pick up a new one and give it a try. Or there's a couple other things it might be. Dashboard lights been doing anything peculiar?"

"Not that I've noticed."

He slid behind the wheel of the 'bird, leaving the door open, and tried the key himself. Nothing. He pumped the pedal and tried again. Again nothing. A dead mule is a dead mule no matter who's at the reins.

He popped the hood open, braced it with the rod, and peered inside. He jiggled some wires. "Battery isn't corroded, but it could still be bad. Or it might be the alternator or spark plugs. How old are they?"

Not as old as my wrinkles, but probably as old as the

polyester pants I was wearing. "Good question. How about the rotor? Is that there?"

"The rotor?" Hanson turned to look at me, surprised, then laughed. "Ivy, if you know about rotors, you probably don't need me."

"Actually, I couldn't tell a rotor from a radish," I admitted. "I just remember reading about it somewhere." In a mystery novel, where the detective removed the rotor to disable the villain's car and keep him from escaping. But men tend not to give much credence to knowledge gleaned from mystery novels, so I didn't mention this.

"Unless someone's deliberately removed it, it couldn't be missing here. They don't just fall out. But I can check."

"Please do," I said. One-time car mechanic's helper Brad Ridenour would surely know how to remove a rotor, although I didn't explain that to Hanson.

I watched as he stretched over the big engine and pressed a couple of clips to remove something I could only identify as a thingamajig. It's a little late in life, but one of these days I'm definitely going to learn more about the interior workings of vehicles.

Hanson peered inside. "Rotor's right here under the distributor cap where it should be."

"Oh. Well . . . that's good, then."

"Might be a clogged fuel filter. I'll check. Although that shouldn't make everything go as dead as it is."

While Hanson was checking that out I circled the car, wondering if there was something other than rotor removal that Brad might have done to disable the engine. Or the problem could be something not directed at me personally, of course. I've heard of a snake or skunk or other small creature getting into a car's inner workings. I got down on my knees and warily peered underneath.

I know very little about the underside of vehicles, but I

know enough to tell that what I saw underneath the old 'bird was not a normal part of any vehicle. Neither was it a skunk or snake. Although my throat suddenly felt as if a rotor might be lodged in it.

"Hanson, you'd better take a look under here," I croaked. "There's something—"

"I doubt anything down under there could be the problem. I still think it's probably the battery—"

"Just look," I interrupted.

He got down on his knees beside me, grunting a little as he did so. A second later he floundered backward, leaving a trail like a heavyweight worm in the loose gravel and yelling, "Get away from the car! Now!"

The panic in his voice sent me scrambling too. I backed off about ten feet, and then he yanked me to my feet and shoved until we were both a good sixty feet away. He stood there panting. His broad face had reddened from the sudden exertion, but now his skin was turning an ashy shade of pale.

"There's something fastened to the car under there," I said, although he obviously already knew that.

"Dynamite."

"Dynamite?" I yelped, even though that was what it had looked like to me too. "You mean like a car bomb?"

"I'm no expert, but that's sure what it looks like to me. Several sticks of dynamite. Probably wired to go off when the car started. All that saved you, and me too, is that the car didn't start."

I'd thought the old 'bird not starting was a minor disaster. Something to grumble and fret about. Instead it was a blessing.

The Lord's protection comes in unexpected forms. Sometimes it's a dramatic answer to prayer. Sometimes it's unanswered prayer. And sometimes he works through the mundane situation of an old car that won't start and a neighbor who can't find his jumper cables. *Thank you, Lord!*

"You got enemies in the Mafia or something?" Hanson muttered. He pulled a handkerchief out of his pocket and swiped it across his face.

No, no Mafia. But I had enemies.

The murderous Braxtons, who'd sworn to make roadkill out of me. Someone in that multitalented clan undoubtedly knew all about dynamite and car bombs, and dynamite would be readily available through Drake Braxton's land development and construction business. I'd thought they didn't know where I was, that I was safely in hiding, but I could very well be wrong. Maybe, for them, I was right out in plain sight.

Or it could be probable murderer Brad Ridenour. The man who'd wanted to "talk" to me about something. A man who'd worked for a mechanic in his youth and probably knew enough to figure out how and where to plant dynamite. I couldn't think where he'd obtain dynamite on short notice, but he definitely knew where I lived and what car I drove.

And, for all I knew, maybe some of the other suspects in Leslie Marcone's murder were after me. I was almost certain Leslie's ex knew who I was, although he'd pretended not to. Maybe he figured he'd better get rid of me before I came up with something to prove to the police he was involved.

When you've raised the ire of more than one set of bad guys, it's hard to know for sure who's after you in any given situation.

"You want to call 911 or shall I do it?" Hanson asked.

He had a cell phone clipped to his belt, and I was feeling so shaky I wasn't certain I could dial numbers if I got to the phone in the house. In theory, I knew the Braxtons were after me. In theory, I knew Brad Ridenour needed to get me out of the way before I blabbed. But this was no longer theory.

This was three-dimensional dynamite reality: someone had honest-to-goodness tried to blow me and the Thunderbird to smithereens. "You can call."

He made the call. His voice sounded like rusty springs, and he had to clear his throat several times, but he did a credible job of explaining the situation and giving the address. Then we just stood there looking at the two vehicles facing each other with hoods raised, like metal combatants ready to take a bite out of each other.

I wasn't certain the dynamite mounted on the old 'bird wouldn't spontaneously explode, and apparently neither was Hanson. He obviously did not intend to go back and move his pickup out of the danger zone. So we just stood there silently watching and waiting. I could see nervous sweat standing out on Hanson's face. I could feel it running down my own ribs. I figured together we were making enough moisture to affect the humidity level on a weather report.

# 30

Finally, after what seemed like hours but was surely no more than a few minutes, we heard sirens. Hanson was still so pale that I tried to lighten things up.

"Still interested in trading your motor home for the old 'bird?"

He looked at me as if I'd told an off-color joke at a funeral, and I hastily switched to apology.

"I'm really sorry I got you involved in this. I had no idea it was anything but a minor repair problem."

"A car bomb isn't the kind of thing you think will happen in Woodston. You have any idea who'd do this?" He sounded both scared and bewildered, as if he still found the situation inconceivable. "It doesn't look like a practical joke or juvenile stunt."

"I . . . uh . . . might have some ideas."

Another odd look. *What sort of person,* it asked, *knows people who plant car bombs?* We'd been huddled together, but now he inched away from me as if he thought I might be wired for demolition too.

Two cars from the county sheriff's department screamed down the driveway a minute later. Spotting our two vehicles, one officer braked so hard that the car behind almost rammed into him. Four officers jumped out. I didn't recognize any of them.

"Okay, everybody stay back," an officer yelled.

A superfluous order at the moment, since Hanson and I were the only two people present and we were already hiding behind the big black walnut tree. Within a few minutes, however, the situation changed. People showed up, seemingly materializing out of nowhere, just as they had over at Leslie's place. They gawked at the yellow plastic tape an officer started stringing in a wide circle around the area and looked speculatively at the vehicles with gaping hoods, everyone asking everyone else what was going on. A fire truck arrived, then an ambulance, both with flashing lights and wailing sirens. A bomb threat obviously gets top priority from all emergency services.

None of the officers approached the two vehicles. The ones who weren't stringing up the warning tape appeared to be searching for something in the trees and bushes and yard. The booby-trapped Thunderbird and the innocent pickup were as splendidly isolated as two slabs of roast beef at a vegetarian party.

While the officers were securing the area, I picked a middle-aged officer and gave him my name.

"The Thunderbird is mine, and this is where I live," I explained with a gesture toward the house. "When I came out this morning, the car wouldn't start, so Mr. Watkins here came over to give it a jump start with his pickup. But he couldn't find his jumper cables, and then we discovered the dynamite attached to the underside of my car."

The officer looked at me doubtfully, as if suddenly suspecting they may have stormed in with a gangbusters reaction to what might be the wild imagination of a little old lady who watched too many crime shows on TV. "You're sure it's dynamite, not just something like, say, a loose muffler hanging down? Or a piece of paper sack or something caught underneath the car?"

Hanson stepped up. "It's dynamite, all right. At least four sticks. I've worked in construction, and I can tell dynamite when I see it. And I was down there practically looking it in the eye. I'd guess it's wired to go off when the engine starts, but lucky for us the engine wouldn't start."

The officer's patronizing attitude changed as he turned his attention to Hanson. The questions he asked now were no longer doubting. Where, exactly, was the dynamite fastened to the car? Had Hanson seen any wires attached to it? I was relieved yet annoyed. I wasn't totally invisible to the officer, but I may as well have been. Once, he asked Hanson, "When was the car driven last?" as if I were incapable of answering for myself.

"I drove it last night. I got home about 10:30," I snapped. "Are you going to do anything or just leave the vehicles sitting there until they explode on their own?"

It was a more tart question than I'd have asked if the deputy's attitude hadn't suggested that my gray hair and wrinkles meant my mental capacity was a few points short of a turnip.

"We're waiting for a bomb squad from the state police," Deputy Simpson, as he'd identified himself to Hanson, said.

"What were the officers looking for out in the bushes?"

"Sometimes terrorists set up secondary devices intended to take out anyone investigating the scene."

Would the Braxtons or Brad Ridenour or Shane Wagner

261

do that? I doubted it. They just wanted to make hash out of me. But I didn't know that for certain, of course.

"What happens when the bomb squad gets here?" Hanson asked.

"Depends," Deputy Simpson said. "Last year we had a pipe bomb incident, and they set it off right there in the vacant lot where it was found. They have a special device for—"

"You mean they might blow up the dynamite right where it is, while it's still attached to my car?" I gasped.

"I don't think so, especially considering that the house is fairly close. But they can't risk lives just to save an old car. So if they decide they can't disable it safely, they might have to detonate it in place."

I had the impression he'd be thrilled to see the old Thunderbird blow. I was beginning to long for Sgt. Yates and his inscrutable eyebrow.

"Ivy says she may have some ideas about who planted the dynamite," Hanson offered.

"Oh?" Officer Simpson looked me over as if suspecting I'd come up with names of ladies from my knitting society with whom I'd squabbled about the luncheon menu.

"She's the person who found the body of that woman who was murdered not long ago," Hanson added. He nodded toward Tara of the Ozarks. "The woman in the lake."

"Is that so?" Deputy Simpson regarded me with greater interest. Apparently being the Lady Who Found the Body gives one a certain credibility even if one is possum-gray and semi-invisible. Perhaps I should add this qualification to my resume.

He flipped his notebook to a fresh page. "And these persons might be . . . ?"

"Will Sgt. Yates be back soon?" I asked.

"Should be back by this afternoon or tomorrow. He had a bad tooth and went into Fayetteville to have it extracted."

I was reminded that police officers aren't always dealing with life-or-death crises; sometimes they just have bad teeth like the rest of us. Two more sheriff's department cars arrived.

"I'll wait and talk to him then."

Deputy Simpson, who a few minutes ago had acted as if my speaking capabilities rivaled that of a stump, now frowned with obvious annoyance that I *wasn't* talking. "We'd prefer to have the information now—"

"I'll wait."

Reason one was that I trusted Sgt. Yates more than I did this man who couldn't even ask me directly when I last drove the car. Second reason was a fresh jolt of awareness about what this news about Brad's relationship with Leslie was going to do to Tammi and Skye. For all Tammi's bubbly, exclamation-point personality, she really loved the guy, as did Skye. Was it fair that they get hit like a bomb exploding in their faces when the police came to question or even arrest Brad for murder and/or car bombing?

It was, of course, going to be a devastating personal bomb for them whenever it went off, but maybe it would help if Tammi had some warning ahead of time about Brad's involvement with Leslie. I wouldn't mention my suspicions that he could be involved in the murder as well, of course. Or that he may have planted dynamite under my car. That was police business. But if I could just do something to prepare Tammi for the devastating revelation about Leslie . . .

Perhaps, if I talked to her, Tammi could even persuade Brad to go to the police about the relationship. Then, if he wasn't guilty of murder, just infidelity (and I cringed when I found myself putting that *just* in front of infidelity, because infidelity is definitely not a *just*), maybe it wouldn't have to become public knowledge and the family relationships could somehow be salvaged.

"Did you see anyone around the car between when you last drove it and this morning?" Deputy Simpson asked, finally directing a question to me.

"No, but I'll discuss it all with Sgt. Yates. He's already familiar with . . . the situation." Part of it, anyway.

Deputy Hanson looked as if he'd like to set off a small explosive device under me, but I just stared back at him and held my ground.

Two more vehicles arrived. The parking area was large, but space was getting crowded. A couple of deputies moved the sheriff's department cars out of the way to make room for the new arrivals. One of these was a car, the other a pickup pulling a trailer with what appeared to be a huge ball on it. Both car and pickup bore state police logos. The big ball baffled me.

"Bomb squad," Deputy Simpson said. He went over to join the growing number of official types gathering near the new vehicles.

After a brief discussion, two men from the bomb squad returned with him to where Hanson and I were standing. They questioned both of us further, going into considerable detail with Hanson about the dynamite.

My big question was, of course, were they going to make mincemeat out of my old 'bird. Finally I asked.

"Right now, from what you and Mr. Watkins have told us, it sounds like a relatively unsophisticated explosive device. We have X-ray equipment we use in some instances, but that probably won't be necessary here since the dynamite is readily identifiable. We'll send someone in to take a look, and if we can safely disable the bomb where it is, we'll do it."

I felt marginally more hopeful. He sounded like a reasonable man. Definitely competent. But he hadn't, of course, assured me they wouldn't blow up car and all. I wondered how my insurance company would feel about a claim for a car detonated by a bomb squad. I suspect something such as this tends to raise one's premium rates considerably.

Two guys from the bomb squad suited up in padded gear that looked suitable for space exploration. I hadn't encountered this in my mystery novel reading. When ready, another officer lifted the yellow tape protecting the area, and the two men lumbered toward the cars.

"Suits must be heavy?" Hanson suggested.

"Something like 110 pounds." Deputy Simpson spoke importantly, as if pleased to be able to show off his knowledge on this subject. "The men can spend only about 20 minutes inside a suit because of the weight and because it's made of a special, nonbreathable type material that sometimes causes blood pressure to go sky high."

I wasn't even in a bomb suit, and I suspected my blood pressure was careening around up there in the stratosphere.

"Can these suits really protect them if the dynamite actually blows while they're up close to it?" I asked.

"I've never actually seen the suits in use when a bomb went off," Deputy Simpson admitted. "I'm sure they offer considerable protection, but still . . ." His voice trailed off as if he also had some doubts.

And scared as I was for me and the old Thunderbird in all this, I was suddenly much more scared for these two men. I didn't want to have to find out whether or not the suits worked under full explosive attack.

*Protect them, Lord, as you protected me!*

The two men carried out their inspection slowly and deliberately. In spite of the bulky suits, they both got down on the ground. Their bodies blocked the view of what was going on under the car. Everyone outside the yellow tape was silent and motionless, as if any sound or movement might set off the dynamite. I found I was holding my breath.

Several minutes went by. No actual clock was ticking,

but I could feel one ticking inside me. Or maybe it was my heartbeat. Tick-tock, tick-tock.

Maybe the thing was rigged so that if anyone so much as touched it, it'd go off. Maybe it was on a timing device rather than connected to the ignition, and the time was any minute now . . .

Then one man stood up. The other one still on the ground gingerly handed him something.

"That's the dynamite," Hanson breathed.

I could see the dangling tape that had held the reddish sticks of dynamite to the car. And a length of cut wire.

The two men walked back to that big, ball-shaped thing on the trailer. The man not carrying the dynamite opened a door on the ball. I was surprised. I hadn't realized it had a door. The man in the protective suit placed the dynamite inside. He closed the door.

The whoosh of released tension among watching officers was palpable. The silence of held breath turned to a babble of voices.

"The big ball is a protective container for hauling an explosive device. The walls are about this thick." Deputy Simpson held out his hands in a knowledgeable gesture, but they still had a giveaway tremor. "They'll take the dynamite off to some safe place and detonate it."

I went all saggy with relief. I'd rather have seen the old 'bird blow sky high than have anything happen to those two men, but I had to admit relief that the car was still in one piece.

"Now what?" I asked.

"I'll check," Deputy Simpson said.

I had hopes they wouldn't take the Thunderbird away, that they could look for fingerprints or other evidence right here and at the end of the day I'd still have my old 'bird. Those hopes fizzled when Deputy Simpson returned to say the car would be towed into a secure warehouse for processing.

"Will the bomb squad do that?"

"No. Our department will handle it."

"How long will it take?" I asked.

"Hard to say."

The pickup pulling the big ball departed. I wondered where they'd take the dynamite. I had to admit, now that it was safely removed from the 'bird, I wouldn't mind seeing it blow myself. But no invitation was forthcoming.

A tow truck arrived. A deputy got in Hanson's pickup and moved it out of the way. A few minutes later the tow truck, with my Thunderbird strung up like a hunk of beef on a hook, disappeared down the road, leaving me with only a paper in my hand to signify that it was in their custody now. Deputy Simpson returned to suggest that, since the person who planted the bomb was still unidentified, I should leave the house and stay away for a few days.

"I wish we could offer you guards and protection, but we just don't have the manpower." He sounded apologetic. "Perhaps you could stay with friends for a few days?"

I nodded. I felt as unsteady as if I were trying to walk that narrow beam Sandy does gymnastics stunts on, shakier than during most of the action. Because now I was thinking of the danger not only to myself and the car but to Sandy too. So many times we'd ridden in it together, and whoever planted that bomb hadn't cared if I wasn't the only one who blew up.

People, already pushed back to the property line by the deputies, dispersed. Police cars, fire truck, and ambulance departed. Except for Hanson's pickup, the yard was empty. At some point rain had started falling again, but I hadn't noticed it until now.

I shivered, partly from the cold rain, partly from leftover

nerves. It was really true. Someone had tried to blow me sky high.

Hanson held out a palm, catching the rain, and I remembered the leaking roof he'd been fixing.

"You'd better get back to your roof. Thanks for coming over."

"I can stay for a while. In fact, if you don't have someplace to go, I could come over and sleep on your sofa tonight. You and Sandy definitely shouldn't be alone. I could bring my dad's old rifle—"

"Thanks, but as soon as Sandy gets home we'll go to a motel or something. We'll be fine," I assured him.

"Well, I'll go on home and see if my patch job on the roof is holding up, then. But you call if you need anything, okay?"

I thanked him again. I wondered if the Big Brad would be giving the news about my car bomb on his early TV show. And what his expression, always so suited to the occasion, would be if he did so.

"I guess we can be grateful for the bad battery," Hanson added. "If not for that, you, me, and the old 'bird would all be scattered around here in shrapnel-sized pieces."

Bad battery . . . or a good Lord? I knew the answer to that.

"You might consider telling the Lord thanks for that bad battery," I suggested.

Hanson gave me a startled look, as if he hadn't considered that angle, then nodded. "I'll do that."

Now, I realized as I started toward the house, I had to decide. Should I talk to Tammi before I told Sgt. Yates what I knew about Brad and Leslie? I looked at my watch. I felt oddly drained. It seemed a week since I'd walked out to the car, intending to spend the day on a leisurely drive, but it was only late afternoon. Sandy wouldn't be home for quite a while yet. She had a team meeting and practice at the gymnastics studio after school.

I'd missed lunch, although the hollow feeling inside me wasn't hunger. The thought occurred to me that I didn't have to decide right now about talking to Tammi, because I was at the moment quite without transportation. I didn't feel it was something I could discuss over the phone, and I had no way to get over to her place.

Although there might be a solution to that problem . . . And I had to call DeeAnn and Mike anyway. They had a right to know what was going on.

DeeAnn answered on the third ring. It still astonishes me that I can dial *Hawaii*. I can remember back to when it took a couple of long-distance operators just to call a few states away.

I gave DeeAnn as non-sensational a version as possible of the day's doings, although having someone plant dynamite under your car tends to come off as somewhat sensational no matter how you put it.

DeeAnn didn't fall apart or go into hysterics while I was telling her. She is not the hysterical type. But the waves of fear rolling through the phone felt bigger than anything hitting the Hawaiian beaches.

"Sandy was never in any danger," I emphasized. Though it was a weak comfort, given the circumstances, and we both knew it. Because nothing about future danger was guaranteed. "I—I think the Lord was looking out for both of us."

"I'm sure he was, but . . ."

But we both knew about those unexplainable times when tragedy happened.

"DeeAnn, I'm just so sorry about this. If I'd really thought my coming here would put Sandy or any of you in danger, I'd never have done it. But I thought . . . Well, apparently I was wrong." The thought of anything happening to Sandy

269

sent tidal waves of fear rolling through me. "Look, how about I send Sandy over to Hawaii just as soon as I can get her on a plane?"

"Oh, my goodness. In all this, I forgot that I have something to tell you too. In fact, I was going to call you later today. We're coming back to Woodston!"

"To visit, you mean? Or to pick up Sandy?"

"No. Home to stay!"

DeeAnn went on to explain that the company's deal on a site for a manufacturing plant there on Oahu had fallen through, and the company had decided to give up the venture. "So now it's pack up and move everything home again. We weren't planning to make a rush deal out of it . . ." She paused, then added emphatically, "But that's changed now. Now it's going to be a real rush deal. A week or ten days at the most."

"Are you disappointed you won't be living over there?"

"Oh, in a way. It's lovely here. But Woodston is home. Now Sandy will be able to graduate from there, and it'll be safer for you with all of us living together."

I'd have to think about that, considering the events of today. But later.

"Sandy and I will go to a motel as soon as she gets home, okay? And we'll stay there until you and Mike get here."

"Have Sandy call me as soon as you get to a motel, will you?"

"Will do."

"The Braxtons did this?" DeeAnn's voice had a surface steadiness now, but I could feel the fear lurking underneath. I could also feel her already leaping into packing and moving mode.

"It was probably the Braxtons. But not necessarily." Honesty made me add, "I may have . . . irritated a few locals."

DeeAnn waited, but I didn't elaborate, and finally she

sighed. "Ivy Malone, for a sweet, harmless little aunt, you do seem to get yourself in an unusual amount of trouble."

I decided I couldn't deny it, so I skipped to another subject. "One more thing. Until I get the 'bird back I need something for transportation—"

"Use whichever one you need," she said promptly, referring to the SUV and the Buick in the garage. "The keys to both are on that hook by the kitchen door."

"Thanks, DeeAnn. I'll be really careful with them."

"Just . . . umm . . . don't irritate any more car bomb people, okay?"

"I'll do my best."

So now I had transportation and was back to the problem of Tammi.

It would surely be a horrific blow for her to learn about her husband's infidelity from the police. Yet more than infidelity was involved here. There was murder and attempted murder . . . my attempted murder. There was also the possibility that, if I told Tammi about the affair, she'd immediately rip into Brad with more than exclamation points. He might then realize he was in jeopardy on bigger charges, take off for South America or other parts unknown, and escape justice.

As it turned out, however, I didn't have to decide whether to contact Tammi. She called me.

# 31

Actually, at first I didn't know who was calling, just that it was a woman sobbing and gasping and choking as she struggled to say something.

"I think you have the wrong number, but maybe I can do something to help?" I asked anxiously. The woman sounded on the verge of hysteria. Or collapse. If I could find out who she was trying to call . . .

"Oh, Aunt Ivy." Choked sob. "It's me, Tammi."

"Tammi! Hon, what's wrong? Are you sick? Has something happened to Skye?"

"No." Sound of blowing nose. "Oh, Aunt Ivy, I just had to talk to someone . . . and I didn't know who . . . and then I thought of you!" Another burst of tears.

"Is it Brad? Has he been hurt or something?" May the Lord forgive me, but right then I was hoping something had happened to the rat.

"Oh, yes, it's Brad!" Sudden flash of fury breaking through the tears. Then more sobs. "I—I don't know what to do! I just found out something awful . . . I can't believe it . . . I don't want to believe it . . . and yet I'm afraid it's true."

So. The buffalo chips had hit the fan. Tammi knew about Brad and Leslie. How had she found out? And had the knowledge of his infidelity expanded into a suspicion of his involvement in Leslie's murder? No, I didn't think so. Right now, Tammi was simply trying to deal with this first shock of Brad's unfaithfulness. The worst might be yet to come.

"I'll come over and we'll talk and see what can be done," I said quickly. "Until I get there, you just . . . oh . . . fix a cup of tea and snuggle up with Baby. Okay?"

I wanted to add something soothing like, "Don't worry, everything will be okay," but the knowledge that everything probably wasn't going to be okay stopped the false words. "I'll be there as soon as I can," I said instead.

I started to put the phone down, but a second thought suddenly grabbed me. What about Brad? He surely wasn't home now, or Tammi wouldn't be calling me. But was he apt to walk in? The man may have tried to kill me this morning, and I'm not as brave as Daniel boldly joining the lions in their den. I didn't want to find myself with Brad in *his* den.

"Is . . . uh . . . Brad going to be coming home anytime soon?"

"He's at the station." Tammi's voice sounded stronger now, as if her tears and shock were beginning to harden into fury. "He won't be home until after the late news. And when he does come home I may meet him at the door with a . . . a butcher knife in my hand!"

"We'll talk," I said quickly. I figured Tammi was mostly bluster, but you never can tell. A woman scorned and all that. Maybe she would grab a butcher knife. "Don't do anything rash, okay?"

"Oh, Aunt Ivy, how could he have done this?"

"We'll talk," I repeated. Another second thought on my

part. "What about Skye? She'll be getting home soon, won't she?"

"She won't be home until late. There's a practice for graduation ceremonies. She's going to be one of the girls holding the arches. It's a very special honor. We're so proud of her."

"Oh, that's nice." An inane comment, I realized even as I said it, considering the bomb that was about to go off in Skye's life. But we could tackle Skye later, after Tammi had herself more under control. At least Skye wouldn't come strolling in while Tammi was having hysterics.

"It'll take me a few minutes to get there. My car is . . . out of commission, and I have to get DeeAnn's car out of the garage."

DeeAnn's Buick started right up, and I pulled into the Ridenours' driveway a few minutes later. The drapes were drawn, as if Tammi was trying to keep the world shut out. Or maybe trying to keep the ugly knowledge within from escaping into the world. There was no car in the driveway.

I rang the bell. Muffled words that I took to be "Come in" came from inside, and I opened the door. Tammi and Baby were huddled on the sofa. Crumpled tissues littered the floor, and Tammi was just pulling another handful from the box. Puffy folds framed her bloodshot eyes, and mascara streaked her blotched face. Her usually fluffy hair was flattened in places, corkscrewed in others. If a dog can look troubled, Baby surely did. His mistress's distress obviously distressed him. His soulful brown eyes never left her face.

There was an oniony odor in the air, as if she'd been cooking. Diet and exercise books covered the coffee table, that huge one open to a recipe page.

I rushed to her and put my arms around her. At least as best I could with half of a 260-pound dog draped over her lap. She dabbed her eyes with a tissue. I was 99.9 percent sure what was wrong here, but I wasn't going to jump in just in case I was mistaken and this was some other disaster. It could be that Brad had plunged them into financial disaster by buying a Lamborghini. Or decided to leave TV and politics to take up designing flashy ties.

"You think you know someone," she said, the hurt in her voice coming through in spite of the tissue pressed against her mouth. "You trust him with your life and your heart and then . . ."

"Maybe you should tell me exactly what this is all about."

She looked up at me reproachfully. "Oh, Aunt Ivy, you know what it's about."

Okay, it was definitely Brad and Leslie. "How did you find out?" I asked cautiously.

"I was looking in Brad's desk for something, and I found all these notes and pictures he had stashed away . . ." A fresh flood of tears.

"Of?"

"Leslie Marcone. Some of . . . of him and her together. I found records of where they'd stayed together in motels. They—they were having an affair! But you knew, didn't you?" Now her swollen eyes held accusation, as if she thought I'd withheld information that I should have given her. "You found out when you were working for her."

She phrased it as a statement not a question, and I didn't feel obliged to contradict her assumption of how I'd acquired the knowledge. I didn't want Sandy involved in this. "Does Brad know that you know?"

"Not yet." The threat in her voice said he soon would, however.

So where did we go from here? "The . . . relationship is obviously over now. Perhaps . . . ?" I left the *perhaps* open-ended, on a cautiously upward swing.

"You think I should just try to let it go? Never let him know I found out? I do love him so much, you know. And he has been so sweet and caring lately. I—I might be able to do it." She sounded hopeful as she lifted her swollen face to me again. The bloodshot eyes were suddenly beseeching. "You wouldn't tell anyone, would you?"

I wanted to assure her, say, "No, I'll never tell. The secret is safe with me." But I couldn't do that. Gently I tried to explain. "Tammi, there's a murder investigation going on, and it was your husband's—" I broke off, squeamish about using some ugly word. "Your husband's friend who was murdered. I'm going to have to tell Sgt. Yates what I know about their relationship."

"But why? This is none of his business! It has nothing to do with Leslie's murder!"

"The authorities need to know everything they can about all aspects of Leslie's life." Neither did I honestly think Tammi and Brad could have a happy married life with this kept hidden between them, like something turning blue and moldy in the refrigerator.

"But if you tell Sgt. Yates, he might think Brad had something to do with Leslie's murder! There'll be terrible accusations and an investigation. Every newspaper and TV and radio station in the state will jump on it!" She sat up straighter, clutching Baby to her as if he were a big pillow. "It would mean the end of Brad's political chances! It might even mean the end of his news career. And Skye. Think what it might do to Skye!"

Exactly what I was afraid of. Yet the suspicion I couldn't escape, the suspicion that Brad might be more than unfairly accused of Leslie's murder, that he might actually have done it, apparently hadn't stabbed her yet.

"I'm sure, if you stand by him, as other wives have done in situations such as this—"

"So you are going to tell Sgt. Yates about their affair." She sounded scornful, as if this were an ugly character flaw newly exposed. "Maybe you even think Brad killed her, and you'll tell Sgt. Yates that too." More scorn. She gave Baby another hug, then pushed him off her lap and stood up.

"I know that someone tried to kill me today. I found dynamite planted under my car. It was rigged to go off when the car started."

Her dark eyebrows lifted in startled astonishment. "This is why you had to use DeeAnn's car? Because someone put dynamite in your car?"

"Yes. The bomb squad removed it, but then the sheriff's department took the 'bird away for examination. I don't know when I'll get it back."

"But who would do something like that? It doesn't make sense. People who set car bombs are in the Mafia or something!" She sounded quite aghast. Then the expressive eyebrows widened. "Surely you don't think Brad—"

"At this point I don't know what to think. I'm almost certain, from something Brad said when he came home last night, that he knows I'm aware of his relationship with Leslie. He may have decided he had to get rid of me before I could tell anyone. For the same reasons you would prefer I not tell anyone."

"Don't be ridiculous," she snapped. "Brad is afraid of firecrackers. He had his hand burned on one when he was a kid. He hates to even light the barbecue. He wouldn't go near a stick of dynamite."

Did I believe that? Tammi could be lying to protect Brad. But the unnecessary details and another hint of scorn in her voice told me she wasn't. I had the feeling this part of Brad's character, with its hint of wimpiness, was a sore point with her, and she'd rather Brad were a man who could toss dynamite around like carrot sticks.

So it was the Braxtons after all. They'd found me. Not a surprise, but still a shock that they really were out to track me down and kill me.

Without waiting for a comment from me about Brad and dynamite, Tammi detoured past me on the sofa and disappeared down the hallway into the bathroom. Her step was surprisingly brisk and firm. Baby followed her. Tammi was, I suspected, a stronger and more resilient person than her adorable butterball appearance suggested. Maybe she could determinedly put Brad's infidelity aside and go on with their life.

I heard water running in the bathroom sink. A few minutes later she returned, her hair fluffed, the blotches on her face receding, a hint of blush and lipstick brightening cheeks and mouth. But she had a hand behind her as if her back hurt. Which well it might, under the circumstances.

Yet it suddenly occurred to me that the oniony smell in the house wasn't necessarily because she'd been busy cooking. Could she have used onions for another purpose? Like to make her eyes appear all teary and puffy and her nose runny? She seemed to have recovered from that teariness rather quickly. But why . . .

"I really can't let you go to Sgt. Yates with this," she said. "With the right guidance, Brad can make it beyond the legislature, all the way to the governor's mansion, and I intend to see that he gets there. With me by his side. I'm putting big money into his political career, and I can't let you destroy it."

"I'm sorry, Tammi, I really am, but—"

I broke off when she pulled her hand out from behind her. She was holding a gun. Pointed at me.

My jaw dropped, but I finally managed to say, "Tammi, don't do something on impulse that you'll regret. I know how much you love Brad, but . . ." I tried to swallow, but my throat was suddenly too dry. The hole at the end of a gun barrel, even a small one, looks like a tunnel of doom. It's even kind of hypnotizing.

278

"I don't do things on impulse. I'm quite organized and methodical, actually."

It took a moment for that to sink in. "You asked me to come over here with this in mind?" I gestured toward the gun. A jerky gesture, since my brain didn't seem to be in close contact with my muscles.

"More or less. Depending on circumstances."

"What circumstances?"

"I was fairly certain you knew about Brad and Leslie, but I thought I might convince you not to go to Sgt. Yates with the information. But since you insist on telling him, I'll have to go ahead with my plan." She tilted her head thoughtfully. "Although I'd probably have gone ahead with it anyway, just to be on the safe side."

"What plan?"

She gave me a you've-gotta-be-kidding look.

"You'll . . ." I gulped, again tried to swallow and couldn't. "You'll kill me to protect Brad?"

She smiled, that dimpled smile that added to her butterball adorableness. "That's almost noble, isn't it? Maybe someday I'll even tell Brad all that I was willing to do for him. He was such a ridiculous emotional wreck after you found Leslie in the lake. I think he even went out there once before anyone knew she was dead."

Brad crashing around in the woods that day I was also at the house, probably as afraid of encountering me as I was of encountering him!

"You didn't just find out today about Brad and Leslie, did you? How long have you known?"

"For some time, actually. I followed him to a motel where he met her in Fayetteville one time." Her smile was faintly superior. "I may be overweight, Aunt Ivy, but I'm not stupid. Oh, and I also know that Skye calls me the Dumpling."

"If you're planning to kill me, I'd rather you didn't call me Aunt Ivy," I muttered.

She lifted a shoulder in an indifferent shrug. "Whatever you say."

"You hate her, don't you? Skye, I mean."

She tilted her head. "Actually, no. Oh, at first I was quite resentful about the situation. That witchy ex-wife of Brad's pawning Skye off on us just so she could take her fancy job in New York! And it was upsetting when Sgt. Yates instantly brought her back when she tried to run away."

"Sgt. Yates, the sweetie," I murmured. How I wished he and his scarred eyebrow would come striding through the door at this moment.

"Then, when I bought the car for her, I thought surely she'd use it to take off and go to her mother."

"How disappointing that she didn't."

"It was at the time, but I feel differently now. Skye and I are getting along much better. Things are going to work out really well for all of us." She'd been talking with a distracted air, as if her thoughts were elsewhere. On this plan, no doubt. Now she focused on me again. She flexed her finger around the trigger of the gun. "Except for you, I'm afraid."

"Tammi, he isn't worth it! Don't mess up your life protecting a man like this. Think about it. Brad was unfaithful, apparently for quite some time. He may have turned into a murderer when the affair became too big a liability—"

"Oh, please!" Small roll of baby-blue eyes. "Brad can't even take a dead mouse out of a trap. He'd never have had the stomach or the nerve to kill Leslie."

"So you think Leslie's ex-husband or someone else conveniently got her out of the way for you?"

"Who cares? She's dead. That's all that matters. Except that I can't let you drag Brad into it."

I thought how irrelevant the Braxtons' determination to

kill me was at this moment, since Tammi apparently had the same goal. And she was now first in line.

"Into the kitchen, please." She jerked the gun a fraction of an inch in that direction.

I didn't move, not because I was brave but because my legs felt like frozen salami. It also occurred to me that if she wanted me in the kitchen, I definitely didn't want to be there.

I eyed her warily as she stood there impatiently waiting for me to move, obviously confident the gun would bring compliance. I calculated my odds of making a run for the front door. Surely she was no expert with that gun. Although, in the confines of this living room, she wouldn't have to be much of an expert to bring me down . . .

"Why?" I said warily.

"Why, what?"

"Why do you want me in the kitchen?"

"The garage is right through that door over there." Another fractional wave of the gun. "We're going for a ride."

"That's an overused line," I muttered. How many times had I read it in a mystery novel or seen it in an old movie? "Very cliché."

"What?"

"Never mind."

"Then get in there."

"No." I hadn't planned the word, and it came out like a strangled gargle, but apparently the meaning was plain enough. To both of us. I repeated it in a stronger voice. "No."

Tammi stood there frowning, her expression annoyed. I could see that, in her reasoning, I had no right to react so stubbornly. A gun in hand demanded compliance.

"You'll just have to shoot me right here," I stated with considerably more bravado than I felt. The coffee table was right behind me. My knees trembled, and I felt a huge urge just to plop down on it. I braced one leg against the corner of the table and forced myself to stay upright and sound coolly distant when I added, "And shooting me here will certainly leave a terrible mess. Even if you dispose of my body, how will you explain blood all over your carpet?"

She frowned again. This obviously was not in her script.

It was not, however, an insurmountable problem. The house had one of those open floor plans in which one room flows into another. Keeping the gun on me, she backed past the dining area and into the kitchen. There she reached into a cabinet and brought out a length of clothesline rope. She marched back to me, holding it in her hand like a lariat. It looked as if she had enough rope there to string me up from the nearest flagpole. I wondered if she'd acquired the rope purposely for me or if it had originally had some other purpose. Not that this mattered at the moment.

"I—I don't know what you think you're going to do, but your plan isn't going to work," I blustered. Baby was still following her like a faithful shadow.

"I'm going to tie you up, and then we're going for that ride."

She had another problem, however. With the gun in one hand, the rope in the other, how was she going to tie me up? Even Superwoman would surely need two hands for such a project. Tammi solved that with unexpected viciousness.

She lifted the gun and crashed it against the side of my head.

Or she would have hit the side of my head except that faithful Baby, trying to get as close to Tammi as possible, pushed up against her legs at that moment. The gun hit my neck—painful, but not the knockout blow she'd intended.

I stumbled backward, reeling but not unconscious. I hit the coffee table, and it tumbled over, spilling its load of diet and exercise books. I grabbed one as it fell and slammed it

282

into Tammi's gun hand. The gun flew across the room. We both lunged for it.

Neither of us got it. Baby, thinking this was some fun new game, lunged with us. He landed right in the middle of us, and there we were—260 pounds of dog, two desperate women, a tangled length of clothesline rope, an overturned coffee table, and scattered books all churning around on the carpet.

A lamp crashed into the melee. The rope tangled around my legs. I tried to kick it free and at the same time stab a finger in Tammi's eye. *Oh, what I wouldn't give for a good Dilly bar stick right now!* A tail swished in my face, and a spike heel—*Tammi, planning to murder me, is wearing fashionable spike heels!*—jabbed me in the calf.

I thought maybe Tammi would yell "Attack!" at Baby, and that would be the end of me, but what she yelled was, "Baby, go away!"

Baby, bless his heart, was obviously not an attack dog. He licked Tammi's face, then mine. He obviously thought this was a great game. He wallowed around with us as if we were three pigs in a mud hole. I got a mouthful of dog hair.

But my flailing arms hit something metal. The gun! I closed my hand around it. I had the gun!

No, I didn't. Tammi slammed her fist down on my wrist, and the gun flew again. Then she was on top me, her legs straddling my midsection, and I was very much aware that she was several decades younger and a whole lot heavier than I was. She picked me up by the shoulders and slammed my head against the floor.

Thank heavens for expensive carpet. The floor was too well padded for the blow to knock me out. But I was dizzy and rattled enough that stars rolled around in my head, and Tammi used the moment to grab the rope and stretch it across my throat, a hand on either side of my neck. I made a choked sound that came out *gurk*.

"C'mere, Baby," she said. "Come do your caterpillar crawl just like you did for the other lady."

*Caterpillar crawl . . . like you did for the other lady.* I was certain those were significant words, but it was difficult to organize my thoughts with a rope cutting off my oxygen.

But I was aware that Baby obediently came and did his caterpillar crawl, right across my face, all the while making little happy-dog sounds.

"There, stop right there," Tammi said, her voice muffled by the barrier of dog. "Good dog. This will work. Though it would've been better if I'd given her something first, like I did the other lady, wouldn't it?"

The big dog body wiggled happily. Baby was delighted his mistress was playing, no longer distressed. At that moment the truth finally slugged me. I'd been a little slow here. But now I knew.

"Brad didn't kill Leslie. You did!"

But I was gasping my revelation into 260 pounds of dog and a faint scent of Eternity perfume.

# 32

Baby stood up, and I gasped for breath. But I got only a minimal gulp of air before Tammi said, "Down, Baby. Lie down again. I'm going to tie her up now."

Baby plopped down on my face again. *This is how Leslie died*, I realized. *This is how she suffocated!* Except Tammi had given Leslie something first, so Leslie wouldn't be aware of what was going on and wouldn't struggle.

But I hadn't ingested anything, and I *could* struggle!

I twisted and squirmed as Tammi did something with one of my hands. The rope tightened around my wrist. I twisted harder and flung myself sideways.

I caught Tammi by surprise, and she tumbled to one side. Baby was still on top of my face. I swatted him in the head. He, who had probably never felt a mean blow in his life, yelped and jumped up, sticking a foot in my open mouth as he did so. I sat up sputtering and coughing.

Only to have Tammi come down on me again. She landed on me like one of those football players throwing himself

on a pile of other players on a Monday night game. I felt
the air go out of me with an *oof*. She straddled my midsection again, spread-eagling my arms until her palms covered
mine and we were face to face, both breathing hard from
the exertion. Plopped across my midsection, she felt a whole
lot heavier than she looked. I don't like to be judgmental
about such things, but the woman really could stand to
lose a few pounds. Although this hardly seemed a prudent
time to point that out. Besides, this new revelation was far
more important.

"You really did kill her," I gasped. Somewhere in the back
of my mind came the dim memory of Sgt. Yates asking me
if Leslie had pets. "You drugged her and then—then used
Baby to suffocate her!"

And dog hairs had showed up in Leslie's lungs in the autopsy, one of the details they hadn't shared with the media.

"The sleeping pills should have been enough to kill her! I
ground them up and fed them to her in high-energy bars I
made. They put her to sleep . . . but she was just lying here
. . . snoring. And I could tell that sooner or later she was going
to wake up." Tammi squirmed, looking over her shoulder
for the rope. She'd lost one high heel in the scuffle, but the
other one dug into my thigh like a spur.

The rope was several feet away. I remembered seeing
people on TV do these amazing flops, arching the back and
flinging an attacker halfway across the room.

I tightened my muscles, arched my back, and flung. I obviously had something to learn about technique, because all
this did was make an insignificant little wave under Tammi.
She didn't, in fact, even seem to notice my heroic convulsion.
I lifted a knee and tried to jab her in the back, but I couldn't
get the knee up high enough. She couldn't take her palms
away from mine, but she whacked me with that high-heeled
spur for punishment.

"The rope, Baby!" she suddenly said urgently. "Over there! Bring the rope!"

Baby tilted his head, tail waving gently, expression curious. He surely wanted to be helpful, but, blessedly, rope was not in his vocabulary. *Was gun?* I wondered fearfully. At this point I had no idea what had become of the gun.

"We seem to be at something of an impasse," I suggested. She'd have to let go of at least one of my hands and lift her weight off me in order to stretch over and reach the rope. During which time I had no intention of meekly lying here.

She yanked my arms closer to my body so she could lift her head higher and so our faces weren't quite so close together. "Not really," she muttered. "I'm younger and stronger. You'll give out first. In fact, you might have a heart attack or stroke any minute now!"

She could be right. My neck hurt where she'd clobbered it with the gun. My vision seemed a little blurry. My heart felt like butterfly wings fluttering in my chest. I was, no doubt about it, in a very bad situation here.

*But safety isn't the absence of danger,* I reminded myself. *Safety is the presence of the Lord.* Maybe some people can remember helpful Bible verses at times such as this. Not me. Only scraps came. *Fear not . . . I am with you . . . never will I leave you.* And God was here, right with me, just as he always was.

The reminder came with a soothing sense of calm, even a certain detachment from the jab of high heel in my leg, the weight squashing my middle, and the almost overpowering scent of Eternity. But, since we were apparently going to be in this awkward position for a while, I figured we may as well talk.

"So, how'd you get Leslie to come over here?" I asked.

Tammi frowned. Her freshly applied lipstick had widened to a clownish smear. "Brad was out of town. I called her up and told her I knew about her and Brad, but I didn't see any need for it to be an unpleasant situation and I wouldn't stand in the way of a divorce. I suggested she and I get together to discuss the situation in a civilized manner. She fell for it, and I had tea and my homemade high-energy bars ready when she got here."

"The ones you'd prepared with your secret sleeping-pill ingredient."

She twisted so she could stretch a foot toward the rope. She still couldn't reach it. I made a lunge—at least as much of a lunge as I could make with Tammi sitting in my middle—at her arm, thinking a hard bite might change the situation. All I got was a mouthful of sleeve.

Still an impasse. We regarded each other warily. The phone rang. Tammi's head shot up. I had the impression that she, unlike Leslie, couldn't ignore a ringing phone any more than I could.

"Maybe you should answer it," I suggested. "Could be important. Maybe it's someone saying they're coming over, and how will it look, you trying to kill a helpless little old lady when they get here?"

Her gaze narrowed, as if the prospect of someone showing up unexpectedly did concern her. Then her expression cleared. "Oh, but if I don't answer, they'll know I'm not home, won't they? And not come over. No problem."

After eight rings—we both counted—the phone stopped ringing.

"So, after Leslie was snoring peacefully, you had Baby lay across her face until she suffocated without a struggle."

"It wasn't quite without a struggle. I had to help hold her down when she started jerking around. But she didn't wake up."

"Then what?"

Tammi frowned, but she couldn't resist telling me. "Everybody thinks I'm so soft and fat and helpless. But I drove her

288

car into the garage, dragged her out there—all by myself—and drove out to her place. That ridiculous house, pretending to be a Southern plantation! Then I dragged her out on the dock, me, the Dumpling!" She sounded proud and pleased with herself. "And threw her in the water. Then I walked, *walked*, all the way home in the dark. I checked it later. It's over seven miles out there!

"The only thing that went wrong was that I had to lock Baby all alone in the garage while I was gone, and he was very traumatized."

I had the impression that Baby's traumatization upset Tammi more than Leslie's murder. I craned my neck and looked over at him. He tilted his head and looked back at me, tail swishing gently.

*Death by dog*, I thought. Baby, who really was a gentle giant, would be horrified if he knew and understood such things. Would Tammi have to leave him alone again when she disposed of me?

I swallowed. Baby's traumatization was the least of my worries at the moment. "So what do you plan to do with me?"

"Lost Lake. There's an old road going around to the side opposite the inn. I drove out there to look it over, and it's wooded and quite isolated. Except this time I'll make sure the body doesn't hang up on something, like Leslie's did. Maybe I'll use some of those concrete blocks out in the back yard to weigh it down. I'd rather it didn't turn up for weeks. Maybe even months."

*It.* It was me. The body. Were concrete blocks traceable? Would the authorities someday figure out they had come from Tammi's backyard? Maybe. Fine lot of good this did me at the moment, however.

"Sandy will be really hurt if something happens to me."

"I'll help comfort her. I think she likes me."

Tammi's palms were sweating against mine. I felt as if my muscles and bones were beginning to stiffen up, as they often did when I was too long in one position. Tammi's position straddling my midsection was awkward, and I could hope her legs might begin to cramp. But I doubted this was something I could count on.

Any possibility of help arriving? Not from Brad or Skye. I already knew they wouldn't be coming home soon.

So Tammi was right. Sooner or later, stronger, heavier Tammi was going to do me in. The thought occurred to me that if she moved her weight up to my chest I might not even be able to breathe.

I hastily discarded that thought, afraid it might somehow ooze from my mind into Tammi's. Something like the osmosis I remembered studying about in school so many years ago.

"C'mon, Baby, come play!" I urged suddenly. I tried to twist and turn, urging him to jump in as he had before. With 260 pounds of dog in the middle of us, anything could happen.

He crouched down on his forelegs and looked playful and eager, but Tammi laughed. "Baby doesn't take orders from anyone but me. It makes Brad furious. But he's my sweetie, aren't you, big boy?"

Baby ambled over, tail waving, and Tammi, always affectionate with him, lifted an arm to reward him with a hug.

And I, I now had one hand free! *Thank you, Lord!* I frantically swept my hand across the carpet and grabbed the first thing I could reach. And then, using every ounce of strength remaining in bones, muscles, ligaments, and cells, I slammed it against the side of Tammi's head.

## 33

Tammi's eyes rolled and bounced like marbles in a hot frying pan, and she collapsed on me like a falling sack of potatoes. I squirmed out from under her dead weight. For a moment I feared it truly was a dead weight, but thankfully, when I felt for a pulse in her throat, I found one. I grabbed the clothesline rope, half afraid she'd suddenly come to and snatch it before I did.

With not a lot of expertise but with a whole lot of layers of rope, I trussed her up like a mummy in progress. Wrists bound behind her back, rope looped down to encircle her ankles, ankles pulled up behind her derrière, rope circled around to bind both her arms to her body for good measure. I tossed in some knots I'd formerly used only for tying fishing flies for Harley.

By that time I was breathing so hard that I had to rest a minute before digging in my purse to find Sgt. Yates's home phone number. His attitude was noticeably grumpy when I first identified myself, as if he figured he didn't deserve a toothache and Ivy Malone all in one day. I hurriedly gave him a condensed version of what I knew about Brad Ridenour and Leslie Marcone's relationship, how Tammi had used a combination of sleeping pills and big dog to get rid of her rival, and how she'd planned to do me in as well.

Long moment of silence.

"You do believe me, don't you?" I asked anxiously. "I know it sounds far-fetched, but—"

"Where are you now?"

"At the Ridenour house."

"Since you're calling me, I assume you're okay? Not in any physical danger at the moment?"

I rotated my stiff neck and shoulders, fingered a spot on my neck that felt like a bump in the shape of Denmark, wiggled my toes, and scraped dog hair away from the corner of my mouth. "I'm fine."

"And Mrs. Ridenour? Where's she?"

"Well, uh, she's lying on the floor. She seems to be, umm, unconscious."

"A fall, perhaps?" I detected a note of sarcasm.

"Well, uh, actually, I hit her with . . ." I kicked the book around so I could read the title. It was that enormous book in which Tammi had been underlining sentences. "A copy of *The Comprehensive Guide to Total Fitness, Diet, and Exercise*." I momentarily wondered if there was a certain irony in this. Knocked out by her own self-improvement book.

"She was trying to kill me at the time," I added defensively.

"I suppose you have a signed confession about what she did to Leslie Marcone? Or maybe you have everything she said on tape?"

"Sgt. Yates, you are being sarcastic. Or facetious," I chided. "Just because I read a few mystery books—"

"Okay, I suppose I am," he muttered.

"I think the synthetic fibers you found under Leslie's fin-

gernails will match the carpet here at the Ridenour house,"
I added. "Your lab reports have probably already noted the
presence of sleeping-pill chemicals in her system. And the
dog hairs found in her lungs during the autopsy will match
Baby's."

"I'll be right over." He sounded resigned.

"I hope your tooth extraction isn't bothering you."

Grunt.

After Sgt. Yates hung up, I located the gun, which was
lying on the floor near the TV. I left it there. I rubbed my
throat where Tammi had tried to choke me and stayed well
away from her. I doubted, when she came to, that with the
way I had her trussed up she could do more than wiggle
her fingers and toes, but I wasn't taking any chances. I felt a
twinge of guilt as Baby nosed her unconscious body and then
snuggled up beside her, nose resting on her shoulder, expressive eyes faintly reproachful. Then a certain fact bombed me.
I'd clobbered Tammi while she was hugging her dog. Which
did seem a bit unsportsmanlike.

It was a small and fleeting twinge of guilt, however. Mostly,
while I waited for Sgt. Yates, I contemplated the strange fact
that Baby had unknowingly helped cause Leslie's death and
then, just as unknowingly, helped save my life.

I was still somewhat dazed, partly from the struggle with
Tammi, partly from the shock of knowing the truth. Brad
hadn't murdered his girlfriend. Shane Wagner hadn't murdered his ex-wife. None of the others of whom I'd been
so suspicious had played any part in Leslie's death. Tammi,
Tammi the adorable butterball, Tammi the Dumpling, Tammi
the chooser of gifts with charming care, had done it. And was
efficiently planning to kill me to hide that fact.

Tammi was just beginning to regain consciousness when
cars pulled up in front of the Ridenour house. They had ar-

rived without benefit of sirens, but I could hear one in the distance. Her fingers twitched and her eyelids fluttered.

I went to the door. Sgt. Yates, accompanied by another officer, came in and looked down at Tammi's rope-bound figure.

"Your handiwork, I take it?" Sgt. Yates inquired.

I had to agree that it was. He did not compliment my technique. "It's her rope," I said. "And that's her gun over there."

Sgt. Yates knelt, looked at my tangle of loops and knots, and said to his partner, "We'll need a knife."

"How about an ambulance?" the second officer asked. He was already bagging the gun as evidence.

"Better call for one. That looks like a rather nasty lump forming on her temple." He leaned closer to inspect the darkening bump. "You pack a mean wallop, Mrs. Malone."

I couldn't tell if that was compliment or criticism, and I prudently didn't ask. With the ropes cut free and replaced by handcuffs, they moved Tammi to the sofa. She was still a little groggy but conscious enough to turn on the charm.

"Sgt. Yates, thank goodness you're here! This woman is demented. She came in here and attacked me!"

"I did not," I said indignantly. "She called me up and asked me to come over here so she could kill me!" I had some exclamation points of my own, and I was willing to use them. "See what she did to me?" I lifted my chin to show the line the rope had left on my neck and my developing bruise.

"She's crazy! You can't believe anything she says. Leslie Marcone fired her! Maybe she didn't just find Leslie's body, maybe she killed Leslie!"

Sgt. Yates's scarred eyebrow lifted meaningfully. "Were we discussing Leslie Marcone?" he asked mildly.

Tammi scowled at him, apparently realizing she may have made a blunder here. But she wasn't about to back down. "Do you know who my husband is?"

"Yes, Mrs. Ridenour, I do," Sgt. Yates said.

"You can be certain he'll let everyone know about this atrocious action toward an innocent citizen," she stormed. Her charm was fizzling rapidly. She struggled with the handcuffs. "This is outrageous! A travesty of justice! And you can expect a lawsuit too!"

Sgt. Yates didn't argue with her. "Tammi Ridenour," he said as Baby pressed close to her, "you are under arrest for the murder of Leslie Marcone. You have the right to remain silent and refuse to answer questions. Do you understand?"

Tammi glared at him through smeared eyeliner. "I'm warning you!"

Sgt. Yates extracted a plastic card from his wallet and started reading aloud the required statement of Miranda rights, although I suspected he'd repeated them often enough to know them by heart.

The second officer glanced at me doubtfully as Sgt. Yates read, although whether the doubt was about my sanity, my possible guilt in Leslie's murder, or my knot-tying ability, I couldn't tell. I gave him my most innocent LOL smile. He did a little double take, apparently just now recognizing me. "Hey, you're the woman with the dynamite under her Thunderbird. I was over there this morning—"

Sgt. Yates stopped in the midst of reading Tammi her Miranda rights. He gave me a sharp lift of scarred eyebrow. "I heard about that . . . That was you?"

"I'm afraid so."

"I suppose I should have guessed," he said in a resigned tone that said *Who else in Woodston would have a bomb planted in her car?* He went back to Tammi's Miranda rights. "Anything you do or say may be used against you—"

"Oh, shut up," Tammi snapped. "I want a lawyer. And my husband."

And by then I suspected Tammi didn't think Sgt. Yates was such a sweetie after all.

The ambulance arrived, and after a brief conference between Sgt. Yates and the medics, they brought in a stretcher. Tammi was still demanding a lawyer and her husband, but then another thought struck her. Her expression changed from anger to dismay. She struggled to a sitting position.

"What about Baby? Baby can't be left here all alone! He's already confused—"

"I'll take care of Baby," I said.

Although she'd intended to kill me, I was apparently not unacceptable as a Baby-sitter. "He hasn't had his supper yet."

"I'll see that he gets it."

They loaded Tammi into the ambulance, which I suspected was a safety move to protect the sheriff's department legally rather than the result of an urgent need for medical attention for Tammi. The second officer left to accompany the ambulance to the hospital. Sgt. Yates said he'd be along a little later.

I watched the ambulance drive away. I wondered if the Big Brad would be reporting his wife's arrest on tomorrow's news. Sgt. Yates was conscientiously making notes in his little book. Finally he flipped it shut and looked up at me.

"You seem to have had a busy day, Mrs. Malone. Car bomb this morning. Capture of a possible murderer this evening. Anything on tomorrow's schedule that I should know about?"

"No, I don't think so," I said, ignoring the facetiousness of the question. "But I did talk to DeeAnn today. She and Mike will be moving back from Hawaii in a few days."

"That's good to hear. Now, if you'll excuse me, I think I'd better notify Brad Ridenour of the situation."

"Would it be okay if I wait here with Baby for a while? Skye should be getting home soon."

"Since from what you've said, Leslie Marcone was killed here, I'm afraid the house is now considered a crime scene. So you'll have to wait outside—"

"Baby and I can sit in the car."

"I'll also need you to come into the office tomorrow and make a full statement."

I nodded. "Did you already know about Brad Ridenour's relationship with Leslie Marcone?"

He hesitated, then, sounding a bit grudging, said, "No, I hadn't yet come across that information." Even more grudgingly he added, "I suppose I should commend you for your excellent detective work."

I decided to ignore the unspoken *But after this, Mrs. Malone, stay out of police business!* and simply said, "Thank you."

Sgt. Yates reached for the cell phone on his belt, then turned back for a moment, eyebrows scrunched into a frown. "Oh, Mrs. Malone, there is one other thing."

"Yes?"

"My father definitely wants to meet you."

# 34

As it turned out, however, I never did meet Pa Yates. He came down with the shingles, and in the meantime I made new plans. And Brad Ridenour didn't report his wife's arrest on TV. Brad's perfectly tousled hair and cleft chin were never seen on the local TV news show again.

The initial announcement by his properly somber-looking coanchor was that he was on an "indefinite leave of absence," no reason given, although listeners undoubtedly connected the "leave" with the news of Tammi Ridenour's arrest for murder and the revelation of Brad's relationship with the dead woman.

I expected the Thunderbird might be held by the sheriff's department for weeks, but in less than a week, while Sandy and I were still staying at the Shady Lane Motel, Sgt. Yates returned it to me. There were still some residues of finger-print powder on the dashboard, but other than that it was in fine shape.

But a week later, when Mike and DeeAnn were home, the

Thunderbird was no longer mine. A different vehicle stood in front of the house now. A vehicle crammed with everything I'd brought to Woodston, plus a big supply of groceries and mystery books from Mike and DeeAnn, a carton of home-made pecan-mint brownies from Sandy and Skye, and a paw print on paper from Baby.

We'd all just finished breakfast at the big dining room table. I crumpled my napkin and stood up.

"That was a wonderful breakfast, DeeAnn. Thank you."

"I wish you'd reconsider," DeeAnn said. Under her Hawaiian tan, she looked close to tears. I patted her hand.

School was out now. Mike and DeeAnn were fully moved back from Hawaii. Skye and Baby were living here with them. Tammi was in custody in Fayetteville awaiting trial or, if her lawyer could manage it, a plea bargain. The fibers under Leslie's fingernails had matched the carpet in the Ridenour house, and the animal hairs in her lungs had matched Baby's.

Skye's mother had balked at Skye coming to New York to live, especially with Baby in tow. Brad Ridenour had slunk off to California, with assurances he'd send for Skye and Baby later. I had my doubts. I'm sure Skye did too. But she was seeing a counselor at church, and, with Mike and DeeAnn and Sandy's help, seemed to be coping with the situation. Baby occasionally wandered around as if searching for Tammi, but mostly he seemed content.

Now, we all went outside. A gorgeous June morning. Sunshine sparkling on the lake. Birds twittering in the trees. I have to admit I felt some apprehension about what I was doing. It was indeed a leap into the unknown. But exhilaration overrode the apprehension.

I opened the door of the motor home. Hanson Watkins and I had traded vehicles a few days ago. I'd had to blink back sentimental tears when I relinquished the old 'bird, but

I think we both figured we got the best of the deal. Hanson had ridden with me several times, showing me how everything worked and helping me get the feel of driving the bulky vehicle. As size goes, twenty-one feet is fairly small for a motor home, but it still felt like a lot of vehicle going down the road.

"You don't have to do this," DeeAnn said. She clutched my hand as if she might physically try to hold me back. "We have no qualms about your staying here with us."

"I know. I appreciate that. But—"

I hesitated, a little embarrassed about the "but." It seemed ungrateful to say, "But I'm looking forward to this. I'm going to go places I've never been, see sights I've never seen, meet people I've never met!" Although, I have to admit, somewhere in the back of my mind was the thought that I might run in to someone I did know out there somewhere. Mac MacPherson would surely be back on the road again before long. So what I said was, "I'll be fine."

"You'll keep in touch?" Mike asked.

"As much as I can."

I had no doubts about who had planted the dynamite under my car, but so far the authorities had not found anything to back up my belief. According to Sgt. Yates, they were investigating the Braxtons, but no arrests had been made. I doubted any arrests would be made. The Braxtons were too adept at covering their tracks. Dix, my police friend back in Missouri, had come up with the possibility that a Braxton niece who worked for the post office may have provided information about my whereabouts, which was an unpleasant reminder of what a wide net the Braxton clan could cast.

I doubted the Braxtons would give up on their plans to make roadkill out of me just because their car bomb plot had failed. If I stayed here, the people I loved might be caught in the cross fire of the Braxtons' vengeance over my sending one of their own to prison.

I figure if I keep on the move, they can't find me.

"You're just going to head off cross country?" Sandy asked. She sounded troubled. "No idea where you're going?"

"Not a clue," I replied. I tried not to sound too cheerful about it.

"But so many things could go wrong," Skye said. "Flat tires and engine problems . . . all kinds of breakdowns! You could get really sick. Or lost on a strange, dark road in the middle of nowhere. Or—"

She broke off when we all looked at her. "Okay, sometimes I'm a pessimist," she muttered. "But to just take off by yourself, all alone . . ."

"I'm never alone. The Lord has been with me all my life. He'll be with me out there on the road too."

Skye smiled. "Yeah, I guess he will." In the midst of all the upheaval in her life, Skye had been walking closer to the Lord these past days. She was learning about not being alone too. She gave me a hug and stepped back.

There were more hugs all around, including a dignified paw and less dignified slurp from Baby. Then I climbed in the motor home. There was a new bicycle strapped on back, a going-away gift from all the family. I pulled the door shut and started the engine. I gave them all a big wave as I headed down the driveway.

Out on the highway, I gave another good-bye.

*So long, Braxtons. Open road, here I come.*

Contact the author:
    Lorena McCourtney
    P.O. Box 773
    Merlin, OR  97532

Visit the website at:
    www.lorenamccourtney.com


Turn the page for a preview of the next Ivy Malone book.

The pickup had been tailing me for at least the last thirty miles. I slowed. It slowed. I speeded up. It speeded up. We were as synchronized as the wiper blades swishing back and forth on my windshield.

Not good.

In the same jittery brain wave, I scoffed at my reaction. No reason to think this was a malevolent Braxton honing in on me like a heat-seeking missile programmed to the temperature of a little old lady in polyester pants. Probably just a cautious driver who didn't want to take chances passing on a curvy, rain-slicked highway.

"No need to get all sweaty-handed and jelly-kneed, right?"

Koop, who never gets sweaty-handed or jelly-kneed, opened his one good eye and regarded me with mild interest. Koop is a stubby-tailed, one-eyed Manx with orange fur and a laid-back disposition. Except for an aversion to cigarette smokers, in whose presence he turns into Psycho Cat. We'd adopted each other at a rest area in Georgia.

Now he surprised me by suddenly jerking alert. He hopped down from his usual spot on the passenger's seat and prowled the length of the motor home, even jumping up on the sofa and peering out the window, stub of tail twitching. Do cats get vibes, like my old friend Magnolia from back home claims she does? Maybe hostile vibes from that pickup back there behind us?

I peered into the motor home's oversized mirror, trying to get a better look at the vehicle. It was a light-colored pickup, not new, not ancient, nothing threatening about it. But wasn't that exactly the generic type of vehicle the Braxtons would choose if they were closing in on me? I couldn't tell if the driver was man or woman, or even how many occupants the pickup had. Neither could I make out the license plate.

"Okay, we'll give them an invitation to pass, one they can't refuse," I told Koop.

Ahead was a straight, tree-lined stretch of highway with a nice dotted line down the center. No other vehicles were in sight. I slowed to a crawl. An arthritic centipede could have passed us. But the pickup didn't. It stayed behind, maintaining what was beginning to look like a calculated distance.

My hands turned sweaty on the steering wheel. What did the driver have in mind? Forcing the motor home into a fatal crash on a hill or curve? Picking just the right spot for putting a bullet through a tire or window?

Oh, c'mon. Wasn't that a bit melodramatic? How could the Braxtons have found me? I hadn't stayed more than a few days in any one place in the last couple of months. I'd contacted my niece, DeeAnn, and my friend Magnolia only by prepaid phone card. I never told anyone where I was heading next.

I glanced at Koop again. Next thing I'd be suspecting he was wired for espionage, sending Cat-o-grams to the Braxtons with a high-tech tracking system implanted behind that scruffy orange ear.

No matter how I tried to pooh-pooh my way out of my fears, however, the hard fact was that the Braxtons *were* out to get me. I'd been instrumental in convicting one of the brothers for murder. Drake Braxton, the leader of the clan, had vowed to turn me into roadkill. They'd already tried to burn my house back in Missouri, with me in it. When I hid

305

out at my niece's place in Arkansas, they'd tracked me down and planted dynamite in my old Thunderbird. Which was when I'd decided hitting the road would be a prudent plan, both for my safety and the safety of my niece and her family. Surely, I'd thought, they couldn't find me if I kept on the move. A rolling motor home gathers no Braxtons.

And I'd rolled steadily during the last few months. From Arkansas to Florida, up the eastern coast, now back inland to this wooded valley somewhere in Tennessee. I'd met wonderful people. I'd met strange people. I'd visited an eclectic variety of churches. I'd been encouraged by the love of the Lord I'd found in most of them. I'd been discouraged by internal squabbles in others. In some congregations I'd been no more visible than a dust mote hanging in the air; in others I'd been welcomed like a wonderful new friend. From other travelers I'd accumulated invitations to visit people all over the country. Never had I encountered anyone I even remotely suspected was stalking me.

Which didn't mean the Braxtons *weren't* stalking me. And had found me. Because, at the moment, this isolated road seemed an ideal spot to commit exactly what they'd threatened: roadkill.

*What now, Lord?*

An immediate answer. A sign! No, not a lightning bolt from heaven. A road sign. Stanley, Population 42.

"Hang on, Koop," I muttered. Just beyond the sign I whipped the motor home hard to the right. At which time I was reminded that motor homes, even smaller ones like my twenty-one-footer, do not take kindly to abrupt changes of direction. It tilted like a vehicular Leaning Tower of Pisa and wobbled for a precarious moment before settling back on solid ground.

My attention was elsewhere. I held my breath as I peered out the window. Would the pickup slither in behind me?

Two guys with machine guns get out and close in on me? No. Without even slowing down, the pickup zoomed right on by.

Oh, happy day! I let out my breath and wiped my sweaty hands on Koop's fur when he jumped into my lap.

Okay, I'd imagined hostile intentions where none existed. Making the proverbial mountain out of a molehill. Or perhaps, in these days of computer-speak, making a gigabyte out of a kilobyte would be more correct. But isn't it better to be on guard than sneaked up on?

Now I had time to inspect Stanley, Tennessee, which appeared to consist of a lone gas-and-grocery and a few shabby houses on the far side of a field. Muddy water puddled the potholes around the gas pumps, a wet flag drooped overhead, and a gray mule peered over a nearby wooden fence. Posters advertising chewing tobacco, Campbell's soups, and, incongruously, a cruise to the Bahamas covered most of the windows on the weather-beaten building. A man in old black work pants, khaki jacket, and a faded red cap ambled out the door.

Given the price of gas and my limited finances, I'd intended to wait until I reached a discount station before gassing up, but the place looked as if it could use some business. I eased the motor home up to the pumps. The man peered up at me through heavy bifocals. Tufts of gray hair stuck out from under the cap that read "Voorhee's Heavy Equipment—We'll Dig for You!" I slid the window open.

"Fill 'er up?"

"Yes, please. Regular. I'll have to unlock the gas cap." I slipped on a jacket and opened the door. The rain had let up, and the air smelled fresh and woodsy, with just a hint of wet mule. I unlocked the gas cap, and he stuck the nozzle in. The gas gurgled. My motor home guzzles gas like Koop gleefully downing his favorite treat, a half can of tuna.

"Nice rain," I offered conversationally. I hadn't talked to anyone except Koop for two days. He's sweet but not a big conversationalist.

The man nodded.

"Planning a cruise to the Bahamas?" I motioned toward the poster.

He gave me a "what-planet-are-you-from?" look, and I felt properly chastised for my frivolousness. When the tank was full, he surprised me by climbing up to clean my bug-speckled windshield, an action I appreciated more than small talk anyway. I went inside to pay.

A gray-haired woman with a perm tight enough to offer the bonus of an eyebrow lift took my money and rang it up on an old-fashioned cash register.

"You folks travelin'?" she inquired as she peered between the posters at the motor home. Unlike the man outside, she sounded hungry for small talk.

"Just seeing the countryside." To divert attention from myself, which is what I usually try to do, I asked, "Is your town named for some special Stanley?"

"Zeke Stanley. Story goes he was the slickest thief and card shark in three states. Could steal yer horse out from under you right while you was settin' on it."

An impressive though questionable talent, but possibly one that would interest my friend Mac MacPherson, who wanders the country looking for little-known places and events to write about in his travel articles. I'd been thinking our paths might cross somewhere on the road, but so far that hadn't happened.

"Course, ol' Zeke eventually got hung for his troubles. Used the same rope he'd just stole from a guy he was playin' cards with to hang 'im, they did. Called poker justice, ain't it?"

I thought she probably meant poetic justice, but perhaps, in

Zeke's case, poker justice was appropriate. The door opened, and the man stuck his head inside.

"Left front tire's runnin' low. I knocked on yer door, but I cain't rouse nobody. Want me to air 'er up?"

Even the woman looked surprised. Three whole sentences in a row.

"Yes, I'd appreciate that. Thank you."

The woman inspected me again after the door closed. "You ain't travelin' alone, are you?"

"Well, uh, yes, I am."

I expected disapproval and dire warnings, but instead she just tilted her permed head curiously. "Don't you git lonely?"

It was a question I'd heard before, and I answered it as I always did. "No, I'm fine. Traveling alone can be a wonderful adventure." I thought about adding, as I'd heard another woman traveling alone say, "My cat's better company than most husbands. Never argues and doesn't snore."

However, dearly as I love Koop, I can't say he's better company than a husband. I also have to admit that, even though I'm enjoying my traveling adventures and the Lord is always with me, sometimes I do get a bit lonely.

"You headed anywhere particular?" the woman asked.

"Not really." The words unexpectedly struck me as more dismal than adventurous.

"What're you doing in Stanley?"

"Just passing through."

She nodded sagely. "That's what most people do in Stanley. Kids, they pick up'n leave soon as they can figure a way to get outta town." She paused, and her old blue eyes went dreamy. "That's what I'd like to do someday. Me'n Tom, git us a motor home like your'n, put pedal to the metal and just go."

"It's the kind of thing you should do while you still have

each other," I advised impulsively. Harley and I had always intended to travel together, but we never got around to it before he was gone.

I put my hand to the back of my neck and rubbed at muscles that were beginning to feel stiff as dried jerky. The incident with the pickup, even if it had turned out to be a non-incident, had left me feeling kind of strung out. I didn't want to drive any farther today. "Is there an RV park around here somewhere?"

"Old man Feister rents out a few trailer spaces. Mostly permanent locals, but he takes in an RVer now'n then. You go to the left at the Y down the road. Little farther on, gravel road turns off to the right. Miser Lane." She giggled, as if the name were an inside joke. "But you gotta watch close. It's easy to miss. Feister's place ain't much, but it's cheap. And there's a nice creek. Tell 'im Annie sent you."

Cheap sounded good. Even with an occasional free night in a rest area or Wal-Mart parking lot, living on the road was costing more than was comfortable on my limited Social Security and CD income. "Okay, Annie, thank you. I'll do that. Were you born around here?" I asked, curious as always about people I meet.

"No. Come from Iowa. Not much to do 'round here," she added, "but we got a nice little church with a potluck every Wednesday night."

"Sounds great." It truly did. Old Man Feister's place, just outside Stanley, Tennessee, was surely the middle-of-nowhere kind of spot the Braxtons would never think to look for me. With a creek and a potluck as a bonus.

"You take care now, hear?" she said as I opened the door.

"You too." I gave her a thumbs-up sign. We little old ladies of the world have to stick together. Maybe we should form an LOLs United.

Outside, Taciturn Tom was running water in a tank for the mule. I waved and got a jerk of his head in response. I started the engine and threaded my way around the potholes. Three miles down the road I took the left fork at the Y. It would be good to stop and relax for a few days.

But a half mile farther on I saw it. My heart shimmied. My toes cramped. My teeth tingled. Bad vibes. Very bad vibes.

It was the pickup, closer now. Dirty white color. A dented fender. Silhouettes of two people in the cab. No coincidence here. They'd hidden and waited to see which fork I took. The orange fur on Koop's back popped up like porcupine quills.

I started looking frantically for Miser Lane. If I could get off the main road, into the safety of people and trailers . . .

Too late. I saw the leaning sign for Miser Lane just as the motor home sailed past it.

It wouldn't have meant safety anyway, I realized regretfully. Because the Braxtons would have my location pinned down, and they'd figure a way to get me.

My only chance was to lose them.

I tightened my hands on the steering wheel, swallowed hard, and did what Annie back in Stanley wanted to do. I put pedal to the metal and went.

# She's not your average crime fighter!

A mysterious disappear-
ance fuels the mutant
curiosity of Ivy Malone,
whose oddball humor, gray
hair, and quirky sleuthing
skills make her unlike
other women her age.
An Ivy Malone mystery.

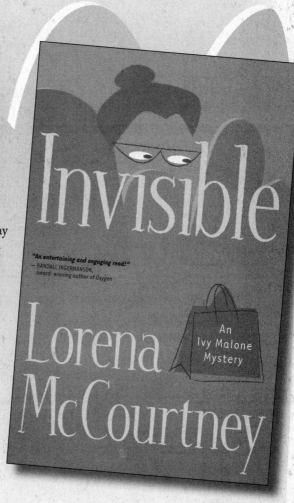

"An entertaining and engaging read!"
— RANDALL INGERMANSON,
award-winning author of Oxygen

Invisible

An
Ivy Malone
Mystery

Lorena
McCourtney

ℛ Revell
www.RevellBooks.com

# A Letter to Our Readers

Dear Reader:
In order that we might better contribute to your reading enjoyment, we would appreciate your taking a few minutes to respond to the following questions. When completed, please return to the following:

Andrea Doering, Editor-in-Chief
Crossings Book Club
401 Franklin Avenue, Garden City, NY 11530

You can post your review online! Go to www.crossings.com and rate this book.

Title _____ Author _____

**1  Did you enjoy reading this book?**

❑ Very much. I would like to see more books by this author!

❑ I really liked_____

❑ Moderately. I would have enjoyed it more if_____

**2  What influenced your decision to purchase this book? Check all that apply.**

    ❑ Cover
    ❑ Title
    ❑ Publicity
    ❑ Catalog description
    ❑ Friends
    ❑ Enjoyed other books by this author
    ❑ Other _____

**3  Please check your age range:**

    ❑ Under 18    ❑ 18-24
    ❑ 25-34      ❑ 35-45
    ❑ 46-55      ❑ Over 55

**4  How many hours per week do you read?** _____

**5  How would you rate this book, on a scale from 1 (poor) to 5 (superior)?**
_____

Name_____

Occupation_____

Address_____

City_____ State_____ Zip_____